H
Agendas

D. Marshall Craig, M.D.

2021 White Bird Publications, LLC

Cover by Matthew S. Craig

Published in the United States
by White Bird Publications, LLC, Texas
www.whitebirdpublications.com

ISBN 978-1-63363-546-3
eBook ISBN 978-1-63363-547-0
Library of Congress Control Number: 2021949716

PRINTED IN THE UNITED STATES OF AMERICA

To my wife, Valerie, and my two sons, Drew and Matt—They are the ones who always push me to try new things in life.

Acknowledgment

Once again, I am tremendously indebted to my wonderful wife Valerie, who continually encourages me to pursue my passion of writing. She always said, “You never know what my husband is going to do next.”

Every parent knows the most honest feedback comes from your kids. I happen to be doubly blessed by my younger son Matt, who gave me editing expertise as well as designed the ideal book cover.

During the year of COVID-19, while I escaped reality by researching about adventures in London, Rotterdam, and Long Island, I was humbled by the real heroes of the world. The front-line healthcare workers, who faced overwhelming odds against the SARS-CoV-2 virus, deserve a standing ovation. We are all thankful to you for our lives and wellbeing.

Last but not least, a special thanks to my publisher Evelyn Byrne-Kusch and her team at White Bird Publications. Without their continued support, my vision for a Dr. Kyle Chandler series would still be only in my head.

Hidden Agendas

White Bird
Publications

1

KANSAS CITY, MISSOURI

Hurry up and wait—the ever present, yet often the raw reality of my job.

Being a trauma surgeon by profession, I guess you could say I chose this life as well as the headaches and back pain that went with it. Over the years, I somehow got used to being pulled in all directions at once and tried to deal as calmly as I could with the situation at hand. But then again, easier said than done.

It was a routine Tuesday evening in early October in the midwestern utopia of Kansas City, my adopted hometown. As expected of any larger US city, Kansas City had its own local chapters of the Nighttime Knife & Gun Club as well as the Drunk Drivers' Bumper Car Club. They practiced their expertise on a regular basis.

Kansas City possessed a unique dichotomy. The city, divided between Missouri's liberal liquor laws, and Kansas's liquor laws likely handed down from the Puritans, with the trauma center right down the middle on Stateline Boulevard.

I moved here after finishing my surgical training in Boston in the fall of 1988. Seven years zoomed by with me spending late hours usually two nights a week at St. Jude Hospital putting automobile accident and gunshot wound victims back together. Over time, I thought I had seen just about everything crazy people try.

I mean, most people think that folks are usually home by 11:00 p.m., maybe even midnight during the week. After all, they need to get up the next morning and go to work. Right?

Wrong.

Seems that one of the veteran members of the Knife & Gun Club decided to exercise his joint membership rights with the Drunk Drivers' Bumper Car Club that very Tuesday evening. According to the triage nurse who called me sometime after 10:15 p.m., a particular gentleman, after multiple cocktails at a local lounge, got into a heated argument with another patron at the bar. That led to each man pulling a 22-caliber handgun and the "Shootout at the OK Corral" ensued.

The prospective dual club member then fled the scene on foot and by chance encountered a fire truck backing into its station after a routine outing for a false alarm. I must admit that this guy was pretty resourceful. He brandished his handgun at the fire truck driver, got all the firemen to back away, and then took off wounded, while driving an almost forty-foot-long ladder fire truck at a high rate of speed. He made it ten blocks before crashing into the corner of a brick warehouse. Dual club membership accomplished.

After his arrival at our trauma institution, proper evaluation was completed in Trauma Room #1. What we had was a twenty-eight-year-old male, BP of 90/50, pulse 132 with obvious multiple gunshot wounds of the abdomen, closed spiral fracture of the right humerus, multiple abrasions and superficial lacerations of the face and chest, and possible laceration of the left lobe of the liver by CT Scan. Just another Tuesday night.

"Dr. Kyle Chandler," one of the trauma nurses I worked with regularly, Bill, said as he arrived in the trauma room at shift change. "Imagine that, you here on what is usually a slow Tuesday night."

"Just the luck of the draw," I said cautiously.

"Anything special you need?" he asked.

"The work up is about done here," I said. "Let's make sure the CT scan hard copies get to the OR. Call the blood bank and have them get those two units here ASAP. And tell 'em to make sure four more units of packed cells are typed and crossed so they're available for later."

"Roger that El Grande Jefe," he said quickly.

After stabilizing the patient with the two initial units of packed red blood cells, this was followed by a lengthy conversation with two anxious members of the KC Police Department to convince them that this nice gentleman was not going anywhere on his own, not with the extent of his injuries. All the necessary arrangements were then made with the OR to proceed to surgery for exploration of this gentleman's abdomen. Finally, I slogged up to the surgeon's lounge to get changed into surgical scrubs.

While I was waiting to get this dog-and-pony-show on the road at this late hour, my cell phone buzzed on my hip. Looking down at the caller's number brought a smile to my face.

"Kyle, my boy, how's life treating you?" the voice on the line blurted out his question in a thick Scottish accent.

I immediately recognized the voice as Ian Griffin, the head of a private investigation firm in Kansas City. I had worked with him on a case for the first time earlier in the year. He was a friend of Sydney Alfred, my deceased wife's uncle who took me under his wing when I moved to Kansas City seven years ago.

It was Sydney who forced me to do something other than work all the time by getting me interested in, of all things, French period antiques. I gained knowledge over time by going to auctions, occasionally buying a few pieces. I would have them touched up by my special refinishing guy Dan, and then auction them off again for a small, but still worthwhile profit. It was Ian who got me involved in a stolen antiques for an illegal stock acquisition case with my employer Columbus HealthCare System last April. This event led me to start a new on-the-side venture of private investigation. Well, it turned out to be more than that, but whatever.

"I'm hanging in there Ian. How about you?"

"So, I guess I haven't convinced you to give up the all-night repair shop putting car crash victims back together then, have I?"

"No Ian, not yet. What can I do for you at this lovely time of the evening?" I said sarcastically. Considering the hour, it seemed to me that Ian probably never slept.

"I've got a situation I want to discuss with you. This morning I received a call from a gentleman in London. It seems this gentleman, a Mr. Clanton Rogers, is some type of wealthy investor and prides himself in discovering rare finds of antique furniture. He was referred to me by Nigel Whittenberg, the antiques dealer in the West End of London who had originally called me in April about the stolen antiques case that you broke open. You know—the one that led to the downfall of your beloved Columbus Healthcare System management team."

My caution antennae started to rise.

"Yes, Ian, I haven't forgotten the case. The one where I almost got permanently sidelined after being beaten to a pulp if not for a heroic ex-Marine who saved my skin from those CHS goons," I said, staring at the ceiling and shaking my head. As if I could forget that fiasco.

"Anyway," he said, avoiding the obvious. "This Mr. Rogers told me that some notable French antique furniture from a private estate in New York was set to be sold by Sotheby's at auction in London. All the pieces from this particular lot were thought to be French originals from the late 1700s. Sotheby's completed the two standard independent appraiser evaluations prior to the auction to certify their authenticity. Mr. Rogers insisted on his own third-party appraiser to evaluate a certain piece of interest to him. His appraiser found the piece to be a reproduction just before it was set to go up for auction. He said his appraiser mentioned it was an incredible copy, too. Sotheby's was terribly embarrassed to say the least. They have their legal department looking into it, but the authenticity of the whole lot has now come into question prior to the scheduled sale."

"Yeah… So, what does that have to do with you calling me?"

"Mr. Rogers wants my firm to look into the matter. He's an American chap and is close friends with the family in New York who put up those pieces for auction in London. Sotheby's won't give him any information about their investigation, but it's looking like they'll be shifting the blame of furniture authenticity to the family in New York who put it up for auction."

"Is that possible?"

"Kyle, you know more about antiques than I do. As you know, in the world of fine art and antiques, anything is possible."

"So, what are you trying to find out here?"

"The family in New York has quietly told Mr. Rogers that they would put out a reward of quite a substantial sum to finding out if the original antiques had been switched for some ultra-premium quality reproductions somewhere in transit from New York to London."

"And you are calling me because...?"

"Well, as a matter of fact, Sydney called me this week and said that you were going to a trauma surgery symposium in London next week as part of your work. Something utterly perplexing; something about abdominal tapping?" He sounded unsure of himself.

"My dubious employer CHS is sending me to a

conference over there as a reward for exposing their crooked CEO a few months back. It's a symposium about studying better ways to diagnose abdominal and chest trauma, but that's neither here nor there," I said. "What does my trip to London have to do with anything with this?"

"Well, I believe my Scottish frugality has gotten the best of me in this case. While you are in London, could you by chance meet with this gentleman briefly to see what the particulars of the case are? And then could you meet with someone from the Port of London Authority about the possible switching of the original pieces for some highly crafted reproductions?" His tentative words hung in the air.

"Whoa there, partner." I jerked to my feet. "I just got through this last episode of investigation drama where I got the bejesus beat out of me when I tried to find out the truth about missing stock certificates. And now you want me to jump right back into the ring and go straight to another twelve-round bout?" I knew my voice grew louder with each word, but…

"I understand you might be a tad gun shy after some of the rough stuff on the previous case. But not only did everything turn out fine, you'll have to admit that you were very good at it. I might go as far to say that you actually enjoyed it."

I refused to respond. Especially since he was for the most part right on the mark.

For some reason, I didn't want to admit that the private investigation work I did for Ian last April was really stimulating to me. I tried to convince myself that I already did my own type of investigation work on finding out what needed to be fixed on the trauma victims I encountered every day at my occupation. But the work that I did for Ian was completely different. It grabbed my attention, and I had been thinking about it off and on since April.

Still, I was hesitant to say yes to Ian because I did get smacked around by some goons on the last case. That situation could have turned out bad for me. It left me with some lower back pain that showed up with long surgical cases in the OR. Or at least I attributed that to the source of the pain.

"It'll be just a couple of short meetings. Just a routine fact-finding mission. Send me a copy of your schedule in London, and I'll work around it to make all the necessary arrangements."

"And no gorillas at my front door trying to turn me into Silly Putty like last time?"

"No reason to worry at all."

I couldn't come up with a reason to say no. And there was that deep-seeded notion of curiosity that would not go away.

"Okay, you win. I'll have my secretary fax you a copy of where I'm staying and the schedule of the symposium. See if they are available to meet in the late afternoons when I can break away."

"Splendid. I'll fax you the info about both meetings. Report back to me as soon as you have a chance when you get home. Same billing as before, and you'll get a cut from the reward the family is offering if you find out anything. Gotta run. Have a good trip."

As I punched off my cell phone, I tried to reason with myself. It'll be just a couple of innocent meetings. What could be dangerous about that? Yeah, but then again, I didn't know any gypsies who could look into their crystal ball to tell me the truth of what was really going to happen.

After the phone call, the surgery front desk called me over the intercom to head on to OR #7. After insuring everything was in place to get started and that the patient was stable, I spent the next three and one-half hours trying to put Humpty Dumpty's abdomen back together again. Even though Hollywood likes to portray that every trauma case is a matter of immediate life and death, that's not usually the case. Just because the patient is not on the edge of life or death, that doesn't make fixing everything in surgery any easier. The truth is that it's a lot of plain, hard work.

No pain, no gain.

After finally finishing the surgery, I headed to the ER waiting area to speak with this gentleman's family about what I found. Not a soul in sight. That definitely lodged a disappointing rating on my "appreciate the doctor" scale. Not to mention the aching back I felt right about now. With the long evening coming to a close, I changed into my street clothes and trudged home to catch some much-needed shuteye. *Maybe better luck next time in the gratitude department.*

I awoke Wednesday morning somewhat disoriented. No surprise there. Six hours sleep after getting home at 4:00 a.m. puts the meter for mental sharpness at about a two on a scale of ten. Wednesday was the day that I usually made rounds at the hospital, and then if it was the first or third Wednesday of the month, I met my deceased wife's uncle Sydney Alfred at his sacred golf club. He had kind of taken a liking to me since I moved here seven years ago. Probably because he had been so fond of his niece Molly. Investments and golf were his passions, and I really learned to cherish our Wednesday get-togethers. We would play golf in the afternoon and then have an early dinner in the board members' private dining room. Today was a third Wednesday of the month, so I decided to touch base with Sydney and tell him that golf and dinner wasn't likely after getting pounded on call last night.

I dialed Sydney's office phone number, getting his ever-efficient secretary on the line on the second ring.

"Good morning, Alfred Investments. How may I help you?"

"Hi, Beverly. This is Kyle Chandler. May I speak with Sydney, please?"

"Oh, hello, Dr. Chandler, so good to hear from you

again," she said in a much slower and now more personally attentive tone.

Beverly was one of Sydney's office assistants. Tall, attractive, divorced, late-thirties. Lots of cleavage. And big-time aggressive.

When I first started playing golf with Sydney seven years ago, she was somewhat standoffish when I called. But when she found out I was single and worked as a physician as my day job, it was like someone blew the horn for the foxhunt. And for her, the chase was on.

From then on, she went out of her way to be nice to me and did her best to suggest that we should get together sometime. Sometime meant just us two alone. Thing about it, she just wasn't my type. I always managed to be polite to her, all the while keeping the foxhound at bay.

"How have you been Beverly?"

"Busy. And yourself?"

"I've been busy also," I said, not knowing what else to say without adding fuel to the fire.

"Well, you know what they say Dr. Chandler," she said as she kept pulling the conversation to her advantage. "All work and no play will make you a dull boy. You wouldn't like that, would you Dr. Chandler?"

I felt like I was on the end of a fishing line slowly being reeled in by Mae West.

"No, I guess not Beverly. Uh, can I speak with Sydney please?"

"I'll get him on the line for you. Come by and see me when you get a chance."

I purposefully didn't say another word for fear she'd take it as a definite yes.

"Hello, this is Sydney Alfred."

His formality always amused me. A real proper gentleman in all regards.

"Hi, Sydney. It's me, Kyle."

"Kyle, my boy. How are you today? Are you ready to take a beating on the links with me this afternoon?"

"That's why I called you, Sydney. I spent last night on trauma call, and it got the best of me. I don't think I could swing the clubs very well today. I'm running on fumes right now. I do look forward to our twice a month golf outings, but I have to pass on today's round."

"Kyle, are you sure about that? I just read a golf article about how to increase the swing speed of your driver and get the same distance as John Daly got at the British Open this year. I'm all set to spring it on you today."

"Maybe so Sydney. To be honest, I'd rather putt like Ben Crenshaw did at the Masters, than swing as hard as John Daly. Anyway, I hope to see your big driver swing the next time we play."

"If you're sure you can't make it, then so be it," he said, sounding slightly dejected.

"Oh yeah, I forgot to tell you that Ian Griffin called me last night. I haven't heard from him since back in April. He told me that you had spoken to him about me heading to that trauma symposium in London next week."

"Oh yes. Ian said he needed you to look into a matter for him while you were over there in England. I thought it would be a marvelous idea to kill two birds with one stone while you were in London."

"Sydney, I gotta admit that I'm more than a little gun-shy about the investigation thing because of last time."

"You'll be fine. Ian assured me that it will just be a couple of innocent meetings and that's all."

"Well, if you say so. I'll be gone all next week, so I might have to work extra the week I get back. It might bump our golf outing that week."

"I doubt it. You'll find a way to make it work. You always do."

"Gotta go, Sydney. I'll call you when I get back."

"Safe travels. Goodbye now," he said as he rang off as proper as ever.

After showering, followed by the requisite amount of necessary caffeine, I decided to call my on-again-off-again-on-again girlfriend Caroline Martinelli. Unfortunately, she currently had me totally perplexed.

Caroline was an unbelievable woman who ran one of the premier antique stores down in the Plaza District. A one-of-a-kind. We met in April when I got involved in the case of stolen French antiques. She saved my backside in a *big* way at the conclusion of the case during the annual CHS shareholders' meeting.

Since then, we started seeing more and more of each other. We met for dinner a couple of times a week and that led to doing new things together on weekends. I was starting to get to know this dynamic, witty woman better and better, and I really felt like she enjoyed getting to know me. As the weeks went by, I thought things were beginning to sail smoothly between us.

Towards the end of June, the nights I was on trauma call got longer and longer. It was beginning to be summer and that meant more trauma victims. In addition, we were temporarily one man short on the on call schedule, so that made it harder on all of the trauma surgeons employed by St. Jude Hospital. That meant me being more tired after work and with less time to spend with Caroline.

About that time things got busy for me at work, she had to travel more for her business. A couple of weeks went by and before you know it, we totally resented each other's schedule. Previously, we had gotten to where we were in touch with each other several times a day. Now it was just a passing call here and there during the week. I decided to see if I could break the impasse.

"Hey, it's me," I said loudly after the loud beep of her phone message machine. "I gotta talk to you soon, so give me a call."

Less than ten seconds after I hung up, she called me back. "Sorry, I was just finishing another call. What's up?" she asked, her tone slightly perplexed.

"Well, as I told you last week, CHS in their continued confusion is trying to make everything kosher with me over the case with the missing stock certificates earlier this year. I leave for the trauma symposium in London this Sunday. I was wondering if we could spend some time together before I leave."

"Well, uh, sure."

"Look Caroline, I know you are kinda weirded out with me right now. Especially since that Friday night a couple of weeks ago where I came to your place for dinner, and we ended up spending the weekend together."

Still a silent pause.

"I don't blame you for feeling that way, really," I said. "It's not like something we planned on happening. It just…happened. But you'll have to admit, it was very special. I know it was for me."

Saying that out loud was kind of big for me. I was not good at expressing my feelings, especially to a member of the opposite sex. Part of that must have been the whole surgeon tough-guy mentality. I do think that I had opened up to her emotionally more before we both got busy, but there was a definite wall of tension that had somehow come between us. I was still interested in extending our relationship together, but I had to find a way to break down that barrier so we could operate on the same page.

After another short pause she blurted, "That's the problem. I thought it was very special. And it scared the living daylights out of me. I already told you that years ago I found out my previous fiancé had been fooling around behind my back right before we were to be married. And I know you're not him. But since then, I've had a big problem completely trusting anyone of the opposite gender on anything more than a superficial level. And that was ten years ago." Her voice rose ten decibels, and I pulled the phone away from my ear.

"Back then, I compensated by throwing myself full steam ahead into my training in antiques in London," she continued. "Then it was the opening of my initial antiques shop here in town. After that, it was moving to my larger store down in the Plaza. All of the sudden you pop into my life and getting to know you caught me by total surprise. We were getting to know each other, share more, slowly, and I really enjoyed that. And then, getting intimate with you…it has me reeling as to where to go from here. Don't get me wrong, I enjoyed being with you. I think about it all the time. I don't know what to do. And there's your insane schedule and my hectic schedule, and I just don't know anything about anything now."

"Caroline, it's okay to be confused. I'm confused. But as Sydney once told me when I moved here, 'you got take whatever pitches they throw at you and keep on swinging.' You are never going to get a hit unless you swing. So, let's try to keep on swinging at the pitches…together. Who knows if it'll work out between us, but we got to give it a fair chance, and that takes time. Fair enough?" I asked.

Another pause.

"You're probably right. And be sure you understand that I stress the word *probably.* Just give me some time to figure out how I feel about all this. What time do you leave Sunday?"

"Sort of early."

"Well, I'm headed to New York tomorrow to meet with potential clients and won't be back until Saturday afternoon. Looks like our schedule conflicts win out again."

"Well, maybe just this time. We'll see," I said. "One other thing I need to tell you. Ian Griffin rang me last night and wants me to look into a small matter in London while I'm there. Some kind of switch of valuable antiques for high priced replications. Do you still have any contacts in the antique world? I need to talk to someone that has the inside scoop."

"Kyle, didn't we talk about this after your case just a few months ago? You were beaten up quite badly, don't you remember? Did you forget telling me how they could have mangled both of your hands and put you out of your real profession for good?"

"Well, I might have said that, but this is going to be just a couple harmless meetings in London. What's wrong with that?"

"I believe that's exactly how it started off last time. Why the sudden amnesia?"

"Look Caroline, I told Ian that I would try to help him as long as it didn't involve any rough stuff. And it's just a couple of meetings. Do you still have any contacts in London who may help me on this one?"

"Well, Dr. Chandler sir, I do speak with my former mentor Sebastian Clarke at Christie's every couple of months. He's still head of Appraisals & Evaluations there and is much in the know of what goes on in that market. If you want, I'll reach out to see if he can meet with you if he's in London next week."

"See if he's available in the late afternoons since I'll be at the symposium in the mornings and after lunch."

"You'll probably have to take whenever he's free. He maintains an unbelievably busy schedule. Beggars can't be choosers."

"Yes, oh gracious kind soul."

"And don't you forget it." She gave a small snicker.

"Call me before your flight leaves from New York? Maybe I can pick you up at the airport if it doesn't get in too late."

"Roger that, Captain. Talk to you then," she said and hung up.

Well, not a perfect resolution. Not great, but it was a start.

2

KANSAS CITY

I spent the rest of Wednesday afternoon mopping up messes and putting out fires at my office. If I had known how much paperwork managed healthcare was going to make me do as a physician before I went to medical school, I might have gone to truck driving school instead. Oh well, I bet truck drivers have a ton of paperwork to fill out themselves.

I had my office assistant fax Ian Griffin a schedule of the symposium that I would be attending and where I was staying in London. As part of the fax, I left him a note that my new cell phone wouldn't have service in the UK, but he could leave a message at my hotel.

By late afternoon, the lack of sleep had me dragging in a big way that not even waves of caffeine warded off. I made it home for an early dinner and crashed on the couch before I could even go through my mail lying on the breakfast table.

On Thursday, I had several elective surgeries both morning and early afternoon that went as well as could be expected. I had a few follow-up patients to see in the late afternoon that seemed to drag a bit, but all in all things went smoothly. My back was aching some but not horribly. Just about the time I told the nurses to head home for the day, I got a call on my mobile phone that turned out to be a pleasant surprise.

"Hello, this is Dr. Chandler." My standard greeting when I didn't recognize the number.

"Kyle, this is Barry down at Imperial Wines and Spirits. How are things?"

"Oh Barry, I didn't recognize your number. How in the world are you?"

Barry was a super guy that I first met when I moved to Kansas City seven years ago. He was about eight to ten years younger than me. After college, his folks were expecting him to move on to law school or business school, but he surprised everyone by immediately buying a run-down liquor store. Not exactly what his family had planned for their only son on the ladder to success.

Barry worked like a bandit to make the store grow and eventually gutted the building to the bare bones. He ended up tripling the size, changing it from a small liquor store into a colossal high-end wine and spirits complex. I first met him at one of my colleague's holiday house parties. It seemed he always came with a new girlfriend that was "the one." Also a big Royals and Chiefs fan, he often invited people over to the store to watch the games on his big screen TV.

"I was calling to see if you're not working Saturday evening, maybe you can come by the store and try some of the new wines we got in today from France. We've had this order in for about four months, and the container finally arrived. I'm closing the store early at 8:00 p.m. and having a few friends try some of these new selections I chose for the fall lineup. I hope you can make it."

"Wow Barry, I really appreciate it. The woman I've been seeing is coming back from a business trip and I need to check with her to see when her flight gets in late Saturday afternoon."

"Well, bring her along, for goodness sake. We should be there until ten or eleven at least."

"That's awfully nice of you to include us. Tell you what; I'll leave you a message tomorrow or Saturday if we can make it. If she gets hung up on her flight home, I just may come by for a bit by myself."

"That'll be great. I know you have a great palate, and I'd like your input on some of these wines to see if I should double down on my next order."

"Sounds good, Barry. Is there anything I can bring?"

"Not a thing. A friend's wife is a caterer, and she loves trying out new things on us, so there will be plenty of finger food."

"Well, thanks for calling and hope to see you Saturday."

"Me too; see you then. Bye."

After the pleasant surprise of being invited by Barry to a wine tasting on Saturday evening, it made me want the weekend to get here even faster. I turned back to the stack of medical charts remaining on my standup dictation cubicle, offices for physicians were totally unnecessary according to Columbus Healthcare System. After a long tussle with the details of each patient and the documentation of their progress, I finally finished my day's dictations.

On my drive home, I wondered why I was letting myself get mixed up with another investigation for Ian Griffin, chasing down irregular antiques transactions. Why was I drawn to that? That's not why I went to medical school. Besides, I nearly got broken into pieces by some big gorillas on that case in April. What kept me being so interested about it?

Deep down, I knew there was the intrigue, a fascination with the case I worked for Mr. Griffin. I was threatened, even assaulted several times, and it still didn't turn me away. I liked what I did for my day job, helping people by putting them back together after accidents. It was very satisfying.

You might even consider it a calling. But somehow it did not give me the same charge as the private investigation work that I was about to take on once again.

The next day was spent seeing patients in the office and battening down the hatches for my upcoming week away from reality. In the afternoon, I received a fax from Ian that meetings had been arranged for me in London on Tuesday and Wednesday of next week. On Tuesday, I was to meet a Mr. Clanton Rogers at the Carlton Club, a private men's club in Westminster at 5:00 p.m. to discuss particulars of the case, at least what was known thus far. On Wednesday afternoon, I would have to find a way to get myself east of London before 4:30 p.m. to the Port of Tilbury in Essex to meet a Mr. Colin Butterworth. He was listed as the senior constable for the Port of Tilbury Police.

Well, that was going to make for an interesting contrast of meetings.

Since it was Friday, it was my turn for weekend trauma on call before leaving town. Most weekend trauma call shifts were back breakers with full pedal to the metal intensity. Every now and then you got lucky, and I finally got lucky for once on this shift. Other than a few minor things to mop up in the ER, there were no real participants from the Knife & Gun Club or the Drunk Bumper Cars Club to speak of. I took it as a good omen of my trip to come.

On Saturday morning, I went to go workout at the health club. By early afternoon, I got a message from Caroline that her flight from New York had been delayed and that she probably wouldn't get back to Kansas City until after midnight. She left me a London phone number and said that she had left a message with her contact Mr. Sebastian Clarke at Christie's that I would be calling to arrange an appointment to meet with him.

I was going to call her back to offer to pick her up super late at the airport, but I decided to not push the envelope too fast. I was trying to make up lost ground with her, so I didn't want some plane flight screw-up to set us back. Since I didn't have to get to the airport super early Sunday morning for my flight, I decided to leave Barry a message that I would make his wine tasting get-together solo. What the hell, why not before leaving town tomorrow?

After finishing my weekend errands, I showered and drove over to Barry's store around 8:15 p.m. The front door was locked so I called his mobile phone.

"Barry, it's Kyle, I'm at the front door," I said when he answered his mobile phone.

"Hey! We're in the conference room in the back. I'll be right up to unlock it for you."

He soon made his way to the front door to let me in. We walked through the large store all the way to the back then down a hallway to his conference room where one end of a large conference table held umpteen dishes of hors d'oeuvres. At the other end stood multiple bottles of wine lined up in groups, with a gazillion small wine glasses. Quite a spread.

There were six other people—two women and four men of various ages all seated around the table. Everyone was eating something and looked ready to start tasting wine. After introducing me all around, Barry got down to business.

"Kyle, all of the people here tonight have helped me in one way or another to make Imperial Wines grow to what it is today," Barry started while looking at me. "I actually brought you in as 'the ringer' tonight, kind of an independent tasting judge. Do you remember that story you first told me about how you learned all about wines?"

"About my college landlady?" I asked sheepishly.

"Yeah. Go ahead and tell everyone here about her."

"Well," I started with some hesitation, "when I was in college, I had an elderly landlady for my last two years. I lived in the top floor of her three-story house. It was really kind of a converted attic. Anyway, she was part wine collector, part philosopher. Her kids were grown and never visited her, and she had all this wine she had collected over the years. She claimed that she had to drink it before it went bad. So, every night after I finished studying, I'd go downstairs to her basement with her and we'd open a bottle. She'd teach me all about the wine we were tasting and the region it was from. Wines from just about everywhere, years and years of vintages."

"How interesting!" one of the women exclaimed.

"While we tasted wines, she had tons of quotes on life she recited to me. One of her favorites was from a well-known owner of a Bandol winery in southeast France. The owner was named Lucie Tempier Peyraud. She was a revered winemaker for a long time and also quite a good cook. Actually, she had a well-known cookbook that came out last year called *Lulu's Provencal Table*. My landlady used to quote her as saying when asked about her secret of longevity, Lulu replied, 'One should only drink wine. Water makes one rust.'"

"Amen!" blurted one of the men at the table.

"I was very fortunate to get to know my landlady. She taught me all the tricks of tasting wines," I continued. "She was one of a kind. I remember another saying she always quoted. It was something like 'great wines, like great friends, are hard to find and impossible to forget.' Since then, I read a lot about wines and keep up from time to time on the different vintages just for fun."

"Wow, I never got that kind of education in college," one guy chimed in. "All we tasted was cheap keg beer."

Everyone around the tabled laughed and wholeheartedly agreed.

"So anyway," Barry said, "I've brought all you guys here to taste a bunch of wines that I have imported from France. I really want everyone's honest opinion of not what is the best of the lot here in front of you. What I want from each of you is what wines are the ones that Joe-Middle-America is going to buy instead of beer, beer, beer."

"What?" everyone answered somewhat together.

"Let's taste some of the wines I have chosen, keeping what I said in mind, and I will explain the method to my madness." Confidence resonated in Barry's voice.

Our host had several of his associates open a bunch of wine bottles and poured them into glasses. All the glasses were marked with a number already placed on individual round trays. Someone then passed out pre-printed sheets to write notes and score for each of the wines. Barry obviously knew what he was doing here.

"Everybody, come up one at a time and grab a tray to take to your seat. We'll taste each wine, one at time, write down our notes, and then I'll explain."

Everyone in the room did as they were told. After about thirty minutes of tasting the wines one by one, Barry finally spoke up.

"Okay people, what do you think? I want one red and one white favorite. Remember, not the best wine, I want the most sellable wine."

We bantered back and forth telling our own opinions of what each of us thought about what wines Joe-Middle-America would like. Surprisingly, we came to a consensus on the red and white that everyone agreed on.

"You sure there's not more to the story? What's all this for Barry?" one of the men asked.

I kept quiet since I was somewhat of an outsider still at this point.

"What this is for ladies and gentlemen," Barry said as he rose from his seat, "is about the future of independent wine stores like mine. Selling high-end vintage conscious wines makes money but is definitely not the future. High volume is the future. Letting huge volume California producers make most the wine gives all the profits to them. If we can establish our own house brand at a slightly cheaper price point, we can steer the local market to us and not them."

"And exactly how do you plan on doing that?" one of the men asked.

"I'm in negotiations now with a number of mid-sized wine producers in France to produce bulk wines for us that we here in Kansas City think will sell big to Joe-Middle-America. All but two of the wines tasted tonight are those bulk wines already bottled that we might be interested in purchasing. The red and the white that you guys chose are both bulk wines."

Everyone looked around the room like they had just been fleeced and not seen the robber coming.

"How are bulk wines going to be cheaper if you have to set up all the bottling and packaging?" another man asked.

"First off, there's newer technology for bulk wine transport," Barry said. "You used to transport all the wine in heavy stainless steel ISO containers that had to be cleaned with each use. Now, there's a newer technology using what's called a Flexitank. They are like a big sterile bladder made of PVC material for one-time usage that can hold up to 24,000 liters. It's much cheaper to make and to transport. I've looked into it and they are made by several companies. One of the largest producers of these bladders is in southern England."

"And the processing of the wine into bottles?" the man asked calmly.

"I've already talked to a friend of mine who owns a manufacturing plant north of town by the airport. He says that he bottles all kinds of liquids, and that they are already set up with all the necessary licenses for bottling all types of alcohol including wines."

I knew Barry to be a sharp guy. It was obvious he had done his homework.

"What I need to do next is find out more about shipping the wine in bulk as compared to shipping heavy glass bottle cases like we do now."

"Is the wine shipped directly from France to the US, assuming it probably goes through New York?" another man asked.

"It's my understanding that almost all of the wines shipped from Europe to America are shipped through either Rotterdam in The Netherlands or London. Those are the two busiest ports over there," Barry said.

"Did you say London?" I innocently joined in the dialogue.

"Yeah. Why?" Barry asked while looking directly at me.

"Well, it just so happens that I'm scheduled to leave for London tomorrow to attend a symposium. Strangely enough, I also have an appointment, totally unrelated to the symposium, to speak with the head constable at the Port of Tilbury east of London for a friend of mine."

"At the port in London?" Barry asked. "I thought you were a surgeon, working on all those nasty car wreck victims? What does the port in London have to do with surgery?"

I hesitated before answering, making sure I didn't get too far over my head here.

"Well, nothing really. It's kind of a long story, but I'm meeting with this port authority person as a favor for a friend. It's about an antiques shipping issue," I replied.

"Wait a minute. Weren't you involved in that big scandal this past spring with Columbus Healthcare System? I remember seeing your name in the paper about how you broke open the case about something with them and black-market antiques," one of the women asked.

"Well," I said. "Newspapers like to sensationalize everything. It was a onetime thing. No big deal."

"I had mentioned before that one of the largest manufacturers of those Flexitank bladders is in southern England," Barry said. "To be more specific, it's just a few kilometers east of the port where you said you have a meeting."

"Uh, huh..." I said.

"Well, do you think you can swing by there and speak with the plant manager? I was going to call him this week anyway to ask him some more questions. Maybe you could check out the plant and ask the questions I have for him to make sure that this company is the real deal."

"I don't know Barry. I have to leave the conference and get a ride way out east to the port."

"What day is your appointment at the Port?" he asked.

"It's supposed to be Wednesday at 4:30 in the afternoon. There will probably be a lot of traffic…" I said with poor conviction.

"Let me call the plant manager Monday morning. I'll set up an appointment with him for you around 3:30 on Wednesday since you'll already be out that way. It should only take about thirty to forty minutes at most. When I talked to him before, the plant manager seemed like a nice guy on the phone. You'll have plenty of time to make your meeting at the port by at 4:30. It'll be a terrific help if you find out more about these bladders for me."

I could tell, like a bulldog clinging to a bone, Barry wasn't going to let this opportunity slide by him.

"How will I know if the meeting is on?" I asked, trying to weasel out of it. "My cell phone won't have service over there."

"Write down the name of your hotel in London for me. I'll get you a message and directions to the plant to the hotel desk mid-Monday. I'll really owe you one if you pull this off for me."

There was no doubt that he was persistent.

"Well, okay, if you schedule the meeting at the plant like you say, I'll give it my best shot," I said, giving in to him.

"Since you're going to be meeting with the port authority person anyway," Barry said all excited, "do you think you could find out some more information for me about the security of bulk wine transport? I can give you a list of questions to ask the constable if that would help you."

"I'm leaving tomorrow morning Barry," I said. "Let me see how cooperative the manager at the Flexitank factory may be before I dive into a bunch of technical questions with the Port Authority that would show that I didn't know what in the world I was talking about."

"That sounds fine. When do you get back to Kansas City?"

"The end of next week. I'll get in touch with you a day or two after I get back."

"That'll work. Thanks Kyle," Barry said.

After a little while longer, I said my goodbyes to each of Barry's friends, left Barry the name of the hotel in London, and left to go home to pack my things for tomorrow's trip. When I finally finished filling my suitcase, I sat there and thought about the whole situation.

First meetings with two gentlemen in London for Ian Griffin, and now information gathering for Barry at two places. Did I really want to get this involved? Was I a surgeon or an amateur private investigator? Just where was all this going?

Where were those unreliable gypsies to tell you your future when you needed them?

3

LONDON, ENGLAND

On Sunday, after what seemed like forever to fly from Kansas City to Kennedy Airport in New York, we landed, and I checked my phone for messages. Caroline had left one message saying she made it home safe and sound and hoped my upcoming week was eventful. Again, not a perfect response, but it was a start.

After an enduring wait in New York, I lifted off from Kennedy Airport and made it to Heathrow outside of London not too awfully late. After a marathon wait to get my luggage, I stood in line for a taxi. The English are so orderly about how they approach things. No bozos cutting in line and cussing out the other waiting passengers like in New York. Here in London, they had an attendant who matched passengers with approaching taxis. Much more civilized, I must admit.

Finally, it was my turn to catch a cab to the city. There was moderate traffic, even on a Sunday evening. Everyone must have been scooting back home to start the workweek grind on Monday. I arrived at my hotel, exited the taxi, and tipped the cabbie well. He didn't say much on the journey into the city, but his face lit up when I presented him with his added tip.

Following a prolonged check-in at the small hotel in the northeast section of Mayfair, I made it to my room where my jet-lagged head hit the pillow in an instant, predictably out for the count after the trans-Atlantic journey.

Upon waking early Monday morning, I went for a short run, then upstairs to shower and change into proper attire for the conference. The symposium was to take place at St. Mary's Hospital, the major trauma center for central London. It was located in Paddington, just north of Hyde Park, about eight to ten minutes by cab from my hotel. After a quick bite to eat at the hotel café, I had the front desk call a cab making it to the meeting right on time.

The symposium was rather formal as compared to those held in the United States, but up to date and informative on some of the newer concepts and techniques of trauma care. Monday's scheduled lectures went a little slow, but Tuesday morning the topics of discussion were quite a bit more interesting. Still, I was rather anxious to break away mid-afternoon for my scheduled Tuesday meeting with Mr. Rogers.

Around 4:00 p.m., I left the hospital meeting room and since it was a rare sunny day in London, I decided to walk to the meeting instead of taking a cab. I headed eastward and then south, skirting the northwest corner of Hyde Park while passing The Dorchester and The Ritz hotels on the way. Both big dollar hotels. Both of them too rich for my blood. I arrived in front the Carlton Club at 4:55, just a few minutes before the scheduled meeting.

Gazing upward at the narrow brownstone façade, it looked like a building that had been a part of London forever. There was no sign anywhere to be had, only an address number. I checked the address on the slip of paper from my pocket. This was the place. I walked up the three small stairs to find a large wooden door with a massive window in it. Next to the door on the left was a keypad and an intercom button. I tried the door. Locked, as expected. I pushed the intercom button.

"May I help you?" A woman's voice came through the intercom speaker in a firm British accent.

"Yes, I am Dr. Kyle Chandler. I have an appointment scheduled to meet Mr. Clanton Rogers here at 5:00 p.m. today."

After a few moments of silence, a buzzer noise came through the speaker, and I pushed open the massive door. I entered and slowly walked to the registration desk. A middle-aged woman with a stern look peered down over her reading glasses directly at me.

"I'm Ms. Shadling. And you are Dr. Chandler?"

"Yes, Ms. Shadling," I said, trying to be as polite as possible.

"Please sign the guest logbook and be sure to note the date and time accordingly," she said as she turned the book around on the counter for me to sign. "Now let's see. Rogers, Rogers," she muttered as she used her right index finger to scroll down her appointment book. "Ah yes, here it is. He's expecting you upstairs in the Thatcher Drawing Room. That'll be up the stairs and to the right, just before the Wellington Dining Room."

"Thank you very much."

I turned to see a huge, bifurcated staircase with ornate polished black and gold ironwork ascending to the floor above. Victorian indeed. I headed up the large bending staircase and turned right at the next floor. I went down the hall where it opened into a large sitting area with chandeliers and lots of portraits of old people on the walls, all men. They must be important club members of years gone by. The room had lots of armchairs with side tables. Stuffy, but not as men's club stuffy as I expected.

Across the room in the far corner sitting in a well-padded wingback chair was a thin gentleman in his late sixties immersed in the London Financial Times newspaper. As I approached him from across the room, he lowered his paper, arose, and straightened his three-pieced tweed suit. He put his reading glasses in his coat pocket and then extended his bony right hand in my direction.

"Dr. Chandler I presume?" he asked distinctly.

"Yes. I'm Kyle Chandler. Nice to meet you Mr. Rogers. Thank you for allowing me to meet you at your nice establishment."

"Oh, I don't belong to this club directly. I'm here in London on some business this week and one of my clubs in New York has reciprocal privileges with this club. They have some fairly nice guest rooms upstairs and the location is convenient for me for this week here in London. Have a seat." He pointed to the adjacent couch.

"Let me tell you that Ian Griffin is an old friend of mine and he highly recommends you," he said.

"Thank you, sir. That's very kind of you. Can you tell me what facts you do know about this unusual situation you've encountered?"

"Ah yes. Ian said you were direct. Now let's see. The family who put this certain lot of French antiques up for sale are close friends of mine for many years in New York and wish to remain anonymous. For particular circumstances, which I won't go into, they chose to have them sold in London rather than in New York. They are well versed in selling antiques as well as artwork and have worked with Sotheby's numerous times in the past without a problem." Rogers tapped his index fingers together as he spoke.

"The pieces had been previously appraised in New York approximately two years ago. They were certified as originals from two different expert sources. According to what the family told me, the antiques included various types of furniture, a few urns, as well as chamber pots typical of the period. The entire lot was padded, packed, and sent by truck to a reputable shipping company in New York. It was then inventoried, repacked in a shipping container, and the container sealed with the proper seal and paperwork."

"I suppose you can get me copies of that necessary paperwork?" I asked.

"That shouldn't be a problem. Then, the shipment was loaded on a freighter and sailed to London without event according to the ship's log. Upon arrival in outside London at the Port of Tilbury, the container was unloaded off the freighter, placed on a truck bed and taken into the city to Sotheby's in the usual manner. There were no reports of any tampering of the seal to the container anywhere along the line of transport."

"Do we have a name of the employee or employees who unloaded the shipment at Sotheby's?" I asked.

"We do not. Sotheby's will not release any information to anyone concerning its employees. But they assure us that all employees are thoroughly vetted and have worked for them for many years."

"Of course," I said.

"Anyway, after the unloading of the lot, Sotheby's went through the usual two standard independent appraisal evaluations prior to auction. Initially, both appraisers were ready to sign off on the lot off as authentic originals. But one of them came back the next day and wanted to run further testing to determine the authenticity of several articles. As you know, I was interested in one of the pieces and I arrived by chance at Sotheby's just about when the one appraiser was explaining his position. It made me cautious, indeed."

"I would guess so," I agreed.

"Well, at that point I arranged for a third-party appraisal at the recommendation of a close friend of mine to come in and evaluate the piece I was pursuing. He spent quite a long time going over the piece and then took three more days of research to reach a conclusion. His final analysis showed the piece to be a more recent replication, albeit an excellent one of a true 1700s French original. I backed out of the auction accordingly."

"Yes, I see. What happened next?"

"Sotheby's got involved and the usual hubris came to the forefront. Next their legal department got involved, and you know what that means. The pointing of fingers began as they claimed that no way it could be their fault. Finally, they issued a decree that the whole lot of antiques was wrongfully declared as originals and that my friends in New York were at fault. Very quaint move," he said.

"Well, that's usually the case when massive Goliath goes against insignificant David."

"Quite so," he said. "Where do you suggest we go from here?"

I put my index finger up to my lips and thought carefully before I spoke.

"As I see it, we have two options. Option one would be to challenge Sotheby's determination that the whole lot was wrongly declared as reproductions instead of originals. I fear that such an option would turn into a total fiasco since their legal department will bog things down forever, despite what financial means your friends in New York may have."

I rubbed my chin. "Option two is a bit trickier but still a possibility. The only real deterrent to being bullied by a large firm is the possibility of losing a client to your strongest competition. Your friends in New York should talk to the representative they have been dealing with at Sotheby's in London. Have your friends tell them that they definitely now have second thoughts with Sotheby's ability to auction French period antiques, and that they are moving the entire lot back to Christie's in New York for proper pre-sale evaluation and handling of such a sale. My bet is that Sotheby's would rather lose the one questionable piece than lose the commission of the whole auction lot of antiques."

"That sounds like our best plan of action at this point," he said. "Should we proceed right away?'

"Give me a few days before you have your friends in New York do anything. I still need to follow up with the chief constable at the Port of Tilbury to look into the possibility of switching original pieces for some highly crafted reproductions at the port. Leave me a phone number where you can be reached, and I'll get back to you as soon as I can."

Mr. Rogers reached into his inner coat pocket and removed a business card and a pen, jotting down a phone number on the back of the card.

"My office number is on the front. On the back is my mobile phone number. Contact me as soon as you know something."

"I surely will. Here is my card if you need to reach me," I replied, likewise writing my cell phone number on the back.

"Happy hunting," he said as we both arose at the same time to shake hands before my leaving.

I nodded as I looked back at him, and then turned around and headed down the stairway. I also made sure to register my exit time in the logbook before leaving.

"Thank you, Ms. Shadling," I said to her as I turned to leave.

The authoritative receptionist again looked down her nose over her reading glasses at me. She offered a minimal nod at best and turned back to whatever important thing she was doing. I know I wouldn't want someone like her bird-dogging me the whole time in London over some silly logbook signature.

Upon arrival outside, I cautiously looked both ways and then quickly behind me. At this point, I was glad that no gorillas had interrupted my brief meeting.

Happy Hunting indeed. We'll see about that.

4

LONDON – FOBBING, ESSEX

The rest of the day went well, as I did a little sightseeing and had dinner in yet another pub. It was certainly different than in the US. The ale was warm, the food was plain, but atmosphere was very enjoyable as the crowd rooted for their regional "football" team on the "telly." Before turning in for the evening, I spoke with the front desk at my hotel about arranging a private car and driver for my use the next afternoon. They assured me that it would all be taken care of as I requested.

On Wednesday morning, I repeated my routine of getting up early for a run, showered, and made it to the symposium with time to spare. The morning lectures were well presented and pertinent to what I saw every day at work. I even wrote down a few things to look into when I got back to Kansas City. Fortunately, the scheduled afternoon lectures were not specifically related to my surgical practice, so I really didn't feel bad about skipping them for my two appointments.

After the morning sessions, I walked outside the main entrance of St. Mary's Hospital. Right on time as they said it would, a man in a small dark sedan pulled over to the curb and hopped out. He was dressed in baggy, old clothes. No formal chauffeur outfit here.

"You must be Dr. Chandler," the gentleman said loudly in a heavy British accent.

Cockney perhaps, but I was no accent expert.

"I am. And who might you be?" I asked a little nervously.

"My name's Alfie. I'm from the auto service your hotel arranged for this afternoon. They told me to say that the password was Trauma."

That was a relief. That was the word I had told the front desk person to relay to the car service. Since my escapade, a few months ago with the missing stock certificates, I'd grown a little more suspicious of any unexpected wayward gorillas, regardless of size.

"Excellent," I said as I started to get in the back seat.

"The back seat is kind of cramped. Hop in the front instead and we'll be off."

I did as I was told and buckled up.

"The hotel told me you wanted to be carted east of the city, am I right?"

"That's correct. I have an appointment at 3:30 p.m. at the Hawthorne Containers factory, which is east of the Port of Tilbury in Essex. Do you know where that is?

"No sir, but I'm sure I can find it."

"Here's the directions from the port to their factory that I got faxed to me," I said as I handed him a folded sheet of paper.

"Take A13 east of the port, go about ten kilometers. Exit south at High Road and then a kilometer and a half until you reach the gate of the left. No problem," Alfie read out loud.

"That meeting should take only about thirty to forty-five minutes," I continued. "Then I have another appointment scheduled with one of the senior constables back at the Port of Tilbury Police at 4:30 p.m. You think you get me to those meetings on time?"

"Traffic's a boozer this time of day. But we got plenty of time leaving this early. I know a couple of byways that will get you there faster with time to spare," he said confidently. "Meeting with a senior constable, eh? Are you some kind of detective or something?"

"No, not me. Just meeting with this officer for a friend of mine. About a shipping issue."

"Sounds important if you made it all the way over here from the States."

"Not really that big of a deal," I said, trying to downplay my task at hand. "Do you know of a place on the way out of town where we can stop for a couple of sandwiches for both of us?"

"I know just the place, governor. It has fish and chips that melt in your mouth," he said as he pulled away from the curb.

We chatted on a variety of subjects as he drove us out of London to more of the countryside east of town. He explained that he and his wife were saving up for something and he appreciated the extra cash he'd make for driving me around. He wouldn't say what it was they were saving for, but I could tell that it seemed important to him. Alfie was a lot more talkative than me, but an altogether nice guy.

When we were out of the city, he stopped his sedan at a small roadside tavern where upon entering, he instantly started up an enthusiastic conversation with the owner that he obviously knew well. We each ordered what we wanted to eat and sat at a booth waiting for our food. He had made good time taking backroads instead of the congested larger byways, so we had time to eat there instead of taking it to eat on the way. The beef sandwich I had turned out to be really delicious, but I was glad I passed on the greasy fish and chips Alfie so heartily enjoyed.

After I paid the bill, we resumed our journey eastward. We drove past the exit to the Port of Tilbury and traveled a few more kilometers until we reached the turn off to go south.

When we exited the main road, we went a short distance, and the factory was there just like Barry said it would be. Their company sign was next to a large gate with a guardhouse on the left. It fronted a moderate-sized compound with a surrounding high wire fence with razor sharp barbed wire on top.

Ominous. Looked like they weren't too keen on visitors.

We turned into the entrance as Alfie eased his sedan up to the guardhouse. As we stopped, Alfie rolled down his window and turned to me to like I was to talk to the guard instead of him since this was my deal. I leaned over to speak through Alfie's window and told the guard I had an appointment with the plant manager, a Mr. Garrolo, at 3:30 this afternoon. The guard looked at his clipboard and made a check to his list. He handed us two visitors' ID cards, told us to clip them to our shirt collars to be visible at all times, then instructed us where to park our vehicle when we drove up next to the plant buildings.

After the guard pushed the button to lift the gate barrier, Alfie pulled through the gate and drove down the road towards a larger building on the left. He parked by a single door. Ten to twelve autos were parked in the surrounding lot.

"You stay here. I'll be back in twenty to thirty minutes at most, "I said.

"Whatever you say, governor."

I exited Alfie's car and walked up to the door pulling it open. Inside was a reception area with a middle-aged woman speaking on the phone. As I walked in, she gestured with her index finger for me wait as she finished her phone call.

After hanging up the phone, she gave me a big smile. "Good afternoon, how may I help you?" She spoke with a strong English accent.

"Hi there, my name is Kyle Chandler. I have an appointment with your plant manager, a Mr. Garrolo, at 3:30 this afternoon."

"Yes sir, he's in his office expecting you. Let me show the way." She rose from her chair and then asked, "Can I get you a cup of tea?"

"No ma'am. Thank you for asking." I followed her down a hall to an office on the right.

As I entered the room, the man staring intently at his computer screen instantly arose and offered his right hand across the desk to me.

"Welcome Dr. Chandler, I'm Ben Garrolo, plant manager. Have a seat," he said pointing to an armchair in front of his desk.

"Thank you, Mr. Garrolo, for seeing me on such short notice."

"I've spoken with your friend Barry Rosenberg by phone multiple times in the last two weeks. He's quite thorough and approaches his business with exhaustive detail. He expressed an interest in importing wines from France to the States using our new bladder technology."

"Yes, he has a growing wine and spirits business back in Kansas City and is a really sharp guy. I've got to say that in this situation, I'm only the messenger to convey the information you give me about your product to him to see if it is the right fit for his growing enterprise."

"I thoroughly understand, Dr. Chandler. He mentioned that you were a doctor. What kind?"

"I am a trauma surgeon. I put people back together after car wrecks and other accidents. I'm here at a trauma surgery symposium at St. Mary's Hospital in London."

"Sounds ghoulish. I'm not the strongest stomach when it comes to blood." He chuckled, patting his rotund midsection.

"It's an acquired taste I assure you," I said with a small smile.

"Let me go through this packet of information that we give to prospective customers," he said as he handed me a thick packet of printed information.

This manager seemed to know his stuff about their product that was transforming the bulk liquid transportation industry. He spoke for ten to fifteen minutes covering the entire subject of his product and where the company was headed. He stated that the bladders were made here at this plant and then constructed in their frames inside each container at a warehouse in the Netherlands before leaving to be filled at wineries in France.

He mentioned how Hawthorne Containers was owned by the conglomerate Evolution Industries in New York. He said their cash infusion into their company really had started the upward progression of the company's stock price.

I smiled and tried to look interested. Fine business details were not my strength.

"Could I have a look around the plant before I go; see how you make the bladders?" I asked innocently.

"I'm afraid that is one thing that I cannot do for you Dr. Chandler, particularly due to British labor safety regulations. I would get into boiling water with the labor unions if you were allowed out on the factory floor, even with a hard hat and goggles."

"That's okay Mr. Garrolo. I won't take any more of your time. You've been very helpful, and I'm sure Barry will be impressed with the details of your operation."

I stood, shook the plant manager's hand, and headed down the hallway towards the reception area. Before I reached it, I thought of one more question to ask Mr. Garrolo. Should I go back and bother the busy plant manager? Following a moment of deliberation, I figured why not. After all, I had come all this way to see him for Barry. Holding my packet of information, I turned around and headed back down the hallway towards his office.

Just before I reached the entrance to his office, I heard Mr. Garrolo saying loudly on the phone, "Are you sure we are out of them?"

I stopped in the hallway waiting for him to finish his phone conversation before interrupting him.

"Well, if we are out of the extra sleeves, then we're out of them," he said. "We'll have to wait until the next shipment comes in Friday before we can go back to adding on the extra compartment to the bladders. I'll let you know when the shipment is in route."

I decided that he was too busy to bother. I turned around and made my way to the reception area again. As I walked to the front door, I wished the receptionist a good afternoon and made my way back out to Alfie's sedan.

"How was your meeting?" Alfie asked earnestly.

"It was about as I expected. Their company seems to be on the rise. The plant manager knew his stuff. My friend back in the US who asked me to talk to them should be satisfied with their product."

"You know, looks can be deceiving," he said as he started his auto.

"What do you mean?" I asked him.

"Nothing. Shall we go?" he asked.

"Sure. On to the Port of Tilbury," I said as Alfie turned the car around to head to the gate exit.

"Whatever you say, governor."

When we arrived at the guardhouse, we gave the visitor ID cards back to the guard. Unlike before, we drove in silence to our next destination.

Looks can be deceiving. What was that all about?

5

PORT OF TILBURY, ESSEX – LONDON

We arrived at the Port of Tilbury Police Department just shy of 4:30 p.m. As we drove to the main gate, we told the guard that I had an appointment with the Senior Constable of the Port of Tilbury Police. After checking his appointment list, he let us drive through.

"There you go my good man," Alfie said as we rolled into the parking lot.

"Thank you very much. If you could wait right here. I don't know how long this meeting will take."

"No problem, sir. I might catch a few winks in the process if you don't mind," he said as he pulled his cap down and leaned back to relax.

I left the sedan and strode up a few stairs to the front doors. Upon entering the building, there was a large partition wall and a thick glass window with a microphone built into it. Behind the counter, a pleasant administrative assistant looked up at me.

"May I help you?"

"Yes. My name is Kyle Chandler and I have an appointment with Senior Constable Colin Butterworth at 4:30 p.m."

Looking down at her appointment book, she said, "Yes, I have you down right here. He's away from his desk at the moment but should be back momentarily. Could you have a seat until he returns?"

I gave her a nod with a pleasant smile and had a seat on one of the metal chairs. Standard government issue. It was the kind that was meant for police interrogations to make the suspect as uncomfortable as possible so that he would want to confess. Oh well.

After about ten minutes, a broad-shouldered policeman with a large frame came through the secure back door, took off his overcoat, and pointed to the assistant at the front desk. She turned and spoke through the microphone to me.

"Chief Butterworth will see you now. If you will step up to the secure door, please."

I did as I was told. A loud buzzer sounded, and I pushed the heavy door open. I stepped forward where a younger constable pointed for me to walk through the metal detector. As I did, of course the buzzer went off.

"Please empty all of your pockets including your cell phone," he commanded. Once again, I did as I was told, and he finished by waving an electric wand around all parts of my body to check for anything suspicious.

"You're all clear. Please follow me."

I gathered my things and followed him to an office that opened up on large windows overlooking the port. Behind the desk was Chief Butterworth vigorously writing on some typed pages.

"Have a seat. I'll be with you in a jiffy," he stated as he pointed to the chair in front of his desk.

Once again, I did as I was told. This was starting to be a repeating theme.

"Sorry for the delay. It couldn't be helped," he said as

he arose from his chair and extended his hand across the desk in my direction.

"Not a problem, Chief Butterworth," I said as I stood and shook his large hand.

"And how may I help a gentleman who has come such a long way?" He eased back in his large office chair.

"Well Chief, I came here to speak with you at the advice of a close friend of mine concerning some valuable French period antiques. I'm sure you are familiar with the recent inquiry from Sotheby's about a certain shipment from New York—a specific lot of French period antiques that were shipped to London to be auctioned at their main facility."

"Yes. I've got the file right here before me. I've been through a thorough interview with their legal department more than once recently," he said, a scowl on his face.

"I understand. Would you mind if I asked you some additional questions about their inquiry?"

"If you must," he responded flatly.

"On the afternoon of the fifteenth of last month the container shipment arrived at this facility from my client from New York, first stopping at the Port of Rotterdam three days prior to that."

"That is what the manifest states," Chief Butterworth said as he glanced down at paperwork on his desk.

"Upon arrival here, all containers from that specific freighter were disembarked portside, divided, and directed to their next destinations, is that correct?"

"That is correct, according to the paperwork in front of me."

"Chief, who runs all this vast complex?" I asked.

"The Port of Tilbury was privatized in 1992 by Firth Ports Limited based out of Edinburgh. The Port of Tilbury Police is still responsible for all of the security."

"Can you explain to me the procedure on how the container holding the French period pieces in question would be unloaded and then reloaded for transportation to

Sotheby's?"

"Certainly. Let's take a walk, and I'll give you the tour."

We grabbed out coats, and I had to sign a visitor roster with the date and time for their records. Chief Butterworth gave me a visitor badge to clip on my coat for all to see and a hard safety hat to wear. He then led the way down to one of the docks. When we arrived next to a freighter, he began to explain.

"Prior to unloading the container off the freighter, its seals and ID number are checked against our master list by the crew shift foreman aboard ship. Once the container has been signed off to be unloaded, a crane unloads it onto an awaiting empty truck bed. The container is then driven into a nearby warehouse. Inside that warehouse, the seal is recorded by bar code and opened by the warehouse chief. The individual wrapped pieces are again checked against the master list and each piece destined for, in this case Sotheby's, is individually scanned by bar code and loaded onto a waiting Sotheby's truck."

We next walked into an adjacent warehouse.

"Sotheby's insists having one of their senior security officers present in each transfer, and he double checks the unloading against his own shipment list," he said as he pointed to the unloading crew. "After completion of the shipment with additional packing, Sotheby's places a new seal with a new bar code on it. Once their truck leaves our facility, at this point the goods are under the receiving party's jurisdiction."

"So, the possibility of switching original pieces which are individually wrapped with ID number and bar code, for replications is close to nonexistent," I said.

"As you know, it's not impossible, but highly unlikely. Security is extremely tight getting onto and inside this facility. As you might not know, The Port of Tilbury Police is the oldest police force in this country, over 200 years old. We do have many occurrences during the year of attempted illegal contraband through our port. And I can say with thirty-three years of experience, very, very few instances get through our surveillance."

"What are some of the ways that smugglers, I guess you would call them that, try to avoid getting detected?"

"I can attest that I have seen just about every possible way known to man of getting contraband through illegally. Some of them genuinely creative I must admit," he said, smiling. "Stuffed inside automobile panels, hidden in stuffed animals, inside the intestines of live animals, welded inside electronics, hidden in food, including canned or dry goods One guy tried to hide drugs in the engine of an automobile at the bottom of a large grain shipment. The stories are endless."

"I get your point."

He turned to leave the warehouse. We retraced our steps back to the dock where several containers were getting their loads inspected prior to their containers going onboard a freighter. One of the containers had the rear doors open with an inspector on a mobile bucket truck searching the contents. He was carefully looking over a filled, large bladder within a frame occupying nearly the entire volume of the container.

"What exactly is that huge bladder looking device?" I asked the constable.

"That's one of the newer ways to transport large volumes of all types of liquids. It's called a Flexitank. It's a collapsible one-time use bladder made of tough plastic material that can hold up to 24,000 liters. I believe those containers had their bladders filled with wine at wineries in France. Most bulk wine from there is shipped to China or the US these days. Most of it from France comes through our port on the way to the US."

That was it. That was what I had just discussed with the plant manager. That was the exact wine transport bladder thing that Barry was talking about at the wine tasting in Kansas City. I decided to play dumb and see how much information I could get without sounding too idiotic.

"Really, how interesting. Are they very expensive to manufacture?" I asked.

"I don't believe so. They are supposed to be cheaper to make than the large stainless-steel ISO containers they've been using for years. Plus, you don't have problems having to clean them over and over since they are a one-time use. One of the major suppliers for worldwide use is Hawthorne Containers. They manufacture them at their plant just down the road from here."

"Interesting."

I thought about telling Chief Butterworth the whole thing about my friend Barry wanting to import bulk wine to the US, about just visiting the plant manager where they made these bladders, but I decided against it. Better to keep it simple with my interest only on the antiques shipping inquiry. I had gotten enough information about security at this port from the Senior Constable to ease Barry's mind about future shipping issues.

As I watched the inspector in the mobile bucket truck who was looking into the container inspecting the surface of the large wine filled bladder, an unusual observation entered my mind.

"Chief Butterworth, who puts together these bladders in their frame before they are filled with wine in France?" I asked.

"It's my understanding that the bladders down the road at Hawthorne Containers are manufactured at the plant there. They take the folded bladders somewhere else to be assembled inside the containers with the supporting frame before they are trucked to the wineries in France. Why do you ask?"

"No reason. Very interesting. Well, Chief Butterworth, I've taken enough of your time. Thank you for your information on the shipping security and the informative tour. That should do it unless something new comes to the forefront."

"Let me walk you to the office so you can sign out," he said.

After saying our goodbyes, I walked out front to the parking lot. It was a little past sunset as I approached my driver's parked car. There was Alfie fast asleep in his auto with his head down resting against the steering wheel. I got in the front passenger seat and closed the door. He was still asleep. I gently shook him, and he came to life.

"What?" he said in a groggy state.

"Alfie. Time to go.

"Whatever you say governor."

We zoomed away and made it back to London in record time. I told Alfie about what I had seen at the port while the senior constable gave me a tour. When he dropped me off, I paid him the prearranged fee for his time as well as a tip for his cooperation. He was very appreciative so before he left, I pressed the issue a bit further with him as a new idea struck me.

"Alfie, how you'd like to make a few more pounds in the next few days by driving me around?" I asked as I leaned into his open window.

"That would be bloody brilliant," he responded quickly. "Me and the missus sure could use the extra cash. Let me call me the boss, but I'm sure he'll give the thumbs up."

"Give me your card, and I'll leave you a message about what time you need to be here to get me in the morning. I'll prepay you in the morning for your time the next couple of days."

"Whatever you say, governor."

I went up to my hotel room and had a decision to make. The trauma symposium was supposed to end at noon tomorrow. My flight out of Heathrow was scheduled for tomorrow evening, finally getting back to Kansas City Friday morning. I didn't have to be back at work until the next Wednesday morning. I had previously planned on spending Monday and Tuesday in Kansas City catching up on paperwork and chores.

After visiting with Chief Butterworth, I was fairly satisfied with the conclusion that there was no way to switch the French antique originals with reproductions once they had been shipped to London and then to Sotheby's. The security guidelines at the port here were so stringent that it would be a very low probability for a switch of the original antique piece for a forgery to occur on this end. The switch had to have been made in New York before the antiques were shipped to London.

The reason I needed to stay a little longer was not the antiques case that Ian had me tracking down in London. It was something that Alfie had said when we were leaving the Flexitank plant that was really jabbing me at the back of my brain. It really should have meant nothing to me.

But it did.

After a moment of weighing my options, I got on the hotel phone and changed my flight to late Sunday afternoon. Changing my flight wouldn't make me miss any days at work I reasoned. I called down to the front desk and asked if I could extend my stay until Sunday. They were more than willing to take my money at a higher weekend rate, of course. That gave me from after the symposium on Thursday afternoon to Sunday afternoon to get a better grip on things here.

I then left Ian a message on his phone that I would check in early next week after I got back. I said that there would be a few more expenses on my account to file with him. I also called the number Caroline gave me and left a message for Mr. Clarke at Christie's that I would be coming by after lunch tomorrow for a brief meeting if he had a minute open in his busy schedule.

I always said that if you are going to do something out of the ordinary, it's better to ask for forgiveness than to ask for permission.

6

ST. JAMES'S, LONDON

On Thursday morning, I repeated my routine of an early run before grabbing a bite to eat and heading to the symposium. I had left a message with Alfie last night to pick me up to take me there. He was right on time as prescribed. The lectures for the final symposium day were more than a little flat, and I was ready to leave when the noon hour concluded the session. I started walking southeast in the general direction of Christie's. On the way, I grabbed a sandwich at local deli and took it with me.

As I was eating my sandwich while sitting on a park bench in Hyde Park, I kept wondering, *Why do I keep thinking about those large shipping bladders that I saw at the Port of Tilbury? What is so confounding about a large fluid container? I had enough information about them to give to Barry, didn't I?*

So many loose ends.

It was another clear day in London, so I decided to

make my way to Christie's on foot. It took a good thirty to thirty-five minutes walking to reach the upscale section of St. James's near The Mall. Along the way, I passed lots of expensive shops and discreet private clubs. The people around this section of London must all have rich relatives to afford this kind of lifestyle. I knew that this was way out of my league.

When I reached the large stone façade of Christie's on King St., I stepped up to the large wooden doors and pushed the intercom button.

"How may I help you?" a pleasant but heavily English accented female voice called out from the speaker.

"This is Dr. Kyle Chandler. I'm here to see Mr. Sebastian Clarke, the Head of Estates, Appraisals & Valuations," I said back at the speaker.

The door lock buzzed so I opened the wooden door and proceeded towards the receptionist.

"Could you point me the way to Mr. Clarke's office?" I asked with a forced smile.

"Take the lift up to the fourth floor." She pointed down the hall. "When you exit the lift, turn right, and go all the way to the end of the hall. Is he expecting you?"

"I believe so," I mumbled as I quickly walked down the hall to the elevator. I didn't really tell a lie, just a little mistruth that I didn't have an exact scheduled appointment time.

After following the receptionist's directions, I arrived at the end of the hall to an ornate carved door with an intricate design of stained-glass windowpanes. I opened the door and confidently stepped up to the clerical assistant's desk. The woman pointed her index finger upward indicating for me to wait while she finished her phone conversation.

"Good afternoon. I am Dr. Kyle Chandler here to meet with Mr. Clarke," I said as soon as she hung up.

"I'm sorry, I don't have you down for a scheduled appointment," she said, scanning her appointment book.

"You'll have to call back and make an appointment sometime in the future. Mr. Clarke has a very busy daily agenda scheduled weeks in advance."

"I previously left a message stating that I was visiting from the United States and needed to discuss an important matter with him. Is there any time at all this afternoon that is available for me to meet with him?"

"As I stated before, he has a very busy agenda today just like every day. There are no openings available for you to meet with him. If you would please..." she said as the door behind her to Mr. Clarke's office opened.

"Mrs. Blake, what time am I scheduled to meet the curator of the Wallace Collection this afternoon? Oh, hello there. I'm Sebastian Clarke," he said as he stepped forward with his hand extended.

"Nice to meet you. I'm Kyle Chandler. I left you a message concerning a certain private matter that I would like to discuss with you."

"Ah yes. You're the gentleman Caroline Martinelli rang me about last week. She said you would be calling. You're a surgeon. Trauma surgery or something of that sort?

"Mr. Clarke," his assistant interjected. "You're going to be late for your one o'clock meeting."

"Yes sir, that's me," I said a bit loudly to get back his attention. "But I need your advice about a completely different subject. French period antiques."

"Well, let's have a short chat right now before I have to leave. Mrs. Blake, have them pull my car around back and then call my one o'clock appointment. Tell them I'll be there in ten minutes. Step into my office Dr. Chandler."

I followed him back into his office and stood in front of a large wingback chair as he made his way around his desk to his chair. It was like I stepped into a hoarder's haven. There were stacks of books, magazines, piles of notes everywhere. On his desk, crammed in bookshelves, on the floor, on side tables.

"Excuse the appearance, I've just a few projects I'm

working on at the moment," as he spread his arm in a motion around the room. "Have a seat."

We both sat, and I began my inquiry before his assistant could return to tear him away.

"First off, I appreciate you giving me a minute of your busy schedule. I don't think Caroline probably told you any of the details, but I am investigating for a friend the possibility of a specific lot of French period antiques being switched for high quality reproductions. Ever seen or heard of such a thing?"

"Ah, yes, Caroline Martinelli. How is she?" he asked as he veered away from my question. "We chat every couple of months. Sounds like she's doing quite well for herself in her new store space. I'm afraid I gave her a bit of a shock throwing her into the lion's den when she was here beginning her training. She adapted quickly and took to it like a duck to water. She said you were looking for leads to what you just mentioned in her phone message last week."

"Yes sir, she is doing quite well in her business. Now about the possibility of switching antiques?" I emphasized knowing my time with the absent-minded professor was short.

"Well, characteristically, most French period pieces up for auction these days come from private collections or wealthy patrons in London, New York, Paris or any of the larger cities throughout Europe. They are transported by a variety of methods, although shipping by truck over land is still the least expensive." He twisted a gold pen in his fingers as he explained.

"On the Continent, most shipments end up at the Port of Rotterdam since it's one of the busiest ports in the world," he said. "I'm not that familiar with that port's shipping security procedures, but those shipments do make their way to us through the Port of Tilbury in the UK. I am quite familiar dealing with the Port of London Authority for many years. And I will tell you that the chance of switching items in a container or switching containers at the Port of Tilbury is almost nonexistent with the current security precautions in place. We send our own representative out to the port with our own bar code tagging system to double check each shipment inventory with the port shift supervisor."

"And these employees are well vetted for this kind of duty?" I asked.

"Most certainly so. Several have our highest security level qualification. Many have been with us over twenty years and have become quite knowledgeable in all types of antiques, artwork, and antiquities."

My suspicion antennae quietly went up while maintaining a blank poker face.

"And once you take possession of the shipment at the port, what happens next?"

"Each piece of the shipment is logged in by a hand-held scanner and transported by truck directly to our secure holding area on the first floor here at Christie's. Each piece is then photographed, catalogued, and transferred to the planned lots for future auctions. Each holding area is specifically adjusted to temperature and humidity levels required depending on the type of goods present."

"And there is limited access to employees to these holding areas?"

"Most assuredly so," he said proudly. "Mix-ups are not tolerated at *this* auction house."

"I already interviewed one of the chief constables at the Port of Tilbury, and he was quite informative about security procedures for receiving and cataloguing pieces for transfer to the larger auction houses, such as Sotheby's."

"Yes, well I'm sure they do a fine job also," he said with a grin and a hint of sarcasm in his voice.

"Caroline indicated that with your vast experience in fine art and antiques, as well as your connections in the auction world, that you might possibly have a few guesses who could pull off such a swap of original antique pieces for high quality reproductions."

"Dr. Chandler, I have worked with the Fine Art and

Antiques Division of Scotland Yard on various theft cases for many years, but I don't pretend to know more about potential art and antiques criminals than they do. If there was such a switch that occurred in this or any case that involved one of the major auction houses, it would have to be most certainly from within. And that would be very difficult with all the security procedures in place these days."

That pretty much sealed the deal with me that the switch of the antique piece in question had to have been made in New York before the antiques were shipped to London. I could tell that I was starting to bark up the wrong tree, so I decided to cut my losses and wrap it up.

"Well, thank you so much for your time, Mr. Clarke. It's been a pleasure speaking with you. I'll be sure and tell Caroline hello for you." I stood to leave.

"Yes, please do. She is quite a unique individual. It's rare that you find someone who is a fast learner who can adapt to a changing situation on the fly. I really don't probe into other people's lives, but you would be making a large mistake by letting that woman get away," he said with a twinkle in his eye. "You should go by and see her previous landlord while you are here. A Mrs. Iris Kettleman. Very nice lady. She occasionally rents out the upper rooms of her small flat not too far from here. Rents only to top quality people. I got Caroline in touch with her when she first arrived. They really hit it off together despite the difference in ages. I believe it's north of Piccadilly in Mayfair, just north of Green Park."

"That would be great," I said, somewhat surprised.

"Ah yes, here's the address."

He copied it down from his overstuffed Rolodex onto a slip of paper and handed it to me. "Thank you again sir."

"Good luck on your search. I hope you find what you are looking for. Mrs. Blake, I'm off," he screamed as he headed out the door in front of me.

Yeah, I sure hope he was right about my search.

7

MANHATTAN, NEW YORK CITY

"Is there anything else I can get for you Mr. Hauser?" the executive assistant asked before turning to leave the large corner office suite.

"No, that will be all for now Mrs. Pennington," the hard driving CEO said.

"Remember, Mr. Sawyer from Security is still holding on line two."

"Right," he muttered.

Not enough hours in the day with too many opportunities to grow and sell so many companies beyond belief. That was how Philip Hauser approached each day. He had taken the helm of the conglomerate Evolution Industries in New York four years ago. Since that time, he had expanded the company's holdings, bought many profitable companies, and sold off the dog companies that were dragging down the bottom line.

When Hauser took over almost four years ago, he knew

right then and there that if someone had to control how business was to be conducted, it might as well be him. Forget all those pantywaists with their consciences. The art of business was like the art of war. Take your opponent by surprise, step on their throat, run right through them, and declare victory before they knew what hit them. He loved it when the business publications called him "the Blitzkrieg of Big Business."

He punched the phone button down. "Philip Hauser here," he said.

"Mr. Hauser, this is Bruce Sawyer from Corporate Security down here on the seventh floor."

"Yes, Mr. Sawyer, what can I do for you?"

"I wanted to let you know that we are going to be installing the updated security cameras at the companies that you recommended at the last budget meeting of the board of directors. It will take a couple of weeks to sync the installed monitors with our central control panel here in this building, but as you already know, we will be able to monitor the security of some our remote site companies from here once the final installation is completed."

"That's wonderful Sawyer. Please keep me informed when the entire system is up and running. Have a good day," the impatient CEO said.

"Thank you, sir," the security chief responded to the click of the phone line being disconnected.

What a struggle it was every day to deal with such inferior intellects like his chief of security. They had such a limited scope of what could be achieved in business. Employees for the most part could not grasp a sense of the big picture of running a business.

Hauser was proud of the previous acquisition of Hawthorne Containers he'd pushed with his company's board. With the additional capital that Evolution Industries infused into this company that made the Flexitank bladders, their investment propelled Hawthorne Containers to be one of the leaders in market share of the bulk liquid transportation industry. Hauser knew that the demand for the one-time use flexible bladders for bulk liquid transport was steadily increasing. Especially in the wine import industry. This demand was definitely driving the stock price of Hawthorne Containers upward.

Hauser smiled to himself knowing he could turn unnoticed opportunities into gold just like Midas. If the world only knew the real truth.

The CEO believed that in business, like any relationship, it always paid to be two steps ahead of whomever you dealt with. He thought that would be the case in relationships with the opposite sex, but he found out in that particular exercise there were no rules that made any sense.

Hauser had been married to a daughter of a prominent New York businessman at the beginning of his ascent to the top of the business world several years ago. It was a carefully calculated relationship where he played all the right moves like an established chess master. First, the courtship of the daughter and then the family. Dinner in the City during the week and summer weekends at her parents in the Hamptons. Union with a gorgeous offspring of a prominent New York family checked all the boxes in terms of status and position.

Hauser's matrimony put him in prime position to sprint to the front of the line of the power elite in the business world of New York. The premeditated relationship brought him all the right clubs, the right connections, and the potential access to in-law financial backing.

For the first couple of years of the marriage, the busy CEO could tolerate his wife's dalliance in multiple charitable organizations. Hauser would silently put up with the increasing number of society events that she kept dragging him to. He even enjoyed the occasional sexual escapades that at first he dictated. But as time wore on, not even the uninspiring physical contact with that woman would keep his attention. Unfortunately, he found out that a socialite wife that did not bow down to his ever-demanding high profile schedule was not an asset to his determined business ascension.

After an eventual nasty divorce settlement, he knew that the only way to make it to the top of the food chain was to stay continually ruthless and leave female relationships scattered where they fell along the way. Building his business empire came first. Money would lead to power. That meant his approach to his personal social life definitely had to change from then on.

Hauser kept an exquisite apartment on the Upper East Side, but since his divorce, he made it a point to never bring female companions to his residence. There was no way that that he was going to let one of them interfere with his business or his domicile. On the occasion where he needed temporary female attention, he had a list of several young, attractive social climbing women to pick from. Each of them would drop whatever they were doing to be seen in public with him and be treated lavishly at a moment's notice.

Hauser's system for this routine was polished beyond belief. He would usually meet his choice for evening companionship at some high-end restaurant that normally took weeks to months to get a reservation. Hauser had an insider in the restaurant industry that could get him in wherever he wanted to dine on short notice. The CEO used this connection to his extreme benefit.

Just another advantage to being two steps ahead at all times, he mused to himself.

After a lengthy show of expensive wines and fine dining, he and his evening companion would catch a cab to one of the luxury hotels where he would be greeted at the door by name. From there, they would personally be shown to one of the special suites that luxury hotels held back from the general public. After opening a bottle of vintage champagne that was already chilled in the suite, the rest of the evening would consist of whatever Hauser dictated. Nothing extreme, but all for the satisfaction of a well deserving CEO he reasoned. The best part was that the whole evening was usually written off as a necessary company expense.

For Hauser, completing the self-serving tryst would not be the end of a productive evening. In most cases, he would wait until his companion had fallen asleep in the bedroom. The driven CEO would then take his briefcase into the other room and analyze spreadsheets on potential takeover companies until the wee hours of the morning.

Hauser continued to stay true to his tenacious climb in the business world. There was no way the competition, extraneous women, or social functions were going to keep him from success when it came to business matters. No way. Ever.

8

MAYFAIR, LONDON

After leaving Christie's, I stopped into a local pub to plan my next move. After ordering a pint of ale, I took a deep breath. In order to move forward with what to do next, I needed to step back from the current situation and reassess my options. As I concentrated, I wrote the following on the back of a bar napkin:

Fact #1: I was supposed to be staying in London Thursday afternoon through Sunday afternoon to figure out for a client if and how a shipment of French period antiques got tampered with and partially switched to very high-quality reproductions.

Fact #2: I had talked to the necessary port authorities, as well as an antiques expert at Christie's, and had run up against a dead end against any likelihood of container tampering at the port here in England.

Fact #3: There had to be an alternative way for someone to get to the antiques in transit and switch them for reproductions. Most likely it was before they left New York. But how?

Fact #4: I had gathered information for my friend Barry about this amazing way to transport large volumes of liquids using a large type of bladder that I had spoken with the manufacturer about and also observed in person at the port.

That's clear enough; right?

But why did these liquid transport bladders create a constant nagging suspicion in me that something about this was *just not righ*t? Are real private investigators bothered by such thoughts I wondered? Somehow, two and two here was not equaling four.

I pondered on these facts for a while and decided that maybe on the way back to my hotel I would stop off and try to speak with Caroline's previous landlady that Sebastian Clarke spoke so highly of. But what good what that do?

Plenty.

According to Mr. Clarke at Christie's, this elderly landlady adored Caroline when she stayed with her during her training in London years ago. If I went and visited this nice older woman, maybe I could find out more about Caroline. Find out what Mrs. Kettleman thought about her. Whether Caroline was the real thing. Not just for now, but possibly forever.

Did I actually just think that? I hadn't even let such thoughts like that enter my mind in such a very long time. Not since Molly.

I decided that I should track this former landlady of Caroline's down and see what information I could get from her to help me decide about Caroline. There was this gut feeling in me that it felt was going to lead to something.

Leaving the pub, I found a red phone booth on the street and left a message on Alfie's phone machine that I wouldn't need him until later in the afternoon. I said I would call him back then.

I took off walking and made my way to Green Park, past The Ritz, and then down Piccadilly until I got to White

Horse Street. Turning right, I walked past office buildings until I entered an all-too-retro neighborhood of Mayfair. Instead of posh men's clubs and fancy five-star hotels, it was a place of small local businesses trying to make a go of it. I checked the slip of paper for the address that Sebastian Clarke had given me. After walking a little further, I ended up in front of a bright red painted door of a residence that was in between an Indian restaurant and a dry cleaners, with a hair salon next to that. A complete oddity of mixed cultures.

I pushed the intercom button and got the voice of an elderly, but forceful woman.

"Can I help you?" the voice asked.

"Yes ma'am. My name is Kyle Chandler and my friend Caroline Martinelli wanted me to come by and say hello to you while I was in town. She misses you terribly," I said for a dramatic but not so truthful ending.

There was a pause of a few seconds.

"Step closer to the door," the voice said as I looked up at the security camera bearing down on my uncovered face.

I heard a loud buzzer sound and pushed the door open to enter into a small but tidy landing. From under the stairs facing me, a door opened, and a small but spry elderly woman came out to greet me, ambulating with a cane.

"Hello, I'm Iris Kettleman," she said in her clipped British accent as she extended her hand.

"Hi there. I'm Dr. Kyle Chandler, a friend of Caroline Martinelli's. She wanted me to come by and see how you were doing."

"Well, come on in and have a seat by the fire," she said as she turned to make her way back to her apartment.

I followed her slow gate through her front door and into what one in the 1800's would call a parlor. She collected herself in her chair by a smoky peat fire as I took a seat on a couch with the back covered with doilies.

"So, Dr. Chandler, what brings you to London?" she asked.

"I came for a medical conference, and since Caroline knew I was coming, she wanted me to stop by and see how you were doing." I said. The half-truth niggled at my conscience.

"Caroline was one of my most favorite lodgers that I have ever had here since my Stanley died in the Battle of Britain in 1940. He was a pilot in the RAF. A natural born airman. We had just gotten married when he was called up to duty that spring. Since his passing, I've rented out a room to select borders now and then to make ends meet. Sebastian over at Christie's referred her my way a few years ago. I believe it was in 1986. I would have been around sixty-four years old then."

I can't ever remember last week, much less years ago. How does she remember the exact dates of her tenants and how old she was then?

"Well, as you probably know, when she moved backed to the States she started her own antiques store. Since then, she's moved to a newer, upscale location and is doing quite well," I said with false enthusiasm.

"I knew she would do well. Such a smart young lady. And exactly how do you know Caroline?" she asked with a strong intent of motherly protection.

"Uh, we're just really close friends."

"Hmm," she said, giving me a look of suspicion.

I wasn't going to divulge anything just yet about my true feelings for Caroline to this sharp septuagenarian.

"And what kind of medicine do you practice in the US?"

"I'm a trauma surgeon. I put people back together after automobile accidents and the like."

"Well, that's nice. I'll bet that keeps you busy."

"Yes ma'am."

Then out of the blue she asked, "Have you ever been married before Dr. Chandler?"

A prolonged pause began between us while she looked me straight in the eye.

"Yes ma'am, I have. Why do you ask?

"Just curious. For Caroline's sake."

Another prolonged pause. Then, for some uncontrollable, strange reason I decided to tell her a part of my life that I usually kept locked far away all to myself.

"I understand your protective concern, Mrs. Kettleman. My wife Molly and I met when she was at Harvard and I was starting my second year of surgical training in Boston. We both were super busy but became inseparable. We married the next year. Her folks were from an East Coast blue blood family, going back generations to the Mayflower, but she didn't play the part at all. She was working at a nonprofit after her graduation until I was to finish my surgical residency. After that, we were planning to come to London for a year so she could go to the London School of Economics."

"You don't say?"

"Yes, ma'am, but her folks were not real happy that their daughter had married down socially, as well as holding her back from her career because of my surgical training."

Her look at me was intense, but she uttered nothing. I decided to proceed.

"But then something happened, and things changed. I was in my final year of surgical training in the fall of 1987. I was at the hospital working when I received a phone call from a state trooper that my wife had been involved in a head-on motor vehicle accident with a drunk driver who crossed over into her lane. Pronounced dead on arrival at the hospital. She was four months pregnant with our first child. A son I never got to meet," I said quietly.

"I'm so terribly sorry," she finally said.

"Thank you, but it's something I've tried to bury deep in the back of my mind. To be honest, I don't know why I just told you all of this. I never tell anyone this."

Another awkward pause.

"So, your husband was a pilot in the Battle of Britain? What type of plane did he fly?" I asked, changing the subject.

"He flew a Hawker Hurricane fighter and switched over to a Spitfire when they became more available to the RAF."

"He must have known the southern England region pretty well to navigate through all the strange conditions they had to fly in."

"Oh yes, my Stanley grew up near Canterbury on the southeast coast of England," she began. "That's where the Germans would fly over from France on their runs to London in the fall of 1940. He knew that area like the back of his hand. He fought a lot of air battles out over that area that summer and fall. He would also accompany bombers over the Channel on their bombing runs to Germany."

She blinked. "He even knew of one or two out of the way airstrips in German occupied Holland near Rotterdam where fighter pilots low on fuel could land under the cover of darkness," she said. "The port there in Rotterdam got pretty beat up by the Germans with all the bombing they did. But he said that the area south of the port somehow made it through. On rare occasions, the RAF pilots would refuel there with the help of the underground resistance and head back the long way around to England. He'd call me at the end of the day when he got back to the base to tell me of his exploits. He was something..." she trailed off.

"Really? Airstrips in enemy territory?"

"Sure. The Germans didn't have radar back then and didn't know the British had it along the coast. I'll bet those airstrips are still used today by smugglers and the like if you fly low enough below radar."

This quaint English senior was really a piece of work. And this triggered a sudden idea.

"Mrs. Kettleman, what do you know about smuggling goods into or out of the country?"

"Oh, when I was growing up my father had a pilot friend before the war that would take things over to France and Holland. He would trade them for wines, cheeses, and the like to avoid all the tariffs. It was pretty common back then."

"And you think it could still be done today?" I asked.

"Given the proper planning and the right price, I guarantee it's being done as we speak," she said.

I smiled to myself about how unique this elderly woman was about her convictions.

"Well, you've been most informative, Mrs. Kettleman. It's been a pleasure chatting with you. I'll be sure and send your love to Caroline when I get home."

"It's been nice talking to you Dr. Chandler. I'm sorry about prying into your previous tragedy with your wife, but as I've experienced heartbreak also, life goes on. Caroline is very special to my heart. She's so good about staying in touch with me by phone or letter. She's like the daughter I never had. I wouldn't ever want her to be hurt, so take good care of her for me. And let me tell you one more thing... She's the one you better not let get away."

"Yes, ma'am. I'll give it my best," I said as I stood and gently shook her hand.

Oh, my goodness. First Mr. Clarke, and now her. Better yet, I had this woman named Genesse who owns a great BBQ joint in Kansas City a few months back tell me the exact same thing about Caroline.

Way too much coincidence.

9

WEST END, LONDON

After leaving Iris Kettleman's flat, I found a red phone box and rang up Alfie. Within ten minutes his sedan pulled up curbside.

"Where to now, governor?"

"Alfie, how long does it take to fly from here to Holland?" I asked.

"Well, that depends, commercial or private?"

"You tell me."

"Well, if you take the larger commercial airlines, you'll have to go through Heathrow or Gatwick and that takes all day. There are a few smaller airports out east but very limited flights."

He glanced in the rear-view mirror. "Now if you go private," he said, "it's much quicker, especially if you leave from one of the smaller airstrips east of London. It just so happens that my cousin, Burt, is a commercial pilot and flies a small plane all the time out of a smaller airport east of here.

He shuttles people all the time across the Channel over to France and Holland on business. He takes me over there on occasion for close to nothing if he has a seat or two open."

"No kidding?"

"Sure. Should I give him a ring?"

"Would you?" I asked.

Alfie didn't have a cell phone, and mine didn't work for international service, so we went back to the red phone box with a bag full of coins he pulled out from under his seat. After going through the operator and inserting what seemed like a hundred coins into the pay phone, he finally got his cousin on the line.

While Alfie chatted with his cousin, I tried to justify to myself why I should be going over to Holland. Was it what the plant manager said about the bladders being constructed into the containers in a warehouse in the Netherlands? Did I really have to see for myself that there was nothing more to it? Or was it the intrigue of possible smuggling that could still be happening today at an airstrip that Iris Kettleman hinted at?

I just didn't know.

I waited patiently as Alfie and his cousin Burt caught up with family pleasantries. His cousin had just gotten back from a flight from France, but said it was too late to leave anywhere today. He said he had two seats open for a flight scheduled to the airport at The Hague first thing in the morning. He said he could bring us back midafternoon at the same time he dropped some clients off in Amsterdam. That would give us a couple of hours to scout around near Rotterdam if we rented a car at the airport. I told Alfie to tell Burt that I'd pay full fare for the both of us. Burt told Alfie that we were good since it was his cousin with a friend.

Bingo. Now, I just needed a plan of what we should be looking for.

Once he got off the phone I said, "Alfie take me to the nearest large public library so I can look up a couple of things."

So off we went until he eventually pulled his sedan over to the curb in front of a large stone building with a wide staircase leading up to the entrance.

"You wait here while I go look up a few things," I said as I got out of his sedan.

"Whatever you say, governor."

I went up the stone steps, through the large front doors, and made a beeline for the librarian's desk. A kind elderly lady patiently listened to what I was looking for and led me to some rows of book stacks in the back of the large first floor room.

I figured the two unanswered questions that I needed to find out before our excursion tomorrow, that truthfully made no sense were: Where was the Hawthorne Containers warehouse in Holland, where the bladders were constructed? And was there still an airstrip anywhere in the vicinity around Rotterdam or Amsterdam like Iris Kettleman had said?

After scurrying around multiple areas of the library for what seemed like forever, I had at least located a few facts to start with. Hawthorne Containers was an English company that was owned by the large conglomerate corporation Evolution Industries based in New York City. Its total sales of the one-time use large bladders had taken off in the past three years. Its largest customers were wine importers that shipped bulk wine from France to mainly China and the US. Most of the shipping on land was done by a sister trucking company also owned by the parent conglomerate Evolution Industries.

It was difficult to get specific details about their supply chain because exact information was limited, but the company's annual report only confirmed the facts I already knew.

Looking through old newspapers, I had found an earlier article in the London Financial Times of an interview with Hawthorne Containers' president about the company's rapid growth. In the article, the company's president was quoted with only one short sentence about the company's recent success. However, the company's parent owner, Evolution Industries, had its CEO Philip Hauser gush on and on for more than four paragraphs of lavished praise. That raised a red flag.

The article mentioned the plant east of London but didn't give an address or mention anything about any warehouse outside Rotterdam where the bladders were assembled into containers. I tried several other resources in the reference section of the library to locate where this warehouse Mr. Garrolo had mentioned might be located. No luck.

I then searched in the geography section of the library for all types of maps of Rotterdam and its surrounding area. I made a copy of one map showing two different areas south of the port at Rotterdam that looked like airstrips with adjacent large buildings that could be warehouses.

Not great, but at least it was a start.

I looked into information about where most of the shipping was headed to the US from the Port of Tilbury. It was almost exclusively to New York. I found some information on the Port of New York shipping terminals just in case.

I also did a fair amount of research of this new technology of the Flexitank liquid volume containers. Since recently switching from a rubber-based container to one made of PVC, these were now lighter and brought the cost down considerably. Because they were a one-time sterile use, they didn't have to worry the vigorous cleaning those heavy ISO metal tank containers that were used for many years. More information to give Barry.

Going back and reviewing the complex annual report again, I got to the section listing the company's major investors where my eyes happened to glance down the list of major stockholders of Hawthorne Containers. At the top of the list were all the corporate executives including Philip Hauser, but towards the end of the list in small print was the name of a trust listed as MAW Trust, Inc.

Wait a minute. I knew that name.

Just to make sure, I tracked down some other financial references and finally found it.

Bingo.

The reference listed MAW Trust, Inc. as a charitable trust with the President and CFO as Tremont Williamson, with Bain Capital in Boston. MAW were my deceased wife's maiden name initials. And Tremont Williamson, he just happened to be my former father-in-law.

Ah yes, Tremont Williamson, with an East Coast lineage and a-nose-in-the-air attitude. MIT graduate, top of his class at Harvard Business School, long time investment guru in Boston at Bain Capital. He did a stint a several years ago in LA as a CFO executive. Third-row seats at the Academy Awards every year. He returned to Boston as a gentleman professor to teach ethics at HBS. Tremont was the main one who disapproved of Molly marrying me. He said it would "hold her back from her destiny."

My mentor Sydney was his older half-brother who had left Boston years ago for Kansas City. Sydney had mentioned to me that Tremont still managed several funds at Bain on the side. The best I could surmise, they were not the closest of half-brothers.

Why, of all the companies out there to invest in, did Tremont pick this one? And it looked like he was using my deceased wife's still existing trust as the mechanism for investing in Hawthorne Containers.

Something wasn't right here.

I gathered up all the notes I had taken as well as the copy of the map I had found and headed out of the library. Upon exiting the front doors, it surprised me that it was getting dark outside. I must have stayed in there longer than I had thought. Good chance that Alfie had probably given me up for lost.

But I was wrong again as his dark small sedan pulled up to the curb in just a few minutes.

"Where to governor?" he asked cheerfully as I got in the front passenger seat of his auto.

"Let me get your thoughts about how we should go about our trip for tomorrow," I said.

We talked in his sedan and discussed a tentative game plan for our outing tomorrow. I told him that I could go at it alone and he could bug out from the trip if he wanted. He said he was all in as long as I would pay him fairly for his time. With that settled, I directed Alfie to find a pub somewhere between here and my hotel that had decent food. I told him the least I could do was to buy him dinner for getting him mixed up in the wild goose chase we were headed into.

"That's bloody kind of you, but I'd best be getting home after I drop you off. On Thursday evenings, the missus gets off work early since she has to work Fridays 'til late. I'll need to take her down to the pub for a pint and watch the replay of last weekend's local football team on the telly. Her brother plays for them now and again. She's a real gamer when it comes to following her local team."

I smiled. Different cultures with similar devotions. Got to love that.

He pulled his sedan over to the curb and pointed to the establishment with the faded painted sign on the red brick wall that read "Red Lion Pub."

As I got out, he said, "Ask for Martin, he's the owner. He used to be a bricklayer but started brewing all kind of ales on the side. Ended up taking over this place that was his father's for many years. His wife is the cook. Have him bring you a plate full of her Chicken Alfredo."

"Italian food in an English pub? Come on Alfie."

"Trust me, you'll never want go to Italy after you eat her cooking."

Alfie sped toward home, and I headed into the pub. It was moderately full for a weeknight. I asked a waiter about Martin, and he said Martin was home with the kids this evening. But he did say Martin's wife was cooking tonight.

He led me to a booth, and I ordered a pint of amber ale and a plate of Chicken Fettuccine Alfredo.

When the waiter brought me my food, I was doubtful to say the least. Oh ye of little faith. The first bite was incredible. The second bite made me a true believer. Alfie was 100% right, an incredible melt in your mouth gastronomic experience. Who would have thought this good of an Italian specialty would be in a local English pub?

When the waiter came to bring me my check, I asked if I could speak to the chef to complement her on her extraordinary culinary talents. He said she was pretty busy right now, but he'd see if she could duck out of the kitchen to say hello in a minute. About three minutes later, a shortish woman with dishwater blonde hair pulled back in a ponytail came striding over to my table wiping her hands on her apron.

"Hello, I'm Sharon," she said as she extended her hand.

"Nice to meet you, Sharon. I'm Kyle," I said as I shook her hand. "I just wanted to tell you that your Fettuccine Alfredo is *the* very best pasta dish I've ever had. Not only here, but also in Italy or back in the US."

"Why, thank you. Are you here visiting from the States?"

"Yes ma'am. I was at a medical conference here in London. I've also had a few meetings with some people for this side project I'm working on. That's when I met a driver named Alfie who's carted me around while I've been here. He's the one who highly recommended your Chicken Fettuccine Alfredo."

"Alfie! What a character! He's known my husband Martin for ages. He's loyal to a fault, that Alfie. Such a good bloke."

"He seems to be a solid guy. We're going to fly with a cousin of his tomorrow morning over to Rotterdam and back on a little excursion as part of something I'm looking into."

"Really? What's there to see in Holland except for tulips?"

"We're going to check out an airstrip south of the port there in Rotterdam as part of some work I'm doing for a friend."

"I've never been there or to The Hague. Only to Amsterdam a time or two. Now Martin used to go over there on some jobs for days at a time when he was still laying bricks back in the day. He knows that area pretty well. Maybe he could help you find what you're looking for if you like?"

"Your waiter says he's home with your kids tonight. I'll bet he's probably got his hands full right now."

As she turned her head away, she said, "My assistant from the kitchen is waving like mad at me to get back and help her, so I'd better go. Let me get Martin on the phone in the back and I'll have one of the waiters come get you to talk to my husband on the line. He might be able to shorten your search."

"Well, Sharon, it's been a pleasure to meet such a talented cook like you. If you're ever in Kansas City in the US in the future, give me a call. I'll take you to get some of the world's best barbeque," I said as I handed her one of my business cards.

"Doctor Chandler it says here. What kind of doctor are you?" she asked as she stood.

"I'm a trauma surgeon. I put people back together after automobile accidents and the like."

"Oh my. That must be stressful," she said as she sprinted away.

After paying the check, I sat tight until one of the waiters motioned with his index finger for me to follow him. I wiggled in between tables and followed him down a narrow corridor into the kitchen. Small, but very busy. I chased him to an enclave in the back with a small desk and a phone on the wall with the waiter pointing to the phone laying on the desk.

"This is Kyle Chandler," I said. "Is this Martin?"

"Yes, it is. Nice to meet you. Sharon told me a little of

what you're looking for. Exactly where are you headed tomorrow?"

"I'm headed with your buddy Alfie tomorrow to Holland to look for a possible airstrip south of the port of Rotterdam as part of my current investigation." I explained briefly about my investigation side hobby.

"Sounds interesting, to say the least. What are you looking for at an airstrip?"

I was talking on the phone to the husband of a chef that I had just met in a pub across the ocean far from my home. Now that I started to explain the purpose of my search, did I actually think this guy I don't know is going to believe such a far-fetched story?

Didn't matter. Sometimes you just got to take a chance.

"Martin, Alfie's cousin is going to fly us to The Hague tomorrow, and we're going to look for one or two airstrips south of the port in Rotterdam that might have a warehouse next to it. Do you know that area at all?" I said trying to dodge the question of what we were specifically looking for.

"Well it's been a few years, but as a matter of fact I do," he stated to my surprise. "Right after Sharon and I got married, we were staying with her parents. She was desperate for us to get a place of our own. I was a bricklayer then, and I signed on with a company that did a lot of contract work in Holland and Belgium. I would go over for two weeks at a time to work on jobs. A lot of them were not so far from the port in Rotterdam. I do remember one place south of the port that had an airstrip long enough to land a small jet. We were working on a large building there and it seems like planes were going in and out all the time. Mainly for cargo delivery in private planes, not passengers. But I bet it's still being used today."

This was at least a little encouraging to justify my wild goose chase. I asked him a few more questions and thanked him for taking the time with me. As I hung up the receiver, I posed the question to myself, "Now why am I doing this again?"

It certainly didn't have anything to do with the antiques shipment from New York that Ian Griffin had me looking into. And I was pretty sure that we wouldn't find anything unusual even if there was an airstrip south of the Port of Rotterdam. I half admitted to myself that I was doing it for the thrill of it. Plain and simple.

The annual report I read about Hawthorne Containers didn't indicate the location of the warehouse. But the plant manager at Hawthorne Containers did let it slip to me that the bladders were constructed with their frames at a warehouse outside Rotterdam. That's where they were assembled before being sent to wineries to be filled with wine throughout France then sent to France to be filled. And since Tremont Williamson was in on it financially, then there had to be something else to it. Sure, he took his share of financial risks, but there seemed to always be a payoff assuring him of success.

After thanking Martin's wife Sharon again, I stepped outside the Red Lion pub and looked around to get my bearings. No gorillas in sight, at least not yet.

I started walking back to my hotel thinking about when I should call Clanton Rogers to tell him that I had come up high and dry on the antiques investigation here in London. Like always, I figured there's no time like the present. It wasn't far to my hotel, and I breathed a sigh of relief when I entered the well-lit lobby.

In my room, I placed a call to Clanton Rogers. He picked up and I related my findings from my interviews with Sebastian Clarke at Christie's and Senior Constable Colin Butterworth at the Port of Tilbury. I told him that I was fairly certain that the switch of the antique piece in question had to have been made in New York before the antiques were shipped to London. I suggested that he tell his close friends in New York that they should have an investigator there look into the possibility of the switch occurring there. I explained that it had to be either by the shipping company that originally packed the antiques or the company that repacked them into the shipping container before heading off to London. He reluctantly agreed that this was likely the case and promised to keep me informed as needed. We agreed to stay in touch, and I hung up a bit sad that I couldn't solve the case for him.

Well, even good hitters know that you don't hit a home run every time at bat.

10

LONDON – SOUTH OF ROTTERDAM, THE NETHERLANDS – LONDON

The following morning, I awoke early. After grabbing a cup of coffee to-go in the hotel lobby, I met Alfie's sedan out front before sunrise.

"You sure you're up for this?" I asked.

"Piece of cake, governor," he said without hesitation.

Traffic was light this early on a Friday morning. After about fifty minutes, we arrived at London Southend Airport that was approximately sixty kilometers east of central London. It was a small regional airstrip that handled private and limited charter flights. Alfie said that it had been there a long time, established during World War I. He also said it was a base for fighter squadrons during World War II, similar to what Iris Kettleman had described to me about her husband.

We drove around to a private hanger where we got out

and Alfie introduced me to his cousin Burt. After all the necessary pleasantries, we climbed inside his charter aircraft where Burt's three other charter passengers were already buckled in. All three businessmen looked at their watches, acting like they were already late. After completing the preflight checks, Burt taxied us to the airstrip and before I knew it, we were airborne in the clear Friday morning sky.

After a short time, we landed smoothly at The Hague airport. Burt dropped Alfie and me off at a private terminal before heading on with his three passengers to Amsterdam. We went through a single-laned room—their excuse for an international customs bureau—showed our passports and then hiked over to the main commercial terminal. We grabbed a bite to eat before heading out in search of the car rental booths. After filling out endless forms of paperwork, we secured a two-door sedan from the rental lot and off we went. I let Alfie drive while I tried to navigate from a map of the Netherlands the rep at the counter said would be in the glove box. Only thing is, he didn't say the map would be written in Dutch.

Definitely the blind leading the blind in this case.

According to the information I had gleaned from my short visit to the library, the map I found showed two different areas south of the Port of Rotterdam that looked like airstrips with adjacent buildings. We first headed southeast through the city of Rotterdam, followed by traveling through land that seemed like one canal bridge after another. I forgot that the Dutch had reclaimed so much of their country from the sea. I was starting to see that The Netherlands was a lot more than just tulips and windmills.

After about fourteen to fifteen kilometers into the farmland, we found the first site from the map. No dice. Instead of an airstrip, it was one long canal with a few large buildings nearby. No place at all to land an aircraft, except maybe on water.

On to the next site.

Alfie and I headed west driving alongside a large canal

or a river of some sort onward through more reclaimed farmland. After fifteen to twenty kilometers, I had him pull over to the side of the road so I could try to make some sense of where we were on the blasted Dutch map.

While shaking my head in disgust, Alfie said, "Look at that."

He pointed to a small jet aircraft heading down out of the clouds towards a long narrow island in the middle of the river. It landed and quickly headed towards a single large tin building with high wire fencing surrounding the whole property.

"Alfie, we might have just got lucky," I muttered in fascination. "Let's see if we can get a better look on the other side."

We backtracked to a bridge that took us across the river and stopped about half a kilometer short of the small one-lane bridge heading over to the island. I pulled a pair of small, powerful binoculars out of my coat pocket. The jet had already taxied into the hanger building through the large sliding door that was now closed shut.

"Now what, governor?" he asked.

"We wait."

After about forty-five minutes, the large door slowly opened. With my binoculars on full zoom power, I saw an Asian man carrying a rectangular package wrapped in cellophane about the size of a shoebox down the steps of the plane. He handed it up to another man on the back of semi-truck container and that man handed it to someone else deep inside the container. It was one of five trucks lined up inside.

I recognized that inner steel constructed frame with a large volume of some kind of material inside the truck. It was exactly like the bladder container I saw with Senior Constable Butterworth at the Port of Tilbury. Only, from what I could see, the bladder was deflated. And what they were loading in the front end of the trailer into the bladder surely wasn't shoeboxes of wine.

All at once, an auto roared up from behind, blocking

our rental car. Out popped two very large men in leather jackets. I quickly put the binoculars under my seat.

"Can I see some ID?" Gorilla number one said in broken English with a heavy Dutch accent.

Alfie said nothing and looked at me.

"Why, are you a police officer?" I asked calmly.

"Private security. This is private property, and you are loitering, so I need to see some identification."

"Gentlemen," I said. "We are trying to make it back to the airport to catch a flight and have obviously taken a wrong turn. Could you direct us the fastest way back to The Hague airport?"

"Out of the car," Gorilla number two said.

Both large men simultaneously opened the doors to the rental car and yanked us out of the automobile, throwing us both up against each side of the car. After a thorough pat-down of each one of us, Gorilla number one decided to make his point.

"We don't appreciate people snooping around anywhere near our business, even if it might be a simple mistake. And to make you two understand, we're going to give you a little parting gift to make sure you don't come back anywhere close to here ever again."

And with that, each gorilla landed an abdominal punch that felt like it was shot out of a cannon. I was pretty sure I was the first one to hit the ground because I got a bonus kick to my left flank from Gorilla number one that set my whole belly on fire.

"Stay away from here and don't forget it," he said as they headed back to their auto.

After he took a few steps, he paused, and with my eyes still closed, I heard a strange buzzing mechanical noise before he continued walking to his car.

It must have been ten minutes before I could take a full breath without causing shear agony to my stomach. My trauma surgeon mentality reflexly ran through the possibilities of internal organ damage with probably at least six ways I could be going into hemorrhagic shock on the way to bleeding to death. After regaining my courage to stand, I went around to the driver's side and helped Alfie up.

"I'm so sorry Alfie. Are you all right?"

"This might be just a bit more than I anticipated," he said slowly.

"I agree. Let's get out of here. Can you drive?"

"I think so, governor," he said as I helped him into the driver's seat.

As I struggled around to the passenger side to open the door, from deep in my memory banks my brain spit out the answer to the buzzing mechanical noise that I had heard. The noise was from a camera that the gorilla must have used to take a photograph of my face before leaving.

Not so good for me.

"Wait one second," I said. Despite the unexpected blows, I couldn't resist one more look as I pulled the binoculars out from under the seat.

"Governor, are you loony?"

"Just give me a second." I zoomed in the binoculars as the jet was rolling out of the building and to the airstrip. It had the standard registration tail numbers present, but what caught my eye was the letters up on the front of the plane. Under the English letters were a series of Chinese letters not usually seen on American or even European planes. I knew that from a fellow surgical resident who used to take me up with him while he flew on the weekends during my training in Boston. As the jet raced along the airstrip up into the sky, I figured that it had come a long way from home for such a quick landing.

I directed Alfie across all of the reclaimed farmland back to the airport. On the way, there was not much conversation since I really didn't know what to say. After returning the rental car, we made our way across to the private terminal and waited for Burt to return.

"What next governor?" Alfie finally asked.

"Alfie, you've gotten in too deep with me already. I had

no idea that looking for a warehouse next to an airstrip would get us into any trouble. I'll pay you in full when we get back. I'll figure out some other way to get around for the next two days."

"Don't do that," he said. "I've had worse scraps after football matches than today. The truth is my wife and I could use the dough that I can make during the next couple of days. Besides, this thing today is just a local thing, and I don't plan on being around here any time soon."

"Maybe, but Alfie, what if it's not like you said, just a local thing? That guy that punched me I'm almost sure took a photo of me lying all balled up on the ground before he split. And that's not exactly normal. What if they have your car's license plate number in London? Did you think about that and what that could mean?"

Alfie paused for a few seconds looking out the window over the horizon before answering me.

"I guess we're going to find out now, aren't we?"

About that time, Burt returned from Amsterdam with his three executives and taxied up to the terminal. After filing required paperwork with the airport officials, he led us back onto the plane, and we all strapped in for takeoff. Despite waiting in a line of planes ready to leave, we were finally in the air in the late afternoon back to England.

By the time we landed, went through customs, and got on the road back to London, traffic got pretty heavy as most Friday afternoons in a big city. Fortunately, most people were leaving London for the weekend as we were heading back in towards town. On the way back, I discussed what I had in mind for tomorrow and if he wanted to keep driving me around despite the incident today. He told me he was still all in.

When Alfie dropped me off at my hotel, I asked him to come around the next morning by 8:00 a.m. with his sedan and to keep his eyes open for anyone following him. He agreed and headed off toward home.

Even though it was around 5:20 on a Friday afternoon,

I decided to try to catch Senior Constable Butterworth at the Port of Tilbury on the chance that maybe he hadn't left for the weekend. I had a question or two about the Flexitank containers that were still bothering me. Instead of going up to my room, I headed for the hotel phone area at the back of the lobby by the bar. After giving the operator all my credit card information, she connected me with the security office at the Port of Tilbury.

On the fifth ring, when I was fairly sure everyone had left for the day, a male voice said, "Senior Constable Butterworth's office."

"Is Senior Constable Butterworth still in? It's slightly urgent."

"Who's speaking please?"

"This is Dr. Kyle Chandler. I spoke with the Senior Constable at his office on Wednesday and need his advice on something."

"This is he. I was just heading out the door. What's so urgent?"

Busted.

"Oh, thank you so much for answering. This won't take a minute and then you'll be on your way."

Silence.

"Senior Constable, sir," I said, "When those Flexitank containers get filled with wine, as you said usually in France, where do they go next before being shipped to the US?"

"What does this have to do with the antiques investigation we talked about?"

Busted again. I pressed onward.

"Well, it's kind of complicated. I was following up on Flexitank transport because I have an idea that it might give me a clue to how articles like valuable antiques might get switched in the overall process," I said.

He must have really wanted to head out of the office badly because he didn't take the time to call me on it.

"As we discussed on Wednesday," he said, "the majority of the Flexitank bladders are filled at different wineries throughout France. Most of the bulk wine these days is usually shipped from Rotterdam either to China or the US. The containers going to the United States usually come through our port on their way."

"Are any of the filled bulk wine containers shipped here to be bottled in the United Kingdom?"

"Not very often. There is one new winery processing plant south of London, near Epsom, I believe, that we registered a few months ago. They plan to receive a container of bulk wine about three times a year to make sparkling wine of some sort. I remember because I had to sign the paperwork for them to clear customs yesterday, since they are new. Their truck is taking delivery here starting tomorrow morning."

"Can you tell from the markings on the outside of the container what kind of materials are being transported inside?"

"I can't divulge the specifics of most of our security procedures, but it is well known throughout the industry that most wineries place a separate burgundy colored tag next to the bar code seal to indicate that there is perishable wine inside. This is really only useful when the bulk wine is being transferred in the less expensive unrefrigerated containers during the cooler months of the year."

"So not all containers have this extra tag?"

"Not all, but almost all the wineries put them on every container because of habit."

"I assume that most of the containers to the US are shipped from your Port of Tilbury to New York. Is that correct?"

"Not always, but usually."

"And about how many times a year do shipments go from here to New York?"

"All year. Wine exporting is big business year-round."

"And one last question. About how long does it take for the containers to clear customs in New York before they are transported throughout the country?"

"You'll have to understand that I'm not as familiar with all the procedures of the Port Authority of New York and New Jersey, but I've been told it is anywhere from two to ten days"

"Senior Constable, you've been super helpful, and I hope you have a relaxing weekend," I said as I quickly hung up before he asked any more about my antiques investigation.

It was one more piece of the puzzle that I was still trying to figure out. In addition to why I was pursuing it in the first place.

Without going up to my room, I left the hotel lobby and walked to a pub down the street, watching over my shoulder for anyone suspicious that might be trying to follow me. At the pub, I slid into a booth, ordered a pint and a sandwich, and tried to figure out my next move.

I had a feeling that my curiosity on this one was going to get me into big trouble. Regardless, there must be a way to track these Flexitank bladders once they were drained of wine. Senior Constable Butterworth had said that the containers filled with bulk wine in the Flexitank bladders usually had the burgundy-colored tag on the back next to the bar code tag. If I could find out where the bladder was being emptied of its wine back in the US and follow where the empty bladder was taken, then it just might allow me to find out if there was something other than wine hidden in the empty bladder. Lots of ifs.

That meant that I was going to have to change my return flight from London to Kansas City one more time. This time for a day-long layover in New York to see where the bladders filled with wine were being taken. While it wouldn't delay me from getting back to work on Wednesday, it wasn't the primary reason I came over here in the first place. More importantly, that meant by doing this I had a real chance of me getting in over my head even more than I was already.

If I had any brains at all, I would notify the authorities

of what I saw when I got home and let them take care of things. Then it would be their problem, not mine.

Where was Superman to the rescue when you needed him?

11

PORT OF TILBURY – LONDON

After returning to my hotel room from the pub without incident, I spent the better part of the evening pondering what my next move should be. I was beginning to get more than a little nervous since I had been roughed up several times by lurking gorillas on my case last April. And now a repeat performance today. Maybe I should just forget the whole thing and go sightseeing in London on a pleasant Saturday. Then make my way back to Kansas City, deny to anyone that I ever heard anything about extra bladder compartments at a factory east of the port, and never saw anything at an airstrip south of Rotterdam.

Yeah, right. I'm sure that would be immediately believed by whomever.

If the incident today in Holland with the gorillas was related to what I thought it was, the people responsible would not stop looking for me just because I'd left London. They would make it to Kansas City eventually. What I needed was to find a third piece of evidence while I was still here in London to put the icing on the cake. After a few minutes of jogging my cerebral hard drive, an idea popped out front and center. It was risky, but it just might work.

I decided to make the calls to change my flight from London to New York with a day layover in New York to see where the bladders filled with wine were being taken. Not a safe option, but at least I made a decision.

The next morning came quickly. I got a lot more sleep than I would have guessed. After a brief stretching routine in my room, I showered, dressed, and left the hotel to catch a bite to eat at a local café down the street. By the time I finished breakfast, it was a little before 8:00 a.m., the time Alfie agreed to pick me up. I paid the bill at the café and started walking back to the hotel, with Alfie's sedan pulling up to the curb, just as expected.

"Good morning, governor," he said as I climbed into the front passenger seat. "Are you ready for what you have planned today?"

"Alfie, you sure you want to go through with this?" I asked. "I really don't want to get you involved. What I have planned may not be such a good idea after all."

"Governor, we've made it through this much so far. And I need the cash, so we might as well see how it turns out on the other side, now shouldn't we?"

"Okay, if you're sure. Here's what I have planned," I said, as I began to explain my scheme to him.

My initial plan was to follow the shipping container that Senior Constable Butterworth mentioned offhand in our phone conversation yesterday. He had said that it was scheduled to be trucked from the Port of Tilbury to the winery facility south of London today. He had also said that the winery facility was somewhat new. Because it was new, I guessed that it might not have a bunch of security protocols in place yet. If by chance I could somehow get close enough to get a look at the bladder after the bulk wine was emptied, that would confirm that I was on the right trail.

Alfie headed out of London eastward towards the Port of Tilbury, avoiding the mild Saturday morning traffic by taking backroads like before. Upon arrival to the port, I had Alfie pull his sedan beyond the main gate and off to the other side of the road under a large shade tree where we were less noticeable. We had a fairly good view of the rear of the semi-trucks that were turning out of the port's main gate and headed west back to London.

Truck traffic leaving the port was light at this early hour on a Saturday. By midmorning, the number of trucks leaving was up to four or five an hour. Even with a better view with my binoculars, still no burgundy tags on any container were seen.

We waited, what seemed like forever, discussing various topics between us while comparing things about both England and the US. Alfie was quite informed on a number of subjects, despite him telling me he had to drop out of school in his mid-teens to help support his family. He had tried all kinds of odd jobs to make ends meet during his younger years. I could tell that despite the lack of formal education, he was a go-getter.

Alfie's wife, Katie, had packed us some sandwiches and fruit for us to eat while we were waiting in the car. I asked Alfie how he met Katie and he began to tell me more about himself and his wife.

"I met Katie when I was eighteen years old. I worked odd jobs to get by, and the first time I saw her I got weak at the knees. We started seeing each other and six months later we were moving in together."

"That's pretty young for taking such a big step," I said.

"I see that now, but back then, I was a crazy nineteen-year-old blinded by love. I understand now that we were too young to get married, but as usual, we didn't follow our parents' advice. We ran off to get married anyway."

"How did your parents take it?"

"Mine, well, not so good, hers, not good at all. We struggled financially from the get-go. I was working two to three jobs with no education. She was working a day job and tried to take night classes at school. It was more than a little stressful."

"Marriage always is. It's a commitment that's hard to explain until you go through it yourself," I threw into the dialogue.

"You sound like you've bloody been there before," he said. "Are you still married?"

"No, I'm not. That situation was out of my control. She was suddenly taken from me by a fatal car wreck that wasn't her fault. That was eight years ago. I'm just now crawling out of my shell."

He nodded like he understood.

"Katie always wanted a big family. Lots of kids running around the house. We found out about a year into our marriage that she had some female problems that wouldn't allow her to stay pregnant. We went through a rough period after finding out that she couldn't ever have children. It took several years for both of us to come to terms and accept it. She finally did admit two months ago that she would consider adopting a baby one day when we get a better leg up on our finances. That's a big step forward from where we were," Alfie said.

"Good for you Alfie. Is that the reason you need the extra money?"

"You're a pretty clever bloke. We checked into it and adoptions don't come cheap. Not to mention how much raising kids cost."

We sat in silence for a minute while I thought how I could help this true-blue guy.

"So you trying to dupe me that you being a bloody rich doctor, and you don't have a bunch of girlfriends?" he asked.

"Just because I'm a doctor doesn't make me rich. It's a lot of long hours and a lot of surgery cases done for free."

"Maybe, but what about the girlfriends?"

"It just so happens I met a super woman that really throws me for a loop. We've been seeing each other since

April. The thing is, I still can't figure her out."

"The really good ones do that to you. Believe me," he said.

I just looked at him and nodded. Alfie was just an all-around good chap.

Around 3:30 p.m., Alfie leaned over and said, "I'm going to head down to the store I saw at the corner on the way in to use the loo. I should be back in no time just in case you spot something. Do you want me to grab you a coffee or something else to eat?"

"I'm good, Alfie. Get what you want, and I'll pay you for it when you get back. It'll be good to stretch my legs, anyway."

I got out of the sedan and ambled up to the base of the large tree as Alfie pulled away, keeping my profile partially hidden from anyone at the main gate. I kind of felt sorry for all of the detectives of the world because stakeout work was so unbelievably boring.

Within thirty seconds, I quickly realized how wrong I was about my assumption on stakeouts. Standing there behind the tree looking at the main gate, I felt a cold shiver go down my spine. Well, I don't believe in premonitions like my dad's Aunt Sally did, swearing she could tell when something bad was about to happen. But maybe I should have.

Out of nowhere, a large black car zoomed up from behind and skidded right up next to me, pinning me in. Out popped the same two gorillas that I had the distinct pleasure of meeting at the airstrip south of Rotterdam. And I hadn't forgotten Gorilla number one and his punch to the abdomen, topped off by a kick to one of my kidneys.

"Well now, Dr. Chandler. We meet again," Gorilla number one said calmly as he walked straight at me. "We've done some digging about you since your snooping episode over in Holland. I guess you decided that our suggestions for you to stay away were not persuasive enough for you."

Oh perfect. Now they knew exactly who I was. Even in

a foreign country.

Before I could answer, his patented right uppercut punch to my stomach connected. I fell to my knees, gasping for air.

"Now my good doctor, we are going to take a little ride together." He grabbed me and threw me into the backseat of their automobile. Gorilla number two opened the backseat door on the driver's side and held me down while Gorilla number one pulled my hands behind my back to secure them with a zip tie. He jumped in next to me, slammed the door as Gorilla number two got into the driver's seat. Next thing I knew, off we went.

I slowly struggled upright as we headed to what looked like to me back to London. No one said a word. *Where in the world are you, Alfie?*

Finally Gorilla number one said, "We figured that you and your driver would still be interested in nosing around one the bladder containers, so we followed you two out here this morning. We waited for one of you to take a break before we made our move. And don't worry about your driver, we know all about him, too."

Great. They had not only done their research on me, but Alfie, too. I was hoping Alfie had gotten away before any other gorillas had gotten to him. This investigation scheme of mine was starting to be not so fun anymore.

We stayed on one of the main roads leading into the city and exited into an industrial part of London, with the River Thames still in sight. After multiple turns, Gorilla number two pulled into a driveway leading to a warehouse sitting back from the road. He got out and unlocked the garage door. After pulling it open, we drove in and came to a stop.

"Out you go," Gorilla number one said.

I was partially lifted off my feet as he pulled me out. He thrust me down on a hard wooden kitchen chair with my wrists still firmly secured behind my back. The warehouse was dark except for a single bulb on the opposite wall.

Gorilla number two got back in the auto and backed out of the warehouse while Gorilla number one pulled the garage door closed.

Think Chandler. Think how to outwit these bozos. At least it was one-on-one with the gorillas for the moment. Still not great, but better than being outnumbered.

The memory of almost the exact same situation flashed in my mind. Last spring, I had been seconds away from having my hands broken by a similar gorilla until an ex-Marine martial arts expert saved my bony backside. Needless to say, things right now were not looking so well. I needed to stay calm and think since the Marines were not coming to the rescue here in England.

"Now Dr. Chandler, we need to have a little talk," Gorilla number one said. "We need to make sure that you understand how serious we are about you staying away from any more snooping expeditions, not only right now, but anytime in the future."

I nodded in agreement He pulled out a set of brass knuckles from his back pocket before he continued.

"We don't know what you saw or what you were doing at an airstrip in Holland. And at this point, we don't care. What we want is for you to forget anything you saw or heard until now if you want to make it out of here in one piece. Understand?"

I gave another slow nod of agreement.

While lifting his hand with the brass knuckles in place next to my face he asked, "Who are you working for?"

"I don't work for anyone. I'm a surgeon from the United States, as I'm sure you know from your research. I'm over here in London at a medical conference."

"And what part of your conference was for you to go to a bladder manufacturing plant and then to an airstrip out of the country?"

Oh no. He already knew about my scheduled visit to Hawthorne Containers.

I took a deep breath before answering. I needed to buy

myself some time.

"I went out to the bladder manufacturing plant as a favor to a friend. My friend is a wine importer, shipping all kinds of wines through the Midwest region of the United States. When I told him I was headed to a medical conference in London, he said that he was thinking of starting to transport bulk wine to the US from Europe. He said the company that makes the shipping bladders had their factory east of London," I said. What else could I say to buy some time?

"My friend arranged an appointment with the plant manager and asked me to go there and get information on their product," I said. I tried to swallow, but my throat was bone dry.

"Sure he did. And the airstrip?" the gorilla asked, not lowering his hand with the brass knuckles.

"My driver was headed over to Holland for the day anyway with his cousin. The information my friend gave me said the bladder manufacturer had a plant to assemble the bladders inside of trucking containers south of Rotterdam. Since I was through with my medical conference, I went there with my driver. We got lost looking for the plant, and that's when we ran into you."

"Doctor, do you really think that story is believable?"

"Believable or not, it's the truth."

I did my best to not show even a hint of fear.

Gorilla number one put down his hand with the brass knuckles. I began to think that I might slip by on this one. I soon realized there was no such luck. That's because he walked up to me and violently kneed me in the stomach. I doubled over. He kicked my other flank this time, and I fell off the chair onto the floor. Searing pain like before, now on the other side.

"We'll have to wait and see what the boss wants to do to you," he said as he walked away.

I tried to control my breathing in order to keep from blacking out. The situation here was not looking good.

Why didn't I give in to him and beg for mercy? I just couldn't, that's why.

Ever since I lost Molly, some kind of trigger went off in me. I would not give in to those who decided that I must do as they say, even if they held all the cards. Just like the case I fell into earlier, I wasn't going to let Goliath run over David. Call it blind stubbornness; call it lunacy; call it whatever psychiatrists like to define it. It was not going to happen. Not now, not ever. Even if only one piece of straw in the whole haystack could get me out of this, I wouldn't stop searching for it as my way out.

Gorilla number one pivoted and started back to me. A sharp knock at the warehouse side door drew his attention. He stopped, paused for a second, and made his way to the door. He unlocked it and opened the door a crack to see who was there.

"Pizza delivery," a loud voice rang out. "A large pepperoni with extra cheese, but we were out of anchovies," the voice said.

"We didn't order a pizza. Go away. You must have the wrong address."

"No, the call-in order specifically explained to deliver it to this address to the side door at the warehouse away from the street."

Despite still lying on the floor, that voice finally registered in my brain. A hint of a smile came to my face.

Gorilla number one succumbed to his curiosity and pulled the door open, expecting the smell of a fresh pizza in front of him. Instead, he got a tire iron across his neck and the side of his head. He went down like a sack of potatoes.

Not quite what he expected. Not quite what I expected. Alfie in the nick of time.

"Are you okay?" he asked as he took out his pocketknife and cut the zip tie off my wrists.

"Alfie, you sure took your jolly-good time getting here," I said as he helped me up to the chair. "How did you find me?"

"To be honest with you," he said, "I almost didn't. Now let's get out of here before we get more company than we can handle. Can you make it to my car?"

"Help me get started and I'll make it," I said as he wrapped my arm over his neck and shoulders.

He helped me into the front seat of his sedan, and then we quickly got out of there half expecting someone to show up to spoil our getaway party.

"I had just gotten back in my car," he said, "when I saw a big black sedan cruise by me picking up speed. I knew right away that something wasn't bloody right, so I jumped in my car and rushed to where I left you. As soon as I didn't see you, I made a U-turn and sped off looking for that black sedan. I figured they'd be going back into the city. I caught up with them on the A13 just before they exited. There were now two people instead of one in the back seat, so I figured that it must be you."

"Yeah, well it took me a while to get my breath back to sit up after one of the gorilla's great-to-see-you punches to my stomach," I said, rubbing my wrists.

"I stayed back until they pulled into the warehouse and drove past to park down the street," he said. "I was surprised that the sedan took off again shortly after they pulled in. I knew I had to think of something quick before he got reinforcements."

"Pizza delivery? Really? That's what you came up with?"

"Who doesn't like to smell the aroma of a fresh hot pizza at their door?"

"But you didn't even have a pizza." I marveled at his gutsiness.

"Yeah, but he didn't know that. And besides, it worked like a charm. He was looking for the pizza, not the tire iron."

"Alfie, you are something."

As I looked out the window, I thought about the events of the last few days. They were spinning through my mind like a jumbled fairy tale that kept getting more complicated.

I couldn't keep on pushing the envelope on this investigation that was getting more and more hazardous. The obvious question in front of me was looking me right in the eyes.

What do I do now?

By the time we made it back into the city, traffic had picked up. After making our way through all the cars almost to my hotel, Alfie suddenly pulled over and shut the engine and headlights off.

"What are you doing?"

"Look ahead. Across the street from your hotel is a limousine lane, a space reserved for transportation other than cabs. Only town cars and the like are supposed to park there, waiting for their scheduled passengers to come out of the hotel. There's a white van at the back of the line that's not supposed to be there," he said.

"How do you know this?"

"I bloody drive for a living, that's how."

Did the people who were after me have somebody waiting at every corner I turned?

"Okay, now what?" I asked.

"Well, we can wait all evening to see if they leave, just like we did at the port earlier today," he said. "Or I can pull them off the lookout to follow me while you make a dash for the hotel."

"Alfie, I can't have you get involved like that."

"You got any better ideas right now?"

I shook my head. "And you think you can lose them, so they won't follow you home?"

"Governor, I know all the short cuts of the city like the back of my hand. Didn't I tell you that I bloody drive for a living?"

I paused, trying to come up with something better. Finally, I pulled out my wallet.

"If you really think you can divert them to follow you, *and* you're sure you can lose them, I want you and your wife to get out of town until Monday. Here's some cash." I pulled out and handed him multiple large British pound notes. "Get away to the seaside and enjoy the rest of the weekend on me. Have your wife call in sick at work. Whatever it takes. But neither of you show up at your place until Monday evening."

"Are you sure?" he asked.

"I'm sure as long as you can shake them from here. Give me one of your cards," I said. "If they get ahold of you, you don't know me. Tell them you were only the driver and that you know nothing. Alfie, it's been a pleasure. When you adopt your little boy, tell Katie to send me a picture, and I'll send your son his first set of golf clubs. I promise. I'll be in touch with you in the future; that's for sure."

I shook his hand vigorously and dashed out of the front passenger seat, quietly closing the door as I left. While the situation was tense, I was happy because I knew that I had made a friend with Alfie for life.

I crouched behind a parked car as I watched him pull out down the block in front of my hotel. As he approached the white van, he slowed down and leaned out the window to say something to the driver.

Sure enough, as Alfie pulled away, the white van started up, made a U-turn, and sped up to stay up with him.

After sprinting the last block to my hotel, I tried to slow my breathing as I walked inside and across the lobby toward the receptionist at the front desk.

"Excuse me, I'm Dr. Kyle Chandler, and I'm checking out of your hotel tomorrow," I said as calmly as I could. "I was out all afternoon today on business and I was wondering if anyone came by today inquiring for me."

"Ah, let's see, sir," the receptionist said while typing on her computer keyboard. "Yes, here it is. We have you on the third floor and your account has no messages listed."

"Do you know if anyone came by in person?"

"Well, sir, except for a short lunch break around 2:00 p.m., I've been here since 11:00 this morning and no one has inquired about you since I've been here at the front desk."

"Do you have an ice machine on this floor?"

"Just around the corner," she said and pointed.

"Thank you very much." I headed the direction she indicated.

I really didn't need any ice, but since there was a stack of disposable ice containers on top of the machine, I got some just in case. I stood there around the corner for a few seconds to collect myself. It looked like the coast was clear, so I walked as calmly as I could to the elevator. After inserting my key card inside the hotel elevator car, I punched the third-floor button. On the ride up, I wondered how this "somebody" knew at which hotel I was staying. I was at least a little more assured that no one knew exactly what room I was in.

At least not yet.

That opinion rapidly changed when I opened my hotel door room. I didn't realize that they had tornados in London. Especially ones limited to indoors.

The entire room was a torrential mess. Clothes thrown from my suitcase. Furniture overturned. Bedspread across the room. Everything was scattered everywhere. But why?

I slowly gathered all my belongings. Nothing appeared to be missing. What were they looking for? I had taken my passport with me in my larger travel wallet I used on trips. I didn't have any camera they may have wanted, and I still had my binoculars in my coat pocket. And I didn't lock anything in the room safe. What else could they have wanted?

Should I call the police? That wouldn't keep me from being harmed, especially in a foreign country. At least should I notify the front desk? What good would that do? The receptionist had just told me that no one had been looking for me. To get upstairs to my room, any intruder would have to slip past the front desk and have a key card to make the elevator run since the lobby stairway was locked from the outside. Not good.

So no, I was not calling the front desk.

I was starting to realize that I had stumbled onto something that was way out of my league. From what I saw through my binoculars yesterday afternoon, contraband packages of something were being flown by jet to an isolated airstrip south of Rotterdam. And there were gorillas keeping any wayward eyes from seeing what they were transporting. The packages were hidden in the Flexitank bladders and sent to wineries in France to be filled with wine. Then in all likelihood, the containers were being shipped to the US for distribution.

And what was that *something* in the packages? It was not a stretch of the imagination for me or anyone else. My bet was illegal narcotics.

Why the US? Well, I had learned way too much about narcotics production and distribution from an eccentric professor in medical school. He was really into stopping the increasing distribution of narcotics in the United States since that is where the world's largest narcotic supply was being sold. It was a private crusade he managed to weave into every course he taught in med school. A noble cause, but a losing battle.

I figured that if the drugs were coming on a plane with Chinese letters on it, then most likely they were coming from the Golden Triangle in southeast Asia, one of the two largest opium producing areas in the world. My professor explained that this was where the borders of Myanmar, Laos, and Thailand all came together. This whole region dominated the opium markets worldwide. The other leading opium producing country was Afghanistan, but it seemed unlikely as the source in this instance.

Too much to comprehend.

As I sat in a chair I had up righted, an epiphany came to me. I had been punched into the stomach twice and kicked in each flank the last two days, and yes, each of those areas ached. A lot. But despite all the unexpected physical abuse, my lower back absolutely had no pain. No discomfort whatsoever. Maybe it was because I hadn't been standing for long periods of time over an operating room table. Maybe. Maybe it was something else.

Perplexing.

Was I safe to stay here tonight? On second thought, probably no need to change hotels. If they could do all this, then they'd just follow me to a new hotel anyway. After asking myself all those questions, I decided my only real option was to hunker down in my room and high tail it back to the US tomorrow as planned. But come on, first the fiasco with Gorilla number one at the warehouse today and now this tornado in my room?

Somebody was definitely not thrilled about what they think I might have seen the last few days.

But who is that somebody?

12

LONDON – LONG ISLAND, NEW YORK

After placing as much of the furniture against the hotel room door as I could, I tended to a few scratches on my face and put some ice wrapped in a washcloth on the bruising of my left flank area. While I tried my best to rest, I only tossed and turned for hours upon end. I finally dozed in and out of sleep for a few hours in the early morning. Before daybreak, I called down to the front desk to tell them I needed a cab out front in about thirty minutes. No public transportation for me at this phase of the game.

Next, I showered, repacked my suitcase, and spent a while putting all the furniture back in its rightful place. Down in the lobby, I paid my bill and quickly dashed to the awaiting cab outside. Out front, there were no lingering persons looking my way as best as I could surmise. Before I got in the cab, I did check the license in the front seat of the cab with the photo ID of the cabbie just to make sure I wasn't jumping in with one of the gorillas.

Better safe than sorry.

At Heathrow Airport, I paid the cabbie and quickly hustled inside to get my boarding pass, despite being over two hours early for my flight. After making it through security, I had to find an out-of-the-way place to hide from any roaming gorillas. I looked at an airport map and found my airline's club lounge.

Head down and overcoat collar up, I reached the lounge front door. Because I worked all the time and didn't fly that much, I wasn't a member of any of the airlines' club lounges. As I approached the front desk, my luck had changed—there stood a tired, young lady who had obviously been there most of the night, ready to head home. We started chatting and I laid it on thick about how I didn't have my membership card with me. I offered to pay for a daily pass, but she waived me through.

I took a seat with my bag in the back of the lounge area and acted like I was reading my paperback. About every thirty minutes, I changed locations just to see if the few people in the lounge made notice of it.

Paranoia, sure. Overkill, maybe. Self-preservation, definitely.

Finally, about twenty minutes before my flight was scheduled to depart, I checked the flight departures screen up by the front desk and it said my flight was boarding. Leaving the airline club lounge, I made a beeline for my gate, checked in, and headed down the corridor to the plane. No gorillas in sight.

I took my seat and casually looked around the plane to make sure I was in the clear. We eventually took off, and I tried to calm myself that yesterday's events were the exception, not the rule to this little excursion.

I still didn't have an exact plan to how I was going to pull this one off, but as my favorite President Teddy Roosevelt once said, "Believe you can and you're halfway there."

Upon arrival at JFK Airport in New York, I headed for

the rental car desk, looking in all directions for any inconspicuous followers. After securing my rental contract, I took the rental car courtesy bus to the remote lot and finally found the not-so-fancy economy sedan that I had rented. No Corvette rentals on my managed care salary.

My general, but definitely not set-in-stone plan was to get lucky spotting trucks with burgundy container tags leaving the Port of New York heading east from the port towards some large facility where they would unload bulk wine in large quantities. From my search at the library in London, there were four primary container terminals at the Port of New York and New Jersey. The closest to JFK was in Brooklyn. The other three were in New Jersey, which was too damn far to fight traffic.

As for where they were taking the wine, I figured that with all the growing number of vineyards and wineries out on Long Island, which would be the place for processing the bulk wine. I mean, like Willie Sutton said when he was asked, "Why do you rob banks?" He replied, "That's where the money is."

I know that chasing any truck that had a filled Flexitank as cargo in its container would not necessarily mean the Flexitank was from Hawthorne Containers. But from my research in London, Hawthorne Containers held a really large share of that market at this time. I had to go with the odds in this longshot case.

It was close to dark, and I reasoned that I would never be able to track any truck in the dark anyway. I found a crummy, but still definitely not inexpensive, motel near the airport and chowed down on some greasy fast food at a nearby diner, assuring me of partial coronary artery occlusion at least sometime in the future.

When I got back to the motel, I took an armchair and wedged it underneath the doorknob of the motel room door. I knew logically it wouldn't stop someone if they really wanted in. I reasoned that the men who found me in London could most likely find me in New York. The chair may not stop them if they wanted into my room, but it may give me a few seconds warning. And besides, it made me feel as though I gave it my best shot.

The next morning, I set out long before sunrise. I was surprised how many people were on the road so early on their way to work on a busy Monday morning. I finally made it to the Red Hook Container Terminal in Brooklyn facing out towards Staten Island. I parked adjacent to the outer gate so that I could see the rear of the container trucks as they pulled away from the terminal gate. With my binoculars at the ready for each truck that left with a cargo container in place, I scanned the rear door to see if it had a burgundy-colored tag next to the bar code tag seal. About mid-morning, I was starting to get a little nervous that somebody from the terminal gate guardhouse would come and tell me to get lost, when a truck with a green stripe down the side of the container slowly pulled out of the terminal gate.

I knew that color design from somewhere. I pulled the binoculars up and looked at the rear door of the container. I really couldn't see if there was a burgundy tag on the back door or not. What should I do?

As a trauma surgeon, I knew that sometimes you had to make a time-sensitive diagnosis on limited information. Sometimes you didn't have all the lab results back before you had to act in order to save a life. But this wasn't life or death. So, what to do?

I turned the ignition on and pulled onto the road. I had inconclusive evidence based on a gut feeling. A lot of times that would get you and the patient into trouble. But sometimes, and usually just a few times out of many, it might mean the difference between great and horrible results for a patient. I sped up.

I don't claim to be the smartest physician in the world, but when I had a medical problem to solve, my tenacity usually won out in the end. And that's what I was going to do now. I decided to follow the truck heading to the freeway and then cruise behind him as he turned on I-495 towards the east end of Long Island. So far, so good.

After five to six miles on the freeway, the connection finally regurgitated from my cerebral hard drive. That green stripe down the side of the container was the same as I saw on the five trucks in the metal hanger at the airstrip south of Rotterdam. I never did get the name of the sister shipping company that did most of the trucking for Hawthorne Containers, but two plus two was starting to look a lot more like four.

I kept my distance on the freeway for about an hour until the truck signaled to get off the Long Island Expressway at the sign for Stony Brook. I got off also, keeping my distance, making sure with my continuing fear of gorillas that no one followed me. We snaked our way through the sleepy town of Hauppauge and then into Long Island suburbia. The truck made a turn off the main road down a fairly wooded lane, and I lagged back to play it safe. After half a mile, the truck turned into a huge facility with a massive entrance gate. I had to decide what to do. It was now or never for me.

Showtime.

I inched my rental car up to the guardhouse. The guard with a clipboard made his way out to greet me.

"How can I help you?" the man asked me through my open window.

"Hi there. My name is Kyle Chandler, and I'm from Wines and Vines Magazine. I have an appointment with the assistant winemaker for an interview at noon."

"I'm sorry sir, I don't see you name on the schedule for today," he said, looking at his clipboard. "Is she expecting you?"

"Yes sir," I said, fumbling at my shirt and coat pockets. "I've seemed to have lost the note with the assistant winemaker's name and number."

"That would be Lori Stimpler. She works with the winemakers on both the estate and bulk wine divisions. I'll see if I can locate her. If you'll wait here one minute, please."

And now for the moment of truth. Either she was too damn busy to mess with some pesky reporter where she had no idea of what I was doing here, or possibly just curious enough to why a wine magazine wanted to talk with her. I was banking on the latter.

"I spoke with one of the other winemakers, and he said she must be in one of the barrel rooms and that you could find her there. Turn left at the stop, then all the way down on the end to park on your right," he said as he reached inside the guardhouse to activate the raising of the gate barrier.

"Thank you very much. Have a nice day," I said, smiling back at him as I pulled forward.

I parked where the guard told me and walked inside a large building through an unmarked side door, following the hallway until it opened into a chilly, large open room filled with wooden barrels. The room was one level below the hallway, sort of built into the side of the slope of the property. Looking down at the expansive area, on the far end, I saw an attractive, tall woman dressed in faded blue jeans, work boots, and a black fleece jacket with her dark blonde hair pulled back in a ponytail. She was kneeling while taking samples from several barrels and putting them in a wire rack filled with glass beakers. I went down the stairs and headed her way. She didn't seem to notice me until I was standing right in front of her.

"Are you Lori Stimpler?" I asked.

She quickly looked up at me and then stood. It surprised me that she was as tall as I was. And despite the loose-fitting male work clothes, she was drop-dead attractive.

Seriously.

"Maybe," she said. "Who's asking?"

"I'm Kyle Chandler from Wines and Vines Magazine. I spoke with someone from the marketing department of your winery a while back. He said he arranged for me a 12:00 noon appointment today with you for an interview about your bulk wine making operation. Does that ring a bell?"

It was a long pause before she looked at me to reply.

"Marketing, really? I don't think so. Corporate doesn't like us speaking to the press except in a few rare cases. Now if you'll excuse me, Mister..."

"Chandler, Kyle Chandler."

"Yeah. As you can see, I'm very busy here, so if you'll excuse me," she said again.

"Look Ms. Stimpler, I know you are busy, but my editor wants a finished story from me on his desk by noon tomorrow about your company's take on the current bulk wine market. Let me ask you a few questions while you eat your lunch, and I'll be out of your hair in no time."

"Why the bulk wine market?" she asked. "Most wine magazines just want to focus on the high-end estate wines that drive so much of the profits. While bulk wine is still the workhorse part of wine production, there's nothing sexy, much less interesting about bulk wine."

"Just doing what I'm told. I'm sure you can relate to that in your own way."

I finally had gotten one small sentence through her protective shell of toughness as she barely cracked a smile.

She looked at me for a long moment and then said, "Follow me."

We weaved our way around the barrels and up the stairs. We then headed down a different hallway where she put her samples in a large industrial refrigerator. She dropped by a small cubicle that contained a single photo of her and a Labrador Retriever where she picked up a sack lunch in a brown bag.

I noticed no jewelry on her hands, especially her left fourth finger. Who knows, maybe rings were a hazard in her line of work. I continued to follow her as we ended up outside behind the building under a large shade tree sitting in two wooden chairs.

"Interesting chairs," I said.

"We have several guys who work in our vineyards that make them for us out of used wine barrels. And surprisingly, they're not that uncomfortable."

She sat there a few seconds, kind of like she wondered whether she should say anything at all to me before she started to open her lunch bag. She undid the rubber band on her ponytail then took off her fleece coat since it was warmer outside. Underneath she was wearing a long sleeve tight fitting t-shirt over an unbelievable figure. It had a Henley type collar with the top buttons unbuttoned.

Wow.

"Now what wine magazine are you from?" she asked as she unwrapped her sandwich.

"I'm from Wines and Vines Magazine. My boss wants to do a piece on the current bulk wine industry in the US. He wanted me to get you guys' opinion of the current profitability and where you think that market is headed in the next five years," I said as I tried not to stare at the obvious.

"And why are you talking to me about this? You should be talking to one of the owners to get their overenthusiastic viewpoint, not mine," she said in between slow bites to her sandwich.

"How long have you been a winemaker here?" I asked, trying to get some answers from her.

"A while. How long have you been a writer at your magazine?"

"How is it different working with the bulk wine division as compared to the estate wine division?" I asked, ignoring her question.

"How do you like doing wine industry statistical analysis articles as compared to human interest feature stories?"

It was obvious that I was getting nowhere. This was going to be one tough nut to crack.

She was an Aphrodite goddess in work clothes with the will of steel. Why was she hesitant to reveal anything about what she did and or why she did it? All I wanted was to get a look at the Flexitank bladders after they were emptied of the wine, and she was the obstacle I had to go through. I decided to try a different tact.

"Are you always this receptive to people who are trying to promote the business you work for?"

"Are you always this defensive when people don't give you immediately what you ask for?"

"Only when it involves mashed potatoes or strip poker."

She paused, and then commented with a straight face, "I can understand the mashed potatoes, especially if they are not whipped to get all the lumps out. But why the strip poker?"

"Because it's the only thing worthwhile I know where you win by losing first."

"And you know this from experience?" she asked with a gradually appearing smile on her face.

"Years of research."

"And how did your research include measuring the satisfaction of the winners?"

"By repeated participation in the experiment, of course. Practice makes perfect. Now, changing the subject, how did an independent, headstrong winemaker like you come all the way from Oregon out to the tight knit society of Long Island?" I asked.

"How do you know I'm from Oregon?"

"Lucky guess. Probably the Northwest work clothes ensemble. That and the small OSU sticker at your desk."

"Let me ask you Sherlock. Are you always probing for obscure details about the people you converse with?"

"To be honest with you, Watson, I only look when I'm awake. How long have you been out here on Long Island?"

She hesitated and then slowly let her guard down. "I graduated from Oregon State with my degree in viticulture and enology slightly over six years ago. I worked two years of harvests in Washington and Oregon right after school, and then spent two years after that, working harvests in France and New Zealand before landing here two years ago. Every place I worked made it very clear that a woman would never be able to make it to the top of the food chain, including here. I plan on showing them otherwise."

"And how's that coming along, Athena?"

"Better than you think, Ares. I've been slowly collecting investors over the years to start my own vineyard and eventual winery in the not-so-distant future."

"Ah, also a Greek mythology fan, I see," I said.

"Actually, I'm partial to their Roman names. And for the record, I prefer love, not war."

"Well then, I guess I'll need to forward you some information about my research."

"Only the part about the lab exercises," she said.

I had at least partially brought down the wall of protection she kept around herself, and it was time to scale the rest of it.

"What if I told you that getting information about the bulk wine market from you guys was not the only reason I came here to talk to you today."

"Well that's interesting," she said, "because so far you haven't gotten a single bit of information from me about the bulk wine division we operate here. You're gonna need to dig a little deeper if you're going to make this reporting gig work."

"Well, Lori, what if I told you that I'm not a reporter at all. In fact, the truth is that I'm a trauma surgeon who's on his way back from a medical conference in London. I also happen to do some work for an investigation firm in Kansas City. I'm currently investigating a situation out here on Long Island and I'm going to need your help."

She smiled a fake smile and responded with dripping sarcasm.

"Right. And my real name is Dorothy and as soon as we find Toto, we're going to meet the Munchkins and head down the Yellow Brick Road together."

I pulled out my cell phone and took off my hospital ID card I always keep attached to the cell phone case. Without speaking, I slowly handed it to her. While she was looking at it, I continued.

"I'll go one step further down the Yellow Brick Road to the unbelievable. Lori, what if I told you that there is a good, if not great, chance that you guys are right in the middle of a huge smuggling scheme to transport illegal substances into the United States, and you didn't even know it."

She handed me back my ID card and paused again before answering.

"How do I know that anything you've said is true? I don't even know you. You could be an ax-murderer for all I know."

"Yeah, well, don't worry about that. I don't even think about sharpening my blade until after I eat, but I am getting hungry for lunch," I said.

She waited another moment before replying, still unsure about me.

"You're not joking about the smuggling, are you?" she asked.

I silently moved my head from side to side.

"You're a trauma surgeon? And you're a private eye on the side? No way."

I now slowly nodded my head.

"And just exactly how am I supposed to believe a complete stranger about a bizarre scenario like that? You haven't explained a thing to me."

"You're right. I haven't explained myself in the least to you, so far. Fair enough. But, if I tell you all the details of what I suspect, then that may put you in a not-so-great position of being followed and harassed just like I was in London. And likely to be real soon here to boot. It's up to you."

After a brief pause, she said, "Throughout my travels, I've learned to handle myself pretty well, thank you. I'll take my chances. So give me the details."

I guess she thought she was Wonder Woman. I'll have to admit, she had the same body, only not as quite a revealing outfit.

I proceeded to explain to her the highlights of initially seeing the Flexitank containers at the Port of Tilbury, followed by the flight over to Holland and seeing what I saw at the airstrip south of Rotterdam. I kind of skipped over the nearly bad pseudo-abduction in London and the hotel room trashing because I didn't want to scare her off at this point. By the end of the summary, she had quit eating her sandwich and was leaning back in her chair, staring at me.

"So, what do you think?" I asked, breaking the silence.

"I don't know if I really believe you, or if you should be with Jack Nicholson and the rest of the mental patients answering to Nurse Ratched."

"Okay. That's fair. But what if I said 'Let's go have a look for ourselves' at the container with the Flexitank that pulled up in front of me at your front gate. It's probably being emptied as we speak."

She kind of turned her Greek goddess face to the side while still looking directly at me with her eyes and then slowly nodded.

"I guess that wouldn't be too difficult," she said.

We got up from the barrel chairs and I followed her inside through a labyrinth of hallways until we were at the other end of the compound. We ended up at a roofed outdoor area where a large composition of hoses and pipes were pumping the remaining wine from the Flexitank bladder still in the container of the truck that I followed into the winery.

As we approached the rear end of the container, there were two men present. One was attending to the hose connected to the Flexitank and the other was standing guard making sure no one would be getting close to interfere.

"Excuse me, that's as close as you can come. You'll have to stand back at a distance, please, strict Teamsters' Union rules," the guy standing guard said.

"Do what?"

"Oh yeah," Lori said. "I forgot to tell you. The transport company is the sole agent responsible for the Flexitank and its disposal after the wine is pumped to our tanks. They don't allow anyone, including any of us who work here, to come close to the Flexitank bladder while emptying it. Something about confidentiality of 'intellectual property ownership' as it is stated in one of the contracts."

"You've got to be joking."

"No, it's the real deal. They have a tight security system here. Lots of cameras, laser motion sensors at night, the whole bit. Part of the joys of corporate winemaking."

I stood there wondering what to do next.

"Let me show you around the facility where we do all of the blending of the wines to come up with our final product," Lori said to me just a little too loud, making sure that the guy standing guard heard her.

I followed her inside and over to a window where we could keep an eye out on our two trucker friends outside. We stood away from the window and both watched in silence.

When the bladder was obviously empty, the guy up in the container disconnected the hose and gave it to the guy standing guard, who handed it to some winery worker. Then, the standing guard got into the container with the first guy and pulled the overhead door closed.

How convenient.

"What are you going to do now?" She said to break the silence.

"Well, that pretty much narrows down my options, wouldn't you say? I guess I'll have to follow them until they drop off the empty bladder somewhere."

"And what if they are taking it from here all the way to Alaska?" she asked.

"Alaska of all places, you say? Well, I guess I will finally get to see some of North Dakota and Idaho, which will be good since those are about the only two states other than Alaska that I haven't been to before..." I said.

She looked at me with a scowl.

"What? When did you get so concerned with what might be inside the empty Flexitank bladders except wine?" I asked, as I was still looking out the window with no sign of the container door opening yet.

"Since you indicated that our company just might be involved in the transport of illegal substances without knowing it," she said defensively.

"You know, we've only been best friends for…what do you think…thirty minutes at most? And despite your will of steel stuck in a model's body disguised with male work clothes, you actually have a sense of caring in there somewhere that nobody gets to see. How's that?"

She was taken aback by the sudden presentation of my honesty that she didn't respond at first.

"Caught you off guard, didn't I?"

"Yeah, you did. You really did. And now my turn," she said boldly.

"Okay."

"How come someone like you isn't married already?"

Wow, that one did surprise me.

"I was going to ask you that," I said.

"Sorry, I asked first."

"Well, with my current schedule of me being at the hospital all the time, that's something that will not likely happen in the near future. To be completely honest with you, I've been seeing a fantastic woman back in Kansas City since April of this year. But, let the truth be told, I was married once. I don't usually let that history fact be known to a stunning woman like yourself."

Shaking off the indirect compliment, she plowed forward.

"What happened? Did she leave you because you cheated on her with another woman?"

"Why would you assume that it would be the guy who cheats on his wife instead of vice versa?"

"You might say personal experience, and I'll leave it at

that. So, what happened?"

After a major awkward pause, I said, "Uh, well, she died in an auto accident. Eight years ago. And I'm finally getting to the point of noticing a rare, attractive woman like you without feeling guilty."

She was taken aback for a second by my response.

"Dr. Chandler, I must say that you are the virtual definition of a piece of work."

Just about then, the overhead door rolled up and the two guys were carrying a large, folded mass of the Flexitank bladder. The guy that had stood guard before jumped down and started to call someone from his mobile phone.

"Look, ah, Lori, you've been a great best friend for the last thirty-five minutes. But about the only option I have here is to get to my car and see where they are headed with that empty bladder. Can you lead me inside through your complex to my car before these guys take off without me?"

"Sure thing. Follow me," she said as she headed towards an exit door.

After multiple hallways and several sets of stairs, we came out the unmarked door I first entered through. I got in my rental car, and she leaned down into my open car window as I buckled my seatbelt.

Let me tell you, it took all the willpower that I could muster to not stare at the obvious cleavage staring right back at me.

"Good luck on starting your vineyard and winery. I know you have both the drive and the looks to make it work. I expect to be reading about your award-winning wines soon. If you're ever in Kansas City…" I lobbed the suggestion to her.

"I'll know who I can get with to try some of those lab exercises of yours," she said with a subtle smile on her face.

Ah, the power of youth and beauty. Definitely a strong dual combination.

I turned the car around and pulled up to the exit gate just as a plain white panel van pulled through the entrance side of the gate and headed back towards the container truck. I stopped and acted like I was trying to reach for something under my seat, all the while looking in the rear-view mirror. Just like clockwork, the van pulled up to the rear end on the container and the mass of folded bladder material was loaded in the back of the van. The guy who had stood guard crawled in the front passenger seat, and they turned around heading my way.

I exited the gate and pulled to the side of the road. The white van zoomed past me, and now the unsure process of tailing the van had begun.

You sure you want to do this, Chandler?

13

HOBOKEN, NEW JERSEY – QUEENS, NEW YORK

After leaving the wine processing plant, I kept my distance from the white van as it headed back on I-495 West in the direction of New York City. When we reached Queens, the van turned north towards the Bronx. Traffic was really getting to be a mess this Monday afternoon. I almost lost sight of the van a couple of times but managed to keep it in view the best that I could.

They kept going over the George Washington Bridge to New Jersey, and then turned south like they were going to Newark. Finally, the van turned off I-95 and ended up around dark in the heart "Old Blue Eyes" hometown, Hoboken. After several turns, they pulled into a cyclone-fenced lot, closing the gate behind them, before driving into a large metal building at the back. As I crept up to the edge of the lot in my rental car, I came to realize that they were completely out of view from me.

Perfect. Now what?

I drove past the closed gate and turned around at the end of the block. I nudged the rental car a little closer and shut off the engine. Looking down at the dashboard, I realized I was almost out of gas. To add to the fun, I hadn't eaten dinner and was dog-tired from all the driving in traffic.

And why was I doing this again?

I sat in my car just gazing out across the street to the building where I couldn't see anything at all. Racking my brain for any ideas of what to do next wasn't working. In life, just like in surgery, sometimes you need to wait and see what the situation was willing to give you.

After fifteen to twenty minutes of not coming up with any logical way for me to proceed, headlights came out of the building. Multiple cars came out one after another. I counted four cars with the white van in front. The van and two cars went north and two went right by me heading south. Split decision time. Should I follow one of them?

My intuition told me that the chances of me successfully following one of those cars to its destination was not really good. The fact was I was here right now. So, I decided to go make the best of it.

I turned on the engine and pulled through the open gate driving back to the metal building. As I got out, I knew it was going to take an Oscar winning performance to pull off something like this.

Better now than never.

"Excuse me, sir? Could I ask you a question?" I said as I walked through the open garage door.

A young guy sat on the hood of a sports car talking in a low voice to an elder gentleman dressed in an older-type baggy suit. Both immediately stopped talking, straightened up, and turned to me as I strode in.

"I'm so sorry; I didn't mean to startle you. My name's Jim Buchanan," I said loudly as I walked up and extended my right hand to the older gentleman.

"I'm visiting a friend of mine, and I'm just about out of gas in my rental car," I said as I finished shaking the hand of the surprised older gentleman and now thrust my hand out to shake the younger guy's hand.

"Could either of you tell me where the nearest gas station is located? I would be ever so grateful if you could point me in the right direction to get some gas," I said in a machine gun cadence. "Wow, nice car you got here," I said as I looked at the sports car and then casually over their shoulders around the room. While eyeing the fancy sports car, I saw what I thought was the corner of a briefcase standing up behind the automobile.

"Listen, buddy, do you have any idea of the trouble you may be in walking in here unannounced like that?" the younger man said, refusing my handshake.

"Easy, Dominic," the older man said, putting his arm out to keep the younger man from getting in my face. "How long have you been here?" the elder man asked.

"I saw a light on and so I drove up just now. Like I said, I'm looking for a place nearby to fill up my gas tank."

Dominic looked at the older gentlemen and said, "Lorenzo, we gotta take care of this."

"Let me handle this, Dominic."

The older gentleman turned back to me and paused before he spoke.

"Mister..."

"Buchanan. Jim Buchanan."

"Yes. Mr. Buchanan. Is it safe to say that you are not from New Jersey?" he asked in a thick, somewhat Italian-American accent.

"No sir. Like I said, I'm here visiting a friend of mine."

"Yes. Now, did you happen to see any other cars around here as you drove into our private property?"

"Not that I know of. Like I told you, I saw your light on and just drove in."

"I see," the older man said. "Mr. Buchanan let me

explain something to you. We have a private business we run here. We take it very seriously. Some of our competitors would very much like to diminish our market dominance that took us many years for us to achieve. They will go to extreme lengths to gain an advantage over us. If there is any possible way that you are connected to one of our competitors, then showing up here tonight has put you in a bad situation, both short and long term. Do you understand me?"

"Not completely, but I do understand your concern. And you can count on me one hundred percent that I'm just here to ask where the closest gas station is. Which is where, by the way?"

Lorenzo once again calmly held out his arm to keep Dominic from lunging out on his prey.

"If you leave here and head north six blocks, turn left on Fourteenth Street, and there should be a Shell station open until 10:00 p.m."

"Thank you so much sir. You've been very helpful. You both have a blessed evening," I said as I stuck my right hand out again. Neither man moved a muscle, so I turned and walked to my rental car.

After I left the meeting site, I followed the directions I was given and actually went to the Shell station to fill up with gas. I had to appear like the guy I told them I was, especially if I was being followed on their turf. I decided to go back to the crummy, and still definitely not inexpensive, motel near the airport where I had stayed the previous night. It seemed to take forever to get to the motel from Hoboken. Why do people put up with such traffic to waste so much of their time each day?

When I got to Queens, I picked up some drive-thru fast food before checking back into the same motel. When I got to my room, I took an armchair and wedged it underneath the doorknob of the motel room door. Then I took a long shower and collapsed on the bed too tired to get under the sheets.

While I lay there, the events of the day kept getting replayed over and over in my head. First, the guy standing guard by the Flexitank bladder being emptied at the winery processing center. That was more than a little unusual. And the gorgeous, quick-witted winemaker was pretty unusual, too, I must say.

Next, the secretive transfer of the empty bladder from Long Island all the way to a nondescript location in Hoboken, New Jersey was more than kind of weird. If illegal drugs were packed in that bladder, the four cars and the white van had them well on their way to distribution by now.

And who were the two hoods I spoke with in Hoboken? Probably from the shoot first ask questions later type of crowd. But I hadn't seen anything incriminating other than a closed briefcase while glancing around their building as I was putting on my act with them.

Should I go to the police? That wouldn't help. They wouldn't believe me anyway. Still lots of questions, not many answers. As I drifted off to sleep, there was one decision I did make.

I decided that it would be best to stay put for tonight. Hope that armchair is strong.

14

NEW YORK CITY – NORTH BLUE RIDGE, KANSAS CITY

The next morning, I checked out of the forgettable motel, returned the rental car, and checked in at the airport for my flight back to Kansas City. I looked back over my shoulder throughout the morning just as a precaution. No gorillas on the horizon that I could see.

After getting a bite to eat at some airport food stand, I checked my voicemail for messages. Half of them were from my administrative assistant Janice. We couldn't use the term secretary any longer according to my employer Columbus HealthCare System. It was too belittling they proclaimed. She had worked for me since I started my practice in Kansas City almost eight years ago. Janice was competent, not really excitable, but definitely knew her job description of what she didn't have to do even if she was capable. Lots of things for me to do in her messages, especially since I had been away for a week.

There was one call from Ian Griffin leaving me a message to check in with him as soon as I had a chance. There were two missed calls from Caroline on my call log with no messages left. That was kind of disappointing, especially since I had been gone for a whole week. I guess the olive branch offering before I left didn't take hold as well as I thought it might. I thought about calling her before I boarded the plane, but since she didn't leave me a message with either call, I guess it could wait until I got back to Kansas City.

After a delay in boarding my flight, we finally made it away from the gate and taxied for takeoff. I casually glanced around the plane to see if I could find any lurking gorillas. Unfortunately, this new habit of looking over my shoulder was here to stay for a while.

The flight to Kansas City, despite the self-centered moron sitting in front of me leaning his chair all the way back into my lap, was otherwise uneventful. It was late afternoon before I made it to the airport long-term parking lot. The shuttle bus finally stopped in front of my car, as I was ready to get home at last.

Ah yes, there it was, my Swedish utilitarian chariot. It was an older Volvo sedan that I purchased when I first arrived in Kansas City. It was a modified square metal box on wheels, not an early mid-life-crisis sports car like many of my current contemporary physicians drove. It had rear-wheel drive, which made for challenging driving in the winter, the back-end fishtailing on slick roads. A perpetual lesson in humility.

Despite the super unflashy appearance, it started on the first key turn. Got to love that Swedish engineering. While I let the engine warm up after sitting in the parking lot all last week, I punched out Ian Griffin's number on my mobile phone.

"Kyle, are you back to your crazy schedule of putting

car crash victims back together? How was your flight back?" he asked in his Scottish accent.

"There was a little change in plans Ian," I said. "I'm just now getting in my car at the airport here in KC. I had to stay a couple of extra days in London to follow up on some leads on something else I found while I was there."

"I'd love to hear about it. Could you meet me at the secure tavern I took you to previously, say in about thirty minutes?"

"Ian, I haven't been home for over a week. I really need to sort things out at home before the onslaught at work tomorrow."

"Well lad, I'm scheduled to fly to Chicago early tomorrow morning to meet a new client on what sounds like a big case they'd like us to investigate. I won't be back until the weekend. It'll just take a few minutes to discuss things at the tavern. You know how I feel about saying anything over the treacherous phone lines, even with cell phones," he said persuasively.

I was already beat from all the travel, but he was the one who was paying the bills for my services. Might as well get it done. Besides, maybe he could help me figure out this whole hidden compartment situation.

"All righty Ian, I should be there in about a half an hour."

"Thank you. I'll see you then," he said and hung up the line.

After paying the attendant at the long-term parking lot, I steered my Swedish sedan onto the freeway south on I-29 toward town through the late afternoon traffic. The airport in Kansas City was built way north of town. I guess they could get the land fairly cheap when they were deciding where to put a newer airport. It sure seemed to me like the middle of nowhere.

I vaguely remembered that the secure tavern I had been to with Ian was on the industrial part of town east of downtown. I racked my brain trying to remember the location on my drive into town. The tavern's location finally popped into my head as I exited off the freeway. It was just before 5:00 p.m. when I turned into the asphalt parking lot in front of the ramshackle bar.

From the outside, this place was a dump. Seedy was a more realistic way to describe it. However you wanted to define this establishment, it was popular because I snagged the very last parking spot on the whole parking lot. The thing was, it wasn't even a weekend night with football on the big TV screen.

When I walked in, the owner recognized me as definitely not a regular. Looking straight at me, he motioned his head towards the back where Ian was settled in his usual booth.

As I sat opposite Ian, the owner reappeared asking, "What'll it be?"

"I'll have whatever dark beer you have on tap."

"And I'll stand pat, Tommy," Ian said before the owner could ask him what he wanted.

I slowly looked all around this place, remembering the first and only time I had been here with Mr. Griffin earlier in the spring.

"Thanks for coming. Do you remember this place?"

"Sort of. I remember you telling me something about the owner turning this into a security fortress."

"Exactly. We don't have to worry about being overheard. Now tell me what you found on your travels," Ian said enthusiastically.

"Well Ian, as I explained to you when I called from the airport, the search to see if there was a switch of original antique pieces for quality counterfeits pretty much came up flat empty. Both meetings with the contacts you gave me were very informative. I met with Mr. Clanton Rogers last Tuesday and he filled me in on most of the details of the case. But the information he gave me really didn't help determine if a switch occurred either there or in New York."

"He seemed like a reasonable chap when I arranged the

meeting for you," Ian said.

"Yeah, I agree," I said. "The next day I met with Senior Constable Colin Butterworth at the Port of Tilbury. He must be ex-military because he runs a tight ship. The Senior Constable discussed at length with me about the whole process of security procedures at their busy port. He gave me a mini-tour of the highly guarded facility, which helped me understand their security a lot better."

"That sounds encouraging."

"I had one more interview with a Mr. Sebastian Clarke, the Head of Estates, Appraisals & Valuations at Christie's. I got his name from the woman I have been seeing here in town. She trained with him a while back in London. He is one knowledgeable expert on antiques of all kinds. He pretty much assured me that the larger auction houses, especially them and Sotheby's, have a system of multiple levels of security to prevent tampering of objects up for sale."

"Interesting. Now from your interviews, your conclusion is exactly what?"

"Ian, if there was actually a switch of an original antique piece in this case for a highly convincing fake, it had to have happened prior to the pieces being shipped to London. I obviously don't know any of the precise security procedures that went on in New York before the shipment left, but I do know that it would have been very, very, unlikely that a switch occurred in the UK with all the security procedures they currently have in place. I talked to Mr. Rogers by phone on Thursday, explaining in detail what I found and why I thought the cause was not on this end of the transaction. He seemed to understand."

"Excellent, lad. Good communication is key. In this business, you have to roll with wherever the facts of the case lead you," Mr. Griffin said. "Now what did you find in addition to all of this that led you to stay over there a couple of more days? Or can you tell me her actual name?"

"No, Ian. Despite what you might think, it's nothing like that."

I waited a moment before I decided to tell him my suspicions of the smuggling scheme I came across.

"I need your experienced opinion on how to handle something I might have stumbled upon while I was over there."

"Go on."

"Well Ian, on the day when I went out to the Port, I also had an appointment just east of there that a friend of mine wanted me to go to for him. He's a wine importer and wants to ship wine in large bladder-like containers from France to Kansas City. So he arranged for me to meet with the plant manager at a factory where they make the bladders."

"Then," I said, "while I was touring the Port of Tilbury later the same afternoon with the Senior Constable, on our tour we came across a freight container that held one of those large bladders full of bulk wine. The port inspectors were inspecting the bladder with a crane-like extension with a guy in a cherry-picker bucket looking into the container. With the bladder full of wine, you really couldn't see anything but the full bladder container."

"Interesting. What did that have to do with anything?"

"Well, for some reason, it just didn't sit right with me. The Senior Constable told me a bunch of ways people have tried to smuggle stuff illegally that he had seen throughout his long career. And here was a container full of liquid right in front of us and you barely could see just one end of it."

"And…" Ian said.

"I went to the library there in London the next day to do some research about the bladders and who makes them, who owns the company, what their share of the market is and the like. That led me and my driver to go searching for an airstrip just south of Rotterdam the next day..."

"Wait a minute," Ian said. "How did you get over to Holland all of a sudden?"

"Well, we went there because of something the plant manager at the bladder manufacturing plant let slip while we talked, and then what an elderly landlady I talked to mentioned about smuggling."

"What are you…"

"It's not that important. What's important is that I believe we saw a private jet with Chinese markings land at an airstrip and drop off a bunch of small packets of something. These packets were being placed into trucks with the bladder containers. We were ready to leave but got delayed when two gorillas showed up."

"Kyle, this is getting serious. We need to…"

"Don't worry, we got lucky. They assaulted us, but we were okay."

"Kyle!"

"Anyway Ian, I was pretty much followed from then on and got in a tight situation again with the reoccurring gorillas, so I hightailed it back to the States."

"It's about time you finally used your head. Kyle, really, this is getting dangerous."

"Well, I had to find out if the smuggled goods were coming into the US. I decided to try and follow one of the trucks from one of the ports in New York. I followed one truck filled with one of these bladders of wine out to one of the winery depots on Long Island. After that I followed the emptied bladder all the way back to Hoboken, New Jersey where I think I stumbled onto where they distribute the illegal merchandise."

"Are you sure?" Ian asked.

"I'm pretty sure. The biggest problem now is that I think it might have to do with organized crime."

"Organized crime! Kyle, what have you gotten yourself into?"

"Well, I think I'm in the clear for now. I got out of there quick like and back to Kansas City. They don't know who I am right now. At least I don't think so. Now I just hope the Mafia in New York is not best buddies with the local mob here."

"Kyle, this is no laughing matter. This is serious business. These guys don't play nice. We need to contact the authorities, starting with the FBI. And right away."

"My research shows that the guy who owns the container manufacturing factory is out of New York. He's not going to have any pull all the way here in Kansas City."

"Kyle, you don't know that. We need to contact the authorities."

"Ian, if I tell the FBI what I suspect about this smuggling scheme, that will be followed by countless interviews with the DEA and FBI filled with constant, repeated questioning about why I was in Holland looking for an airstrip in the first place. Not to mention why I was chasing bladders filled with wine in New York. I'll be spending the rest of my life on the run looking over my shoulder all the time in the witness protection program. That's no way to live."

"You have a better idea?" Ian asked.

"I've a vague idea that just may work. Give me some time to check it out to see if it'll work, and then I'll get back to you."

"In the meantime, you'd better keep your head down, lad. And I mean it."

"Will do, Ian. I'll be in touch," I said as I got up to leave.

They say it's better to be lucky than good. I sure hope that's true right about now.

15

KANSAS CITY

I made it home to my condo in one piece and was a bit hesitant to open the door to what I might see. A similar situation of walking in and finding my condo trashed is what started me on this side-career of private investigation in the first place. Upon entering, I cautiously looked around. Everything seemed pretty normal.

I dropped my stuff in the bedroom and ambled to the kitchen to review my phone messages. There were several that could be taken care of later in the week. But strangely enough, there were four calls on the message register from Caroline and no messages left.

A cold shiver went down my spine again. Not a good sign. Caroline wouldn't have me called four times while I was gone and not leave a message. Even if it were just to check in of how things were going.

I picked up the phone and dialed her office phone number. As expected, all I got was her work message machine since it was after business hours. I hung up and dialed her cell phone number. After five rings, it sent me to her voicemail. Another not-so-good sign.

I stood there getting more worried about all the things that could have happened to Caroline when my cell phone rang. The unexpected sound damn near scared me half to death.

"Hello?"

"Hey, how was your flight back Sunday?" Caroline's voice filtered into my ear.

"Are you okay?"

"Yeah, of course. Why wouldn't I be?"

"Well, I just got home from my trip today and there are two calls listed on my cell phone and multiple calls listed on my message machine at home saying you called but left no messages."

"Do what? I left you messages on both your home and cell phone wishing you a smooth flight back and that I was looking forward to seeing you."

"Caroline, I got zero messages from you on both my cell phone and my home phone."

"That's really strange. There must be some mess-up on your voicemail or something. And why did you say you just got home? You told me that you were coming home Sunday evening."

"There was a change in my schedule, and I had to stop off in New York to take care of something," I said, trying to make it sound unimportant.

She paused before she responded to my comment. With that pause, I knew that this situation was going to get complicated really quick.

"Doctor Kyle Chandler," she said, "What do you mean you had to take care of something? You know darn well that by now, I can tell when you trying to hide something from me."

"What are you talking about?" I asked, trying to sound innocent.

"Let's go Kyle. Spill the beans to me right now."

"Ms. Martinelli. Must you know every detail about my life?"

"You're stalling," she said firmly.

Well, I was cornered, and it looked like I was not getting out of this one.

"Remember that I told you that I spoke with Ian Griffin before my trip?"

"Of course. You asked me to get in touch with Sebastian Clarke at Christie's so you could meet with him. I couldn't reach Sebastian, so I left him a message. Did you get to meet with him?" she asked.

"Yeah, I did. He's a super nice guy. A funny coincidence happened when I was talking with Mr. Clarke at his office. He remembered your old landlady in London and how fond she is of you. He suggested I go pay her a visit while I was in town, so I went to her place that afternoon."

"You're kidding! You went to see Iris?"

"Absolutely. She sends her love to you," I said.

"How is she doing?" Caroline asked anxiously.

"Mrs. Kettleman is sharp as a tack for her age. We had a great conversation. She told me all about her husband flying in the war, her affection for you, and even her opinion on ways to smuggle goods into the country."

"Smuggling?"

"It was really nothing. Back to the thing Ian Griffin had me look into. He arranged for me to meet with the Chief Constable of the Port of Tilbury east of London," I said. "It was concerning a case about an irregularity of some shipment of French period antiques. Ian also set up a meeting for me with a gentleman to discuss the case. In the end, it was an innocent meeting that turned out to be nothing. Case closed."

"If it was case closed, as you call it, then why did you have to stop off in New York to take care of something? Answer me that."

I thought I had gotten by explaining that part of my

extended trip, but Caroline was too clever to forget it.

"Like I said, the minor investigation that I was looking into came up empty. And that's all there was to it."

"Okay," she replied. "But Kyle Chandler, I know you too well. There was something else, wasn't there? What else did that inquisitive mind of yours find when you were in London?"

Oh boy. This was going to be like my boy Teddy Roosevelt going up San Juan Hill. This woman was beyond persistent. Maybe that's why I was so intrigued by her.

"Caroline, do you have your cell phone with you?"

"Yeah, sure. It's in my purse. Why?"

"Caroline, let me call you back right now on your cell phone."

"Do what?"

"You heard me. Just hang up and I'll call you right back on your cell phone."

"But Kyle, whatever for?"

"Caroline, just trust me on this one. I'll call you right back on your cell phone."

"If you say so. Bye."

I hung up and waited ten seconds. I then called her on my cell phone.

"Hello, this is Caroline."

"I'm just being careful, that's all."

"Kyle, why are you're being so careful? Is it from something that you found while you were in London?"

"Well, I did happen to come across another strange occurrence while I was there..." I caved in and told her what happened. I proceeded to give her the highlights of my pursuit of finding out about the extra something being hidden in the Flexitank bladders. I will admit, I did leave out a few of the details of the run-ins with gorillas just to prevent any kind of excessive worry on her part. As I explained the perplexing tale, she didn't speak, waiting for me to finish my story before making any comments.

"So, when I got home and checked my home phone

messages, I found calls from you without leaving any messages. That got me a tad worried," I said.

"Like I told you, I did leave you messages," she said. "Why do you think you didn't get them, unless there's another reason you suspect that you're not telling me?"

Time to fish or cut bait.

"I have a suspicion that somebody connected with this situation I was looking into might be interested in my whereabouts. And that somebody just might have the ability to monitor my phone calls and manipulate my phone messages."

"Kyle, you can't be serious?"

"Serious as a heart attack. I pretty much know they are doing it to my home phone. I don't know for sure that they can monitor my cell phone. The thing that worries me the most is that they know that they can get to me through you. They only deleted your messages, not my other messages."

"What does that mean, Kyle?"

"That means that from now on, we'll have to discuss things only in person and not over the phone. We can't have them knowing every single thing about what we do. In the meantime, you're going to have to be double-dog careful about any suspicious people you might see at work, on the way home, at the grocery store, wherever. Until I get a better handle on who's behind all this, we've got to play it safe."

"You've got to contact the authorities about this thing right now. Kyle, I can't spend my whole life looking over my shoulder trying to identify the boogieman. I have a business to run. I have things that I need to take care of. I have a life, too, you know."

"I know Caroline. I will call the FBI or someone tomorrow to see what they think."

"Promise me, right now!"

"Okay, I promise. Caroline, I'm so sorry that I got you into this mess. Trust me; I know how busy your life is. But that's the situation we're in right now, so we just got to ride this one out. Together. Besides, you seeing me every day to discuss things just might convince you that I'm not all bad, at least for a surgeon."

"Don't be so sure of that, Doctor."

"Moving on, have you eaten anything for dinner yet? I can take you to another out of the way place I know where we can discuss this further over dinner. Or we could skip dinner all together and go straight for dessert…"

"Relax, Romeo. I have yet another board meeting tonight, followed by my aerobics class. Maybe later this week."

"Are you skipping dinner then?"

"How do you think I can still get into that little black cocktail dress that you like so much?"

"Caroline, you know damn well that it's not the dress that wows me. It's the shape inside that takes my breath away. So, Thursday then, for dinner?" I asked, trying to wiggle my way into her schedule.

"That'll probably work. Let me call you tomorrow when I can look at my work schedule."

"Caroline, remember what I said about using the phone?"

"Oh, yeah. I forgot. Well, come by my work when you get off tomorrow, and we'll discuss it."

"Okay. See you then," I said as I hung up.

That woman truly had me bewildered, in the most amorous way. Maybe the olive branch pendulum was swinging back to the positive side. I had to think of some method to keep it that way. And that would likely require getting any following gorillas off my back.

Time for a come from behind touchdown, Chandler.

16

ST. JUDE HOSPITAL MEDICAL COMPLEX, KANSAS CITY

Wednesday morning came early as a shock to my system with the onslaught of reality. I had originally planned to come home from the conference on Sunday. That would have given me one day to do chores at home and a day at the office to catch up on paperwork before seeing patient appointments starting today. No such luck.

Now that I had been on the Flexitank bladder wild goose chase in New York and New Jersey, I was going to have to make up for lost time in the office as I went along.

I had decided to come in early to the office to attempt to chip away the Mount Everest sized stack of paperwork in my inbox. On my way there, I used my mobile phone to place a call to see what information about Hawthorne Containers that I could weasel out of my ex-father-in-law.

"Good morning, Bain Capital, Mr. Williamson's office.

How may I help you?" a pleasant, but firm woman's voice asked.

"Good morning, this is Dr. Kyle Chandler. I know that Tremont gets there to the office early on days that he is not at Harvard. May I speak with him please?"

"I'm sorry. I see here that you do not have a phone appointment scheduled, and I'm afraid his schedule, like most days, is completely full."

"Well, why don't you tell him that I have some vital information concerning his present health status that as a physician I have a moral obligation to discuss this with him? Immediately," I said just as quickly as she had answered.

"Hold the line please. I'll see if he's in."

I knew damn well he was in. Tremont always wanted to get the jump on the next guy and went to the office at insanely early hours. And besides, his longstanding secretary knew where he was almost every millisecond of the day.

"What do you want?" the agitated voice on the end of the line asked.

"And good morning to you, too, Tremont."

Silence.

"It's been a while since we've last spoken, but I wanted to touch base with you about a financial proposition that has been presented to me. I figured that if anyone knew the inside scoop, it would be you," I said.

"I only discuss financial information with my limited personal clients."

"I'm sure that you could make an exception for a previous family member of yours."

"Not likely," he said in an icy tone.

Not taking the bait, I bulled forward.

"My financial advisor suggested I should look into investing in an up-and-coming company named Hawthorne Containers. Seems that they are based out of England. The company is producing a product called Flexitank, a one-time use PVC bladder that is used to transport large volumes of liquids, like bulk wine for example. The company is owned by the conglomerate Evolution Industries. Their CEO is a guy named Philip Hauser. Do you know him?"

"As a matter of fact, I do. He's a smart enough guy. He's been successful in acquiring growing companies."

"Do you know anything about this Hawthorne Containers company?"

"Haven't a clue. Tell your financial advisor that he can look up all you need to know about the company's financial status without my help."

"Well, as a matter of fact, he did just that. He found out that a certain MAW Trust, Inc. was one of the major stockholders in the company. And guess who he told me was the President and CFO of that trust?"

Silence from his end of the phone line.

"Now, why would a chunk of Molly's trust be capitalized as an initial investor in an upstart English container production company? That is, unless the president of that trust had some kind of information and knew something that the public didn't?"

"You didn't know what you were talking about when you married my daughter back then, and you don't know what you're talking about now. I make all kinds of investments for all kinds of complicated reasons, and I don't have the time to explain it to you. Anything else?"

"No thanks. Tremont, you have been a wealth of information. Thank you for fitting me into your busy schedule."

"Kyle, like I've told you many times before, we all have our own hidden agendas. Some more important than others," he said smugly before hanging up.

I decided to make a quick call to Sydney before leaving my car to the busy office schedule of the day awaiting.

"Kyle, my boy, are you back from your trip?" Sydney asked.

"Yes sir, I am. I'm about to head into the office and wanted to touch base with you first."

"Are we still on for golf this afternoon and dinner at my club tonight?"

"Sorry, Sydney. You know how much I enjoy playing golf with you and being away from the rat race of the hospital. I'm afraid the office is going to be dominating all of my time for the next few days since I was gone all last week."

"Ridiculous, my boy. They won't miss you for just a few hours of golf."

"Sorry Sydney. I'm going to have to pay the piper for being away last week. But I did want to say that I looked into a matter in London for your friend Ian Griffin."

"Yes, I spoke with him week before last. He explained his situation to me and I told him that he should give you a call since you were headed to England for your conference."

"I figured you had something to do with him calling me," I said. "Next time we meet, I will tell you what I found over there about something that was totally unexpected. For now, I wanted to tell you that it led to me calling your beloved half-brother Tremont."

"Really? What did that scoundrel have to say to you?"

"Not much. I was trying to get some information about a company I had looked into, and he said that he didn't know anything about it. When I challenged him that I found out a trust that he controls using Molly's name was one of the major shareholders, he told me to mind my own business."

"Typical Tremont. I told you that once I left Boston so many years ago, there was no love lost between us. Even though we had the same mother, he was the younger brother who was doted upon by my stepfather. He turned into a ruthless businessman after I left for Kansas City. He would sell our own mother into indenture if it would hand him a hefty profit."

Wow, I didn't know that there was that much friction between Sydney and my ex-father-in-law. They were definitely at different ends of the personality spectrum.

"Well Sydney, I've got to get to the office now. Maybe

dinner next Wednesday?" I asked.

"You're always welcome for dinner with me. Don't work so damn hard."

"Gotta go. Thanks Sydney," I said before clicking off my cell phone.

I had one more phone call to make before office hours started, especially to satisfy Caroline. I looked up the Kansas City local office for the Federal Bureau of Investigation and dialed the number. After being placed on hold three separate times, I was finally transferred to one of their special agents.

"This is Special Agent Rigney. How may I help you?"

"Good morning Mr. Rigney. This is Dr. Kyle Chandler. I am a trauma surgeon here in town at St. Jude Trauma Center. I have a situation here I would like your professional advice on how to handle."

I proceeded to explain to the FBI agent about my trip to the airstrip south of Rotterdam and our welcoming party of gorillas, my following of the wine bladder to the winery facility on Long Island, and last but not least, my chance meeting with the two guys in Hoboken, New Jersey. I threw in a brief version of my suspicion of having my phone messages being altered. I'll have to admit, either he was very patient listen to my longwinded tale or was totally working on something else when I was explaining.

"So Doctor, you did all of this on your own accord?" he asked.

"Yes sir."

"And other than your suspicion about your phone messages, you haven't been directly contacted by any of the people that you suspect are part of this suspected smuggling scheme?"

"Not directly, sir."

"Well Doctor, at this point I highly suggest your local police force here in Kansas City to follow up with your particular situation. If they feel that it should be further investigated, I'm sure they will be contacting us as needed."

"And that's it from your professional viewpoint?" I

asked in disgust.

"I'm afraid so. I can give you the general inquiry phone number for the KCPD if you like," he said, sounding like he was trying to be nice, but anything to get yet another call-in kook off the line.

"That's okay, Mr. Rigney. Have a nice day," I said and hung up.

Some help that was. Back to square one.

My secretary Janice, make that administrative assistant according to CHS, was in a not-so-thrilled mood when she came through the office door right before 8:00 a.m. She made it quite clear to me before I left to the medical conference in London that my return to the office was not going to be pleasant. And as usual, she was pretty much right on target.

Patient appointments began at 8:30 a.m. Once that started, the hoard of people kept coming like a growing tidal wave. Young patients, older patients, some patients with acute trauma problems, others with chronic never-ending problems.

You name it, I saw it.

By the time the flow of humanity slowed to a trickle, I looked up to see the clock on the wall at ten minutes to six in the evening. I missed lunch completely and wore out the three nurses who were helping me in the clinic. Janice stuck her head in my cubicle with a sly grin, holding a stack of charts.

"These are for your surgery cases Friday. You know that you're on trauma call tonight for Dr. Sanders since he took your call while you were out last week, right?" she asked as she handed me the patients' charts.

"Yeah, I figured as much. I'll try to swing by here tomorrow afternoon to work on my inbox stack if I don't get mowed down on trauma call tonight. And Janice, you were a real trooper today."

She paused with a blank expression on her face.

"You better think twice about the difficulty of reentry

before leaving town ever again," she said.

"I'll try to remember that."

One day back in the saddle and I felt like I had never left. I guess physicians were never supposed to leave behind the handcuffs to their profession by going out of town on rare occasions.

As I thumbed through the charts she had given me, my pager buzzed with the number from the Trauma Center on the display. I laughed out loud. Just like clockwork.

I dialed the number given on my pager and as soon as my call was answered, I was promptly put on hold.

"Hello, this is Dr. Kyle Chandler. I just got paged by the ER attending physician," I said after being taken off hold.

"One minute, please," the voice said, and I was shuttled back to the outer space orbit of being on hold once again.

If you counted all the times I called someone at the hospital, I bet I spent a combined total of two to three days on hold when you tallied it up at the end of a year's time.

Finally, a voice came back on the line. "Bill Atchinson, here. Kyle, is that you?"

"Yeah, it is. Hi, Bill. What do you have for me?"

"Well, Kyle, as you know down here in the ER, every day we see the impossible. This case should sound simple, but it will probably leave you scratching your head on how to handle this one. I've got a twenty-seven-year-old Hispanic male with all vital signs stable. He was in an argument with his younger sister this afternoon when she decided to end the argument by stabbing a number two pencil into her brother's right neck just above his clavicle. We know that it's a number two pencil because she was emphatic that's the pencil she was using. The pencil penetrated all the way to the back of his right lower lateral neck without puncturing the skin posteriorly. There is at least eight to ten centimeters of skin stinting posteriorly where the pencil is causing a tent-like configuration above his right scapula. I can't tell if this area is filled up with blood or not. It's the craziest thing I've seen in a while, and I've seen a lot of strange things during my time here."

"Is there any of the pencil sticking out anteriorly?"

"No. She pushed it all the way in, eraser and all. Not much blood in the front, either."

"I don't suppose you've got an angiogram to see what kind of vascular trauma he may have incurred?"

"He's on his way over to special radiology services now. He should be back to the emergency department by the time you get here."

"Bill, I'll be over in a few minutes. Thanks."

I shook my head in wonder. You just never know what you are going to face next in this nutty profession.

After a quick bite from my not-yet-eaten sack lunch, I refused to subjugate myself to hospital cafeteria food unless under the direst circumstances, I headed for the parking garage. On my way there, I left Caroline a message on her mobile phone that I was probably not going to be able to meet her tonight because of work. I said that I would call her again when I knew more.

After transferring my Swedish boxcar to the physicians' emergency room parking lot, I made it to the St. Jude Trauma Center triage desk. Behind the desk wearing a phone receiver headset was Pam, the afternoon and evening shift triage nurse who could do twelve things at once without missing a beat.

"Which trauma room for the neck stabbing victim?" I asked her in a low volume since she was listening to an incoming call at this same time.

She raised two fingers with her left hand, indicating Trauma Room Two, as she wrote down information from the phone call with her right hand.

I walked back to the trauma corridor and entered Trauma Room Two. Not a soul in sight. The x-ray light board was on, but there were no films to be seen. The patient must still be over at the special radiology department finishing his angiogram, I figured.

I decided to have a seat at the highchair behind the small upright desk used for recording patient data in the corner of the room. It felt good just to sit down for a moment after standing on my feet all day.

Within minutes, an emergency room gurney with two nurses and a patient transporter rolled in the room. One of the nurses handed me the patient's chart on her way in.

"Are you Mister... Del la Cruz?" I asked the man as I slowly approached the gurney.

"Sí," the scared patient whimpered.

"I'm Dr. Chandler from the Department of Surgery. *Hablas inglés*?"

"*Más o menos*," he said.

This was going to make it interesting if he could only answer questions more or less.

"*Donde está tu familia*?" I asked in my obvious American accent.

He tried to point with his right hand, but that obviously caused him too much pain. So instead, he pointed with his left hand, indicating that they were outside.

The nurse by the doorway caught my glance with a nod and went to go get one of the family members to translate for us. She returned with a young Hispanic woman who was crying and obviously scared.

"Are you Paco's sister?" I asked as gently as possible.

She nodded slowly, too scared to speak

"What's your name?"

She stared at me, wide-eyed.

"It's okay," I assured her. "We're not mad at anyone. All we are trying to do here is help your brother. Can you tell me your name?"

"Maria," she said softly.

"Maria, have a seat," I said gently as I pointed to a chair.

After she collected herself, I began again.

"Can you tell me in your own words, and take your time, what happened this afternoon?"

With her lower lip quivering, Paco's sister started telling the tale of how they got into a frivolous argument that had been brewing for a while between them. Paco reached out for her and she reacted by stabbing him with the pencil in her hand. He had fallen to the floor, and she ran to call a neighbor to take them to the hospital.

"Can you please tell Paco that I am going to examine him and that I will try not to do anything that will hurt him?"

She translated this in rapid Spanish as I began examining him from the bottom of his toes all the way up to the top of his head, both front and back.

"*Respiración profunda*," I said calmly, and he took several deep breaths while I listened to his lungs with my stethoscope.

After asking multiple questions about his health status, I completed my physical exam and reviewed the lab data on the chart. I turned back to the sister saying, "If you could stay right here with the nurses, I need to see the results of the special test he just had to see if there were any internal blood vessel injuries. I'll be back in a moment."

She nodded sheepishly as I headed down the hall towards the special radiology unit.

"What's up, Jon?" I asked as I entered the film viewing room. Jonathan was one of the radiology techs I had gotten to know over the years after I had taken out his hot appendix on one late December night a few years back.

"Not much, Doc," he said with kind of a laugh. "You're going to have some real fun with this one," he said as he put the angiogram films up on the light board in front of me.

I stepped forward to get a closer look.

What the films showed was a three quarters length pencil, approximately thirteen centimeters in length completely buried in the right neck just above the clavicle. The pencil had somehow missed the subclavian artery and vein right below it and the transverse cervical artery hugging right on top of it. The angiogram only showed the locations of the major blood vessels in relation to the bones. It wouldn't show any specific injuries to the nerve roots coming out of the spinal cord packed in that area. But the patient didn't have any neurological deficits on physical exam to indicate any nerve injury, so that was good.

The real kicker to the situation was the pencil was no longer in one straight piece. It must have entered anteriorly, struck the right first rib, and ricocheted posteriorly causing a partial break in the middle of the pencil. How the break didn't puncture the surrounding vessels was truly a mystery. The question was, how to get both segments of the pencil out without damaging major blood vessels or nerves that were right next to it.

While I was definitely going have to explore the area in surgery, there were a lot of things that could go wrong with so many structures so close together. It was going to take some ingenuity to pull this one off.

In the old days of the Wild West, if some trooper got shot with an arrow through their extremity, they would break off the tail feathers and pull the arrow through. Because of the two still partially connected segments, I couldn't do that in this case without severely damaging internal structures. And that would result in a sudden, bloody not-so-great mess.

While looking at the films on the light board, I realized that the two partially connected segments were not unlike the predicament that my own personal life was currently in. I had two pursuits, one my profession as a trauma surgeon, and the other my interest as an amateur investigator. Both intrigued me in different ways. Just like the pencil segments, the wrong movement of either profession could result in a not-so-great mess. I knew how to fix the pencil segments problem. I wasn't so sure about the dual profession problem.

I grabbed the films off the light board, told Jonathan goodbye, and headed back to Trauma Room Two. When I got there, I told the patient's sister to translate what I was going to say to Paco.

"Tell Paco that he is very lucky. The pencil does not appear to have damaged any blood vessels or nerves in its current location. But we cannot leave it where it is."

She rapidly spoke to her brother in Spanish.

"As you can see on these x-rays, the pencil pieces are very close to these blood vessels." I pointed to the structures on the films now up on the light board. "And it will be very difficult to remove the two connected pieces without causing some kind of damage. He could end up with permanent weakness or numbness in his right arm, as well as circulation problems to this arm in the future."

She started crying again while translating to her brother what I had explained to her.

"Tell him he will be going to surgery as soon as we can arrange it this evening. I want you, Maria, and your family to wait in the surgery waiting room, not here in the ER, so that I can speak with all of you once surgery is completed. Ask him, do you have any questions?" I told her as I tried to be as calm as possible in this not-so-great situation.

Paco looked at his sister and then back at me. He slowly moved his head side to side as his response.

Next, I went through my routine speech about the risks and possible complications of this or any type of surgery, making sure that his sister was communicating all this to Paco. Although stoic, he seemed to understand what I was telling him through his sister.

"Maria, tell Paco that he will not be able to work for at least six weeks after the surgery. Once he's well, tell him that I will take him to this great taco stand I know of that makes the best fish tacos in Kansas City."

Maria translated this to her brother, and he began immediately speaking Spanish rapidly with a large grin on his face.

"He says that there's no way they can be better tacos than the ones he makes," she translated to me.

"We'll see about that," I said as I squeezed his left hand.

I grabbed the films off the light board and headed to the operating room dressing room to see if I could get this rodeo started.

After getting changed into surgical scrubs, I called Caroline again and left a message that I wouldn't be swinging by her work to talk with her due to my work. I made it to the surgery scheduling desk with the films under my arm and my tape player in hand.

"How ya' doing Vicki?" I asked the evening shift surgery desk technician.

"Not so bad, yet. But it's still early, and you know how things can change at the drop of a hat around here," she said.. "You're going to room eleven. The patient should be coming up the back trauma elevator in a few minutes once he's seen by anesthesia."

"Thanks. Hey, is that room big enough to get a portable fluoroscopy unit in there if I need it?"

"Should be," she said. "Do you want me to notify them now?"

"Go ahead and call them," I said. "I'll have the circulating nurse call you from the room when we are about ready for them."

I slowly walked to the operating room. Upon entering, the scrub nurse was opening all the instruments and supplies on the sterile fields set up on multiple tables.

"Are you going to need anything special for this case?" she asked while opening up things without looking at me.

"Have a vascular surgery set in the room, but don't open it. That's just in case we have to repair any torn blood vessels. And you're going to have to wear some lead to protect yourself because I'm going to use fluoroscopy at some point in the case."

Fluoroscopy was a radiological method to view deep structures within the human body that were projected on a computer monitor screen in real time. Because of the continual radiation emitted while the machine was on, any surrounding people needed to shield different parts of their bodies by wearing lead aprons to prevent the effects of excessive radiation exposure.

"Just wonderful," she said. "You know those damn lead aprons get heavy after about twenty minutes on us dainty types."

"Lois, after putting up with me for seven years, I think you can hold your own with just about anyone, dainty or not. And look at it this way, by wearing the heavy apron, you're actually getting paid to work out."

She shot a piecing look to me over the top of her mask.

It was about that time the patient was wheeled into the room with a number of people, including the anesthesiologist. We went through all of the multiple gyrations and precautions to get things going smoothly and safely. The patient was carefully put to sleep and then transferred to his left side downward, right side upward so I could get to both his anterior and posterior right neck areas. I walked out of the room to the scrub sink and donned a heavy lead apron that covered my front from neck to knees. After washing my hands and arms thoroughly, I returned inside and gowned sterilely. The patient was prepped and draped and we were ready to go. It was now decision time.

"Let's see what's behind Door Number One," I said as I injected some Xylocaine with Epinephrine both anteriorly and posteriorly to help numb the area and maybe decrease any cutaneous bleeding. After waiting a minute or two, I made a small incision on the patient's right posterior neck and exposed the pointed end of the pencil. There was a small amount of collected blood, but nothing indicating a major vessel tear.

"And now the elusive eraser behind Door Number Two," I said as I slightly opened the anterior entrance wound, digging slowly until I could see pencil beyond the worn eraser end.

"Now would be a good time to have the front desk get the guys from fluoroscopy in here," I said to the circulating nurse, as I went to the light board to look at the angiogram films one more time.

The problem was the distal fragment had its partially

broken sharp edge right on the surface of the subclavian artery and vein. Any wrong twist or movement might cause it to puncture one or both of the vessels. And that would turn this case into a real quick blood fest.

About that time, the radiology technicians arrived with their large mobile fluoroscopy unit. They draped it sterilely and maneuvered it into position over the right neck.

"Okay, let me get a grip on both fragments and then we'll see what we got," I said to the technicians.

I placed a Kelly clamp to grasp the exposed pencil posteriorly, and then did the same very gingerly on the small exposed knub anteriorly, trying not to move the fragments at all.

"All right guys, fluoro on."

The image on the screen showed the two clamps on their respective ends of the partially broken pencil with a faint outline of the blood running through the adjacent vessels. I very, very slowly twisted the posterior fragment counterclockwise while holding the anterior fragment steady. The pointed piece began to push on the vessels. Wrong direction.

I immediately went back the other way before there was any damage.

"Fluoro off," I said. "Obviously, that wasn't the right direction. Let's try the other direction. Fluoro back on."

Looking at the video monitor, I then twisted the posterior clamp in a clockwise direction ever-so-slowly, and the same thing happened with the pointed piece pushing on the vessels. I back off once again.

"Fluoro off," I said as I took a deep breath. "Okay, guys. We're oh-for-two so far. We've got to separate those two pencil fragments apart to get them away from those subclavian vessels. Let's try twisting anteriorly. Time for option three. Fluoro on."

The technicians turned the real time video of the area on and this time I held the posterior clamp steady and began to twist the anterior clamp clockwise slowly. You could tell that the partial break in the pencil was trying to give way, but it was turning the sharp end of the posterior fragment against the vessels. I responded to this by turning the posterior clamp slowly counterclockwise at the same time, keeping the sharp end of the posterior pencil fragment stationary.

"Come on baby, come to Papa. I'm not going to let you screw up my batting average. Break, but don't splinter," I muttered out loud.

Just then, there was a gentle give, and I immediately froze.

The video screen showed that the pencil did in fact break into two pieces. And the sharp end of the break was still intact on the posterior fragment. Thank goodness.

"Fluoro off," I said and took another deep breath. "That was close, boys and girls. Now let's see if we can get the two cows back to the barn nice and safe-like. Fluoro on."

Again, looking at the video screen, I gently pulled the anterior pencil piece out intact. I did the same posteriorly, being a tad more careful because of the sharp end present. It appeared that there was no further damage to the vessels.

"Fluoro off. It looks like we dodged a bullet, or should I say pencil, on this one. Everyone did great. You techs can split now. Lois, let's rinse these wounds out and then close up," I said to my scrub nurse.

No doubt about it, sometimes it was better to be lucky than good.

After accompanying the patient to the recovery room, I headed out to the surgery waiting room to talk to the family about what I had found. Normally at this time of the late evening, there was hardly anyone in this waiting room. To my surprise when I entered through the door, the place was jam-packed with family and relatives. And every one of them jumped out of their seats, rushing forward to start asking me multiple questions in rapid Spanish.

"*Un momento, por favor. Un momento,*" I said with both of my palms up and out in front of me. "*Mi español no es muy bueno. No bueno. Donde está Maria*?" I tried my best to communicate.

Maria stepped forward with red eyes from her crying.

"Maria, everything is fine. Will you please interpret for me?"

She sheepishly nodded in agreement as I told the entire crowd about retrieving the two pencil fragments and that things looked pretty good for Paco at this point. I stressed that he could not go back to heavy activity any time soon and would be staying overnight for observation as a precaution. I could see the collective relief on the mass of faces as I explained everything to them through Maria's rapid translation. After shaking all the aunts', uncles', grandparents' and even cousins' hands, I headed back to the operating room physicians' dressing room.

Through all long years of the training, all of the insurance headaches and bureaucracy hassles, occasionally I get in a situation like this and realize something.

You know, sometimes what I did for a living actually made sense.

17

COLUMBUS PARK, KANSAS CITY

Anthony "Big Tony" Fanucci had an important decision to make. As head of the Kansas City faction of the La Cosa Nostra, as the organization was formally named by the press, it was his responsibility to make sure that the operation and security of his empire would continue even if something might unexpectedly happen to him. Loyalties and business associates would come and go, constantly changing like the tide of the ocean going in and out. He learned that and so much more from his Uncle Sal. He often thought about his uncle and how he got to where he was today.

Big Tony was born in Brooklyn right before World War II. He was the third son of six children in a family that lived in a two and a half room tenement apartment. His father was a dishwasher in a restaurant bringing home barely enough money to put food on the table to feed his household. Although the economy began to pick up after the war ended, Tony had to quit school at an early age so he could work to help feed his brothers and sisters.

Working as many as three jobs up to sixteen hours a day, he quickly realized that life wasn't fair. Doing all these chores for other people while watching them get ahead instead of him made Tony slowly boil inside. There had to be a better way.

By the time Tony turned seventeen, he'd had enough. It was the 1950s, times were turning around in America, yet he was getting left behind. He was tired of all work and no pay. Tony never saw his working father and his mother was always too exhausted to talk with him. Nobody cared what happened to him. He decided that life was too short to stay at the bottom of the heap.

One day after another frustrating episode at one of his jobs, he went to see a friend's father who owned a food market. Through his unique power of persuasion, he got the friend's dad to call Tony's uncle in Kansas City, Salvatore Fanucci. This was his dad's brother that his father always warned him about. His father made it very clear to never turn out to be like this forbidden relative. Tony spoke with his uncle on the phone briefly, within two minutes had convinced him to have Tony come live with him in Kansas City and begin learning his Uncle Sal's business.

Fueled by the turn of events, Tony immediately ran home and packed his only change of clothes in a small drawstring satchel along with the meager amount of money he had hidden away. As he approached the apartment door, he turned around and gave each of his three sisters a hug. At the same moment, his mother came into the room looking worn out as usual. Although the scene was almost forty years ago, Big Tony remembers the exchange like it was yesterday.

"Where do you think you're going?" his mother said. "Shouldn't you be at work?"

"I was, but now I came to say goodbye to my sisters before I leave."

"Leave? Are you kidding, you have nowhere to go."

"I'm going to seek my fortune Ma, to find a better life," he replied.

"Oh really. And just who is going to offer you a new start on 'Easy Street' filled with money?"

"Somebody who cares about my future," Tony said as he stood his ground.

"Who would that foolish soul be?"

"Uncle Sal, that's who."

Her eyes got very wide open as she stared directly at her third son.

"Do you have any idea what your father will do to you if he finds out that you even spoke with that gangster?"

"Not only did I speak with him, but he also wants me to come live with him in Kansas City."

"Ha! You won't even make it out of New York. You'll be back by tomorrow begging us to take you back in."

"I'll make it. Just you wait and see."

"That'll be the day. You'll end up in prison or dead more than likely, the same as the rest of those mobsters."

"We'll just see about that. Tell my two older brothers they'll have to find someone else to pick on from now on. And Pop, tell him I'll send him a photo of me when I'm famous. That'll be sooner rather than later. Bye girls," he said to his sisters as he walked out the apartment door for the last time.

It took the seventeen-year-old two weeks taking freight trains, hitchhiking, and grabbing rides with freight trucks to make it halfway across the country to Kansas City. He had begged for food, camped with hobos, and even stole items a few times out the backdoor of food markets to keep from starving.

When he finally made it to Kansas City, he looked up the address of his uncle he had written down from the store of his friend's father. It was a high rise near downtown with a doorman out front. Tony walked up to the doorman with his paltry belongings in his hand.

"I'm here to see Salvatore Fanucci," he said boldly to

the doorman.

"Go away kid," the man commanded him.

"I need to see to my Uncle Sal."

"Sally doesn't see punks like you."

"I'm not leaving until I see my Uncle Sal."

"Then you'll have to deal with Bobo there," the doorman said as nodded his head at the man inside the window standing next to the revolving front door.

"Fine," Tony told the man as he walked to the revolving door.

After Tony pushed through the door, the man inside grabbed him by the arm and pulled him quickly to the side. He immediately got his face about two inches from Tony's.

"Where do you think you're going chump?"

"I'm here to see my Uncle Sal," Tony said looking directly into the man's eyes.

"You say Sal's your uncle? Yeah, you and every other punk who wants a handout," the man chastised him still holding his arm.

"Take me upstairs to see him and he'll vouch for me. I talked to him on the phone a little over two weeks ago. He told me to come see him," Tony pleaded.

"No dice. Sal's too busy to see chumps like you."

"Then send somebody upstairs to give him a message from me," the teen demanded.

"And what would that message be?"

"Have the messenger tell Uncle Sal that 'Trudy's boy is here to stay.' He'll understand."

"What the…?" the man said obviously confused.

"Just do it," Tony insisted.

The man waived his hand at a younger man dressed in a suit standing by the elevator. The younger man came over and Bobo whispered something in the younger man's ear. Immediately the younger guy went over, pushed the elevator button, waited until the doors opened, and vanished into the elevator.

A few minutes later, the elevator doors opened wide.

The younger man came out next to a big, burly, well-dressed man leading the way. The man obviously in charge walked right up to Tony and put out his hand to him.

"You must be Anthony. I'm Salvatore, your father's older brother. I saw you only once just after you were born. My brother hated being called Trudy growing up. It would get under his skin every time I called him that. Anybody brave enough to call him that, is good by my book. Follow me," the burly man instructed as he turned and led Tony to the elevator.

From then on, Tony followed Uncle Sal wherever he went. He bought his nephew the clothes he needed and had him stay with him in his apartment. His uncle fed him like a king to put the pounds back on him that he had lost on the two-week odyssey of getting to Kansas City. Thereafter, nobody messed with Sal's nephew. Most importantly, Uncle Sal slowly taught Tony every small detail about his business.

So what was Uncle Sal's business? It was a lot of things. Salvatore Fanucci was the number two guy in the Cicero Mafia family, which controlled all of Kansas City. They were into everything. Numbers, rackets, gambling, casinos in Las Vegas, prostitution to name a few. They had policemen as informants on the payroll. They controlled labor unions. They ran the Kansas City trash removal at an inflated rate. When a major construction contract came up for bid, they always got it. You name it they got a piece of it. Because Tony followed his uncle everywhere, he learned about it all.

As time went by, Tony found out that his uncle was married and had a large house in the suburbs where his wife and three daughters lived. But there were no sons. His uncle visited his house and family as needed, but his Uncle Sal lived in the apartment, conducting all his business there. Salvatore needed someone in the next generation that he could trust. Someone to learn from him starting at the bottom floor.

Enter Tony from Brooklyn.

About a year after Tony had been working for his uncle in Kansas City, he was walking with his uncle one evening up to a nightclub to have a word with the owner. Seems the owner wasn't keeping up payments to their organization for the monthly "entertainment fee" that all businesses had to pay in order to stay open. After they got through convincing the owner to pay up or his nightclub may be involved in "an accidental fire," Tony had an idea that he wanted to share with his uncle.

"Uncle Sal? Do you know someone nearby that has a camera with one of those flash bulbs on it?" the nephew asked.

"I could make a call and have one here in a few minutes. What do you need it for?" Sal said.

"I thought that it's about time we sent your brother 'Trudy' a photograph of me working with you here in Kansas City."

"That's a great idea Anthony. We should get a few of those dames that dance inside to come be in the photo with us. 'Trudy' would love that. Let me make a call."

Within fifteen minutes, a photographer was taking photos of Tony and Uncle Sal arm-in-arm surrounded by scantily dressed showgirls in front of the lighted nightclub sign out front. It was quite a spectacle.

"The photographer said he'll have the developed pictures over to me day after tomorrow. Do you know where to send them?" his uncle asked.

"I don't know if they live in the same crummy apartment anymore. How can I find out?" asked Tony.

"Don't worry," his uncle responded. "I got a friend in one of the New York families that covers Brooklyn. He'll find out where they are."

Uncle Sal got word to his contact in New York about Tony's family. Two days later, the contact phoned Sal and told him the new address. They had moved in Brooklyn. Tony took a copy of the photo and placed it in a large brown envelope. Before he sealed it shut, he slipped a note to his family that read:

> Making good money and new special friends with Uncle Sal.
> One day soon, I'll be famous.
> Your successful son, Tony

A picture is worth a thousand words Tony thought to himself.

There were so many things that Tony learned from his uncle. He realized early that the leader of the family gave the orders and troops followed the orders. No questions asked. He learned that a family member had to learn to follow orders before he could give them. Tony had followed orders as a foot soldier for years before he moved up within the organization. He learned from Uncle Sal that running a huge money-making machine meant a continual manipulation of men and resources. The leader needed reliable troops that he could trust to make the structure of the organization function like it should.

Seven days a week.

Eventually, Tony's importance within the business grew as well as his girth. He became affectionately known as "Big Tony." He got married and had kids but work always came first. His uncle stressed that the only guarantee one could be assured in their business was constant change. Yet, with all the personalities the leader had to deal with, there was one thing always stayed the same: family. Not just the wife and kids, but his "business family." That principle was stressed to Tony time and time again by his uncle.

After multiple changes in his business family throughout the years, he ultimately took over the reins of the entire organization because of the grooming his Uncle Sal had provided all those years. Big Tony made it a goal to train his eldest son like his uncle trained him. He hoped to groom his son Thomas "Tito" Fanucci to one day take his rightful place as the head of the family business when it was his son's time.

As time moved on, Big Tony began to execute his plan to bring his eldest son into the fold of the organization. Make that his organization.

Big Tony tried his best to teach his son about "the code of family" his Uncle Sal had taught him. To teach him about the strict designation of following orders and working your way up through the organization before you could give orders. About the ebb and flow of loyalties, how to stay ahead of what could happen next. About how to change your cash flow as things about your business constantly changed.

The Mafia don did the best that he could to teach his oldest son about how everything in the organization relied upon following orders. Tony initially had a small difficulty getting his eldest son to carry out orders. Eventually, that changed from a minor problem to a major issue. And that issue was his twenty-eight-year-old Tito didn't like to take orders from anyone about anything, particularly from his father.

Loud and brash, Tito was like a bull in a china shop when it came to making tactful decisions. Whatever Tito wanted, right or wrong, Tito would fight until he got it. Subtle manipulation and behind the scenes exploitation were methods that Big Tony's son had no use for. No doubt about it, anybody could tell what was in Tito's hand when he played cards. There was no bluffing in anything Tito did. That was probably the main reason that had kept Big Tony from revealing all the family business secrets to his son so far.

That led the Mafia boss to a new situation Big Tony had recently learned about which seemed even more important to keep Tito from messing up. He had gotten word from his contact in New Jersey that there might be an unknown someone checking into their source for the distribution of narcotics. Narcotics distribution was a huge chunk of their business that brought in most of their income throughout the Midwest. If their source for transporting the narcotics into the US had been compromised, then things could come to a grinding halt.

His contact had told him that they had reason to believe that the person checking into how they sourced the narcotics into the United States was thought to be from Kansas City, of all places. This unknown thirty-something white male had been seen outside of London, in Holland, and also on Long Island in the last week. Big Tony's informants within the airport surveillance security team showed that this unknown person had been seen on an airport terminal security camera as he returned to Kansas City this past Tuesday evening.

Normally, this information wouldn't have been known to anybody other than himself and his right-hand man Carmine Giacomo. But since this unknown person could affect the whole narcotics distribution scheme not only in Kansas City, but nationwide, information like this had a fast way of leaking out to too many people. Family members, business associates, as well as enemies who would like nothing better than to bring the Fanucci family down and would always somehow hear about something like this in an instant. Because of that, he needed to speak with his eldest son to make sure Tito would keep his unfiltered mouth shut about this until he could track down this unknown suspect.

For Big Tony and his business, it was important financially to keep the steady transport of narcotics coming into the country. After all, he was one of the few people who had a good idea of how the drugs were transported from their source to distribution in the US. He had been told that only the heads of the five families of New York, as well as the heads of the families in New Jersey, Chicago, Miami, Kansas City, and representatives in Las Vegas knew anything at all about the narcotics supply scheme.

Big Tony had learned about the details only because of his long-time friendship with the underboss of one of the five families in New York. He didn't know all the exact details of the source origins, but he did know that heroin was grown in The Golden Triangle in Southeast Asia. It was being brought in, as well as cocaine from Columbia via Mexico. He knew the general scheme of how the drugs were smuggled into the US and how typically they were distributed to the different mob outfits across the country from a constantly changing location in New Jersey set up by all of the five New York families.

If the New York families thought that some guy from Kansas City could bring the whole scheme down, it was going to fall on his shoulders to find out who this someone was. Once Big Tony had the suspect identified, the next step would be to take care of him nice and quiet-like. In fact, he expected a call from one of the families' bosses any time now. And that's why he had to talk to Tito soon. To put a leash on him so this thing wouldn't blow up in his face and on everyone else.

18

MANHATTAN

On Wednesday afternoon, Philip Hauser was in his office reviewing the data analysis on several potential companies that might be ripe for a hostile takeover. In the middle of this financial exercise, the CEO's mobile phone rang twice then went silent. In approximately thirty seconds, it rang twice again then went silent a second time. Hauser knew what to do next.

By calling a toll-free number, then pressing a four-digit number, his mobile phone call was somehow routed to an untraceable number floating in outer space.

"This is Newman," the voice on the other end said.

Hauser knew that was not the true name of the party he called but he didn't care.

"Johnson here," Hauser said, giving the correct response to continue the message.

"New information that your business partners may be concerned about your transportation conduit for the product," the voice said.

"How so?"

"My sources tell me that they are concerned about finding visitors at the rendezvous point across the ocean on Friday. Then it is believed a man followed the transport van with the product from Long Island to the distribution spot in New Jersey on Monday."

"Your share will be bumped this week because of the information. Let me know if this gets bigger," Hauser said.

"Roger that. Out," the voice said and was gone.

The CEO sat there for a minute to consider all the possibilities. He had played this side venture very close to the vest. Not even the plant manager at Hawthorne Containers had known the real reason why an extra compartment was being placed all the way up front on the undersurface of the Flexitank bladders. Hell, the plant manager had bought the story that it was being used for a research project to place a device to measure the oxygen levels in the wine through the bladder during its transport.

Hauser knew that the number of people who understood what the extra compartment was used for was less than five. In addition, that was only the transfer crew that put the parcels into the bladders at the warehouse south of Rotterdam when the shipment would be flown in. While he wasn't in charge of the security of the shipment transport, he doubted the hired security goons even got close enough to figure out what they were keeping people away from.

However, he did know that not even the truck drivers who drove the wine-filled container trucks knew they were hauling illegal substances. Hauser knew he damn sure wouldn't trust anybody from his bumbling security force at Evolution Industries with such a responsibility for secrecy, so they were not a source of the leak. Even the partners that distributed the product didn't know all the details of his transportation scheme.

The CEO wondered what his next move should be. It wasn't just to see who could get the most money. He knew money meant power. And he wanted the kind of power that was above and beyond his peers in the business world. Not something any ordinary millionaire could achieve. The kind of power that came with owning an NFL football team, or his own casino. The plateaus only the top one-half percent achieve. These were the goals for which he reached.

It all returned to his basic rule of success in the business world: Always stay at least two steps ahead of your competitors. It was that simple. It was time to turn to his first backup plan.

After considering his options, Hauser punched a number into his cell phone and waited. When the call switched over to a message machine, he said, "This is Brian. Call me back at this number immediately."

Within sixty seconds, a call with a phony number rang on his cell phone.

"This is Mango. You have instructions?" a low-toned voice with a Latin accent asked.

"Proceed at once with our plan for option number one," Hauser said. "I will need you to pick up copies of photos from source "A" and audio tapes from source "B" as we previously have discussed. I want you to courier them personally to me Saturday morning at our backup meeting place at 10:00 a.m. sharp. Make sure you are not followed. I'll arrange for the usual transfer of funds, slightly more since it will be two pickups. Understand?"

"*Sí, señor.* See you then," the voice said before hanging up.

A slight smile came across the CEO's face.

While Hauser's empire at Evolution Industries had grown significantly since his takeover four years ago, it was nothing compared to the untraceable tax-free cash he was making with this hidden transport scheme. The best part was all that cash was being wired by the truckload to a private account in the Cayman Islands. This was business. Business that was way more profitable for him personally than the climbing stock price of Hawthorne Containers. This was his payday.

Philip Hauser told himself that he was too smart and too ahead of the curve to let some uneducated business partners hold something over him. Besides, he hadn't gotten to where he was in such a short time by being timid. He just put into motion the right plan to make those moronic partners, who distributed the product, beg him to keep transporting the hidden products for them. He'd show them they needed him a whole lot more than he needed them.

19

KANSAS CITY

After getting home after midnight, I only got one or two calls during the night that didn't require me heading back to the trauma center. I guess you could say I dodged another pencil. I awoke Thursday morning in kind of a daze as I stumbled into the kitchen to grab a cup of coffee. Only there was no coffee made since I forgot to set the coffeemaker last night when I got in so late. Oh well, I could think of worse things.

By the time I finished showering and ate a bowl of cereal, I decided to go to the hospital and check on Mr. Del la Cruz from last night so maybe he could go home. I headed out of my condominium complex and picked up some much-needed drive-through coffee.

As I left the coffee place on the way to the hospital, I realized that I didn't have my stethoscope in my white physician's coat pocket. It must have fallen out when I took off my coat last night. It had happened like that several times in the past.

I turned my Swedish-style machine around and started home. I probably could have borrowed a stethoscope at the hospital, but you never know where someone else's instruments have been. Or if they ever clean them. More importantly, I needed to be accurate when listening to someone's lungs with a stethoscope that I knew worked well.

As I turned down the street in front of my condo complex, there was a sedan with dark shaded window tinting parked across the street from the entrance. It definitely wasn't there when I left earlier. When I turned right into the complex and approached the security gate, I glanced in my rear-view mirror. I could see through the front windshield that the driver of the car was looking down at a laptop computer.

Wow. Laptops were just starting to get popular, but you really didn't see that many of them around. Especially someone using one in their car. I started to get that hair-raising feeling on the back of my neck again. Something wasn't right.

Acting like nothing was wrong, I drove to my condo and carefully opened the door from the garage into my place. Not a sound. I tiptoed up the stairs into my kitchen. Still no sound. Just then, I suddenly heard my phone message machine being played out loud. No big deal. But it wasn't a new, incoming message.

The message machine was playing the already recorded messages over and over. All by itself. Or was it?

I stood there completely still and listened. When the machine played a message that I recognized as Caroline's voice, the machine deleted it and went on to the next message. What? Then two-plus-two-equals-four clicked in my mind. No wonder I didn't get any of the messages from Caroline when I had gotten home from London. Someone from afar was editing my messages.

What in the world had I gotten myself into?

Immediately, I knew I had to reach Caroline. I found my stethoscope on the floor right where I thought it would be. I zoomed down the stairs and jumped into my car. As I approached the security front gate, I noticed the dark sedan across the street was no longer there.

Perfect, just perfect.

I drove through the gate and headed for the hospital. About halfway there, I turned off into a neighborhood and parked curbside. Not only had I put myself under surveillance with possible consequences, but I had also involved Caroline in the messy picture.

Not good. Not good at all.

I grabbed my cell phone and dialed her mobile number. Five rings and then message machine service came on. I hung up.

Caroline, if you have a cell phone for convenience, why don't you answer it?

I dialed her work number and after the third ring, a pleasant voice answered. "C.M. Antiques, this is Susan. How can I help you?"

"Hi Susan. This is Kyle Chandler. I need to speak with your boss if she's around."

"Oh, hi there, Dr. Chandler. How are you today?"

Susan was a new employee for Caroline when I met her earlier in the year. I had told her that I was going to convince Caroline to give her a fat Christmas bonus at the end of the year, without telling Caroline, of course. Since then, she was always super nice to me.

"I'm just dandy. Can you track down Caroline for me?"

"I think she's on another line with a customer. Can I slip her a message from you?"

Once Caroline and I were officially an item in the eyes of her employees, most of them would interrupt Caroline if I called. That was especially true with Susan because of the hint of the bonus.

"No, that's alright. Tell her to call my cellphone when she gets off her call. And Susan, just a few more months to

Christmas," I said, taunting her.

"I'll tell her. And be sure to put in a good word for me," she said eagerly.

"Will do. Have a good day," I said and hung up.

I decided to make one more call while I was still parked curbside in the neighborhood. After five rings, the recorded phone voice said the caller was unavailable and to leave a message.

"Hey Barry, it's me, Kyle," I said after the noisy beep ended. "I've been busy at work since I got back from London, so I'm sorry that I haven't got back to you until now. I did get to speak with the chief constable of the Port of Tilbury, and he told me a bunch of information of shipping bulk wines through their terminal. We'll sit down together soon, and I'll tell you all that he told me."

"Also, I had a good meeting with the plant manager at the factory where the Flexitank bladders are made," I said. "From what I found out, they have a great product, but I have an immediate concern about something else their company might be involved in. I'll explain it to you later. Talk to you soon, bye."

I headed towards the hospital, and about three minutes later, my cell phone rang.

"What have you been telling Susan to make her keep reminding me about Christmas?" Caroline's voice shot through my phone before I could say hello.

"Just spreading a little early Yuletide cheer to your troops, my dear."

"I've got a feeling that your cheer-spreading is going to cost me a lot more *dinero* than I expected. I take it you were busy on trauma call last night?"

"Sort of. I had an interesting case involving the hazards of school supplies, but I'll tell you about that some other time. I've got a few other things we need to discuss. Pick you up for dinner when you close at six?"

"That should work. Where to this time? Another former patient leading you to one of your Kansas City culinary hidden gems?"

"As a matter of fact, yes. But not the kind of crowd you would expect."

"What kind of crowd do you think I would like?

"You'll have to wait and see."

"At least give me a hint of what we need to discuss so I'll have my rebuttal brief already written."

"Sorry. Like I said before, no details on the phone until we talk face to face. See you this evening, counselor."

"Whatever you say, Doctor Foodie. Bye."

I eased away from the curb, wondering what my next move should be in the drug smuggling scheme I might have uncovered. There was definitely someone interested in my whereabouts since I returned from the conference in London. I had to find out who that someone was.

Do I keep pushing forward, knowing I was outnumbered? Was this whole endeavor futile? Now why couldn't I just give this entire thing up? Way too many clouded questions with no clear answers in sight.

I made it to the hospital and tracked down what room Mr. Del la Cruz had been sent to after surgery. Upon opening the door to his hospital room, I realized that it was likely I was now witnessing the Guinness Book of World Records of the number of family members that could be packed into one hospital room. Every one of those people from last night in the waiting room and more cousins were there four to five deep. After causing them to divide like the Red Sea, I listened to Paco's lungs with my stethoscope and checked his bandages for bleeding.

Through his sister Maria, I explained that we needed to get a chest x-ray to make sure his lungs were fully inflated. If that film looked okay, then he could go home after lunch. I again stressed that he could not go back to heavy activity for four to six weeks and that he needed to call my office for a follow-up appointment next week.

"Does he understand all that Maria?"

She nodded yes and then Paco whispered something in

amazingly fast Spanish to his sister.

"What is he asking?"

"He wants to know when he can show you that his fish tacos are the best you'll ever eat."

I smiled and said, "We'll talk about that when I see you back at my office. You stay out of trouble." I left with a smile on my face that stayed with me most of the day.

I've always said that it's a great sign when a patient starts to think about eating something other than hospital food.

20

MANHATTAN

Philip Hauser was going over the details on some contracts at his office Thursday morning when his cell phone rang. He was about to reach for it after one ring when it suddenly became silent. After a few seconds, the phone rang one time and again became silent.

That was definitely the signal. He knew this call would be coming from them after his informant had warned him of their worry about his end of the bargain.

"Yes?" he asked after two new rings.

"We need to meet. Soon," the gruff voice said.

"Why?"

"My superiors are not happy about what they are hearing about a possible breakdown in your transport system."

"I don't know what you're talking about. There's no breakdown from my end," Hauser said.

Hauser knew the voice but couldn't connect a face with

it. His distribution business partners always tried to have a new contact reach him whenever they wanted something. He guessed they thought it would keep him on the ropes. The veteran businessman knew that an amateur move like that would not let them gain the upper hand from him.

"That's not what my bosses think. Somebody has been keeping tabs on how you get the product into the country," the gruff voice said.

"Impossible."

"Yeah, that's what you think. But my bosses think otherwise."

Hauser finally put a face with the gruff voice on the other end of the line. He had met the olive-skinned man only once when they set up the terms of their secret partnership. He could tell that the Italian American man was not the brightest bulb in the circuit. But the CEO did perceive that the man carried a sense of threatening anger in his voice whenever he spoke.

"We gotta meet. Grand Central Station, thirty minutes," the gruff voice said.

"No, not possible."

"What do ya' mean not possible?"

"Like I said, not possible," the CEO said firmly.

Hauser had determined from the beginning of their partnership to not let these guys push him around. It had worked for him so far.

"I have a busy schedule every single day. I can't just drop everything this second for this. How about this evening?"

There was a pause of silence. "Then Joe's Italian Deli in the Bronx on East 187th at 6:00 p.m. this evening," the gruff voice said.

"No way. That's not going to happen either. It's way too predictable. Too easy to be overheard there. It's got to be someplace less noticeable, where we can get away from the crowd. Can't be anywhere popular."

After another pause, Hauser said, "I've got just the

place. Make it the Dim Sum Palace Restaurant in Chinatown at 7:00 p.m."

"Are you kiddin' me? I wouldn't be caught dead in Chinatown after dark."

"Exactly. That's why it will be the best place."

That brought on another pause from the other end of the line. Hauser knew that had gotten the man's attention.

Fish hooked, challenge over, Hauser mused to himself.

"You better be right about this place," the gruff voice said.

"Don't you worry. It's perfect. And I've got some news that will surprise you," Hauser said as he pushed the off button on his cell phone.

It was so simple to manipulate lesser intelligent beings. Since he had already contacted his courier Mango, he knew he had ammunition on the way if his distributor business partners were trying to pull a fast one on him.

21

KANSAS CITY

Even though I was usually off work the day after trauma call, I had to make up for the time I had spent at the conference. After discharging Mr. Del la Cruz Thursday, I slugged it out at medical records to sign all my charts to keep me off the delinquent list.

Loads of stimulating fun.

Just about the time I was finishing signing the stack of medical records, I found a noxious piece of gum stuck to the end of the phone receiver in front of me.

I mean, come on. Who in the world does something like that, especially since this small area's access was limited to physicians? You spend big bucks and a million years of education to become a doctor and you end up putting your chewing gum on the phone in front of you instead of the trash can right at your feet? Give me a break.

I bent over the trash can underneath the cubicle desktop to get a piece of trash paper to see if I could pry the gum off the phone receiver. Just as I was pulling a piece of wadded up paper out for the gum, I noticed another piece of paper in the trash can that had a small, exposed segment with the word "Martinelli."

Uh oh.

I lifted the partially crumpled piece of paper and pulled it open. The wrinkled piece of paper had the name "Caroline Martinelli" on it. Below that were her address, work address, home and cell phone numbers, and her car license plate number. Also listed were her college credentials, work experience in London, Paris, and Rome, notable business contacts in Kansas City, and civic organizations she was involved in here in Kansas City.

Definitely not good.

Why would Caroline's information be wadded up in this trash can? Because whoever was looking had no further need for the information. And because they had most likely looked at my medical records at this cubicle to find something to use against me.

I folded up the piece of paper, put it in my coat pocket and wondered how I was going to break this to her. Not good at all. I decided to see if maybe I could ease it into the conversation at dinner tonight and see where it would take us.

Face it Chandler, some things just don't make sense.

It was midmorning on Thursday when Big Tony made all the calls he needed to make to keep his businesses running smoothly. While this whole situation with the families in New York was putting a lot of pressure on him, he knew he had to look into this in a big way. This unknown someone who was checking into their source for the distribution of narcotics had supposedly turned up in Kansas City. His Kansas City. They told him he was supposed to fix it. That meant now.

He had decided to tell Tito that in no way, shape, or form was his son was to go after this unknown someone. Tito was too hotheaded for his own good. He must have got that from his mother's side of the family. One dumb move and his son would be spending his young years behind bars working in the prison laundry instead of learning the ropes of the family business.

Tito was supposed to be here at his office right now to talk about this. Where the hell was he?

Just about then, a knock on the door sounded and the heir to the KC Mob strolled in.

"How's it going, Pops?"

"Where have you been? I said be here at ten o'clock on the dot. Not ten after ten."

"Sorry about that. I had to give cousin Paulie a ride to work this morning. What did you want to talk to me about?" Tito asked as he flopped on the couch.

"Tito, I know you think that I don't get you involved in the family business as much as you would like. I know that's a sore spot for you. But I have plans for you. Big plans. Not now, but in the future."

"Then let me get started working with you. Right now. We could really get this business shaped up and start pulling in some real dough if you just let me loose."

"Soon Tito, soon. Still, there's one thing you have to promise me; you will stay away from right now until I get it cleared up. It's very important. You *cannot* go near this situation right now. Not at all. Do you understand?"

"That's great, Pops, but how can I know what to stay away from if you don't tell me what it is? Huh?"

"Tito I've been told recently by our friends in New York there's a guy who has been snooping around in London and on Long Island investigating our dope smuggling scheme. It could affect not only our huge narcotics business here, but also one of the largest narcotic distributions in the US. I just found out from our sources that he's some surgeon, for Christ's sake, right here in Kansas City. We're working on a plan to bring him in, but until we do, you must stay totally away from all of this. Understand?"

"Why all the wasted time of bringing him in? Just go out and whack the guy. Problem solved." Tito said.

Big Tony had to grit his teeth for a few seconds before answering.

"Tito, do you ever think before you speak? We need to bring him in to find out what he knows and who he might have told. Our snitches on the police force don't know anything as of yet. Whacking people doesn't automatically solve problems."

"Okay. But if you want me to stay away, I gotta know who I'm supposed to stay away from. So what's this guy's name?"

"His name is Kyle Chandler. Dr. Kyle Chandler. Works over at St. Jude Hospital as a trauma surgeon. Just keep your mitts off him. We can't have this blow up on any of us. Got it?"

Tito sat there looking at his father like he didn't know how to take care of anything.

Finally, Tito said, "Whatever you say Pops. You're the boss. Anything else?"

"Yeah, phone your Auntie Rose and wish her happy birthday today. And you better be at our house for her birthday dinner by 7:00 tonight. Capiche?"

"Sure," Tito muttered as he got up off the couch and wandered out of the office.

As soon as he got downstairs to his van, Tito knew he was going to show his father what kind of man he was. It was high time for him to start making some of the decisions for the family business. This insult to him about staying away from this doctor guy pretty much convinced him that his old man was finally starting to lose it. Tito knew he was way ahead of his father's generation figuring out what was necessary to stay the rulers of this city.

Tito laughed to himself as he turned the ignition key to his disguised delivery van. Hell, he'd already found out yesterday from his father's informant who this guy was, what he looked like, and the make and model of the old car this bozo doctor drove. The informant had given him a rundown of the doctor's usual schedule and laid it on thick about the antique dealer babe that he was seeing. All of which could be used to get to this guy.

Why not see if he could scope this whole situation out right now? He decided that he would get another set of hands to pull this off. Tito pulled away from his parking spot with a smile on his face. This could turn out better than expected.

He stopped off at a friend's house and honked the horn. After a few seconds, his pal Bobby appeared out the front door.

"Hey, grab your coat. We got something to take care of right now," Tito said.

"What do ya' mean?" the portly guy asked.

"Just get your coat. Now."

Bobby went back in the house and returned with his coat, climbing in the front seat of the van.

"Where we goin'?" the Bobby asked.

"We got to meet somebody. Maybe take him for a ride."

Bobby nodded and said nothing more. He knew not to ask too many questions when he worked with the volatile son of the head of KC Mafia.

After working his way through morning traffic, Tito found the physician's parking lot next to the trauma center at St. Jude Hospital. He cruised around the outside of the gated lot for a little while to see if by chance this Dr. Chandler's car was there.

There it was. That had to be it. Who else in their right mind would be driving an old square sedan like that when he could be driving a sleek ride with all that money he was raking in? Tito pulled over and decided to wait and see.

About ten minutes later, Tito saw a moderately tall, athletic-looking guy in tortoise shell glasses wearing a sportscoat come out carrying his briefcase in his left hand. He was heading towards the totally-not-flashy sedan. That must be the Dr. Chandler guy.

"Get ready," Tito said. "When I block him from getting out of the parking lot, you rush out and see if you can surprise him by opening his door and yanking him out. Force him into the back of the van. We'll take him to one of the safe houses to have a little chat."

The man opened the back door to the sedan and slid his briefcase on the floor of the backseat. He then got in and began to back out of the parking spot, totally unaware of what was about to happen. The sedan pulled up to the exit gate and waited for the gate bar to lift all the way up.

At that moment, Tito pulled away in his van to race up and block the exit from about half a block away. Before he could get there, a large cargo truck pulled out from the side street and stopped, totally blocking the van's access to the street ahead. Tito slammed on the brakes, just missing a collision by inches. The height of the truck blocked any kind of view that Tito and Bobby needed.

"Dammit!" Tito screamed. "Go get him, now!"

Bobby bolted from the van and tried to hurry around the back of the large truck. In a few seconds, Tito saw the Volvo move ahead of the stationary cargo truck and drive away while the van remained totally blocked in.

Bobby returned to the van, shaking his head.

"Sorry, Tito. No dice."

"Just my luck. You couldn't get to the car in time?"

"He had already pulled out of the lot by the time I made it around the truck," Bobby said.

"Stupid truck driver. We'll have to set something up for this doctor guy later," Tito said.

22

DOWNTOWN, KANSAS CITY

I spent the better part of late Thursday morning and all afternoon at the office putting out fires and leveling molehills that had turned into mountains while I was gone to London. All of those necessary evils of paperwork they don't tell you about when you think of applying to medical school. And that damn lower backache had returned even though I hadn't been standing up in the OR for long periods of time. It was bad enough to take a few Advil. What was up with that?

By the time I cleared the majority of work from my inbox, my stomach was rumbling. The clock said a few minutes before six o'clock in the evening. Time to leave the grind behind and go talk with Caroline over dinner about my suspicions.

I made my way across town and parked next to her white BMW behind her store. I called her cell phone, and she said would be right out as soon as she locked everything up.

While waiting in my Volvo, I knew I had to figure out a way to handle this whole investigation into the smuggling thing. And how to explain it to Caroline to keep her out of it, especially considering what I found in the Medical Records' trash can. I was desperate enough to start hoping that divine intervention was a big possibility.

Caroline came out the rear delivery door and got in my auto.

"Where are we going for dinner?" she asked when she buckled her seatbelt.

"You'll see," I said while trying to keep a poker face.

We weaved our way through traffic as we headed north toward downtown. It amazed me how many people were always driving somewhere in Kansas City. Anytime of the day or night. Always in a rush. Never able to take the time to go with the flow. Strange.

When we got to the heart of downtown, we finally found a parking spot amongst all the cars. After opening the passenger car door for Caroline, we walked toward an older warehouse with a large window at street level. A red neon sign simply read "Real Italian Food." A total dive if there ever was one.

"Well, Emeril Lagasse. How did you find this restaurant?" she asked.

"My usual excuse, a former patient. And for your information, it is *not* New Orleans Cajun food. Strictly old-fashioned Italian."

"Aren't you afraid of going in some of these rough looking places?"

"Well, at least I know where to go if I get hurt."

"That's comforting," she said as we went in the front door.

The hostess showed us to a booth in the corner and gave us each a large menu encased in plastic so they could wipe the spilled spaghetti sauce off it. I hadn't been here in quite a while. It was just as I remembered.

Dark atmosphere. Chianti-style straw-covered bottles as candleholders. Red checked tablecloths. Dean Martin singing, "That's Amore" in the background. Some things never go out of style.

"This restaurant reminds me of a place I visited one time when I was living in Boston during my surgical residency," I said. "One evening I drove down to Providence, Rhode Island to visit a friend of mine. He took me to dinner at this Italian restaurant in the part of town named Federal Hill. It just happened to be the neighborhood of the head of the New England Mob."

"Really?"

"Yeah. You drove up a hill on a crowded city street with a large arch over the street. The road stripes changed from yellow to red, white, and green as soon as you drove under the arch to indicate you were now in the Italian-American section of town."

"You're making this up," Caroline said.

"Nope. On the left past the arch, there was a large white house with southern plantation columns that looked really out of place. This restaurant had only two small dining rooms up front with the kitchen. But there was always a ton of cars parked in a big lot out back. That's because there were multiple meeting rooms in the rear with a private back entrance. You figure it out what was going on there."

About then, a young man in his late twenties came over to our table, eager to get the ball rolling.

"How we doin' tonight folks? My name is Frankie, and I'll be you waiter tonight. Can we start you with something from the bar while you look over the menu?"

"I'll have a glass of your house Chianti, and what about you?" I said as I turned to Caroline.

"Just water, thank you," she said.

"Would you prefer sparkling water? We have Pellegrino."

"No, plain water will be fine."

"I'll be back to take you order in a minute," he said as he darted away.

"You didn't ask all about the wine list tonight?" she asked. "I thought you told me that older landlady you had in college taught you all about wines? I was expecting to witness a grandiose debate between you and the waiter over what wine to choose."

"Just because she took me down to taste from her collection in her basement every night doesn't mean I have to use that knowledge every time I go out. A house Chianti will be just fine for Italian food."

"Fair enough, Doctor Sommelier. Now explain to me how you found this hidden gem?" she asked.

"Well, about four years ago, I took care of a nineteen-year-old young lady who was having a lot of problems with abdominal pain that kept coming and going. She had been to all kinds of doctors, and they still didn't know what was wrong. I finally convinced her family late one night that we needed to take her to surgery for what was called a retrocecal appendix. It's really hard to diagnosis from other types of abdominal pain etiologies."

"Sounds way too medical for me."

"Anyway, that's exactly what I found at surgery. I took her inflamed appendix with a big mass of inflamed gunk out and that solved her problem. The family kept saying I was 'the world's best doctor'. I found out later that her older brother managed this restaurant, and her granddad is some bigwig here in town. At the time, it didn't mean much to me."

"And?" she asked.

"And about two weeks later, I'm eating a sandwich at a local place on a Saturday afternoon, minding my own business. From nowhere, an older gentleman in a tailored suit and overcoat slides into my booth opposite of me and introduces himself. He wanted to thank me for taking care of his granddaughter. Says his name is Carmine Giacomo."

"*The* Carmine Giacomo?"

"Right. Better known as the underboss for the Kansas City faction of La Cosa Nostra. He's Big Tony Fanucci's right hand man. As I'm sure you know about him, he's the guy who's always in the news for all kinds of innocent things. Like money laundering, loan sharking, and making trial witnesses disappear right before they're scheduled to testify."

"And he's now your new best friend?" Caroline asked with a grin.

"Something like that. So, he leans over and tells me that if there's anything I need, like if someone's hassling me over something, if a cop gives me a ticket, anything at all, he'll take care of it for me. He tells me that his family is in debt for a favor to me for helping his granddaughter. And he says that I can cash it in anytime in the future."

"Interesting."

"Before he slipped away, he told me that his grandson, the older brother of the patient I took care of, was the manager of this restaurant. The first time I visited, the brother treated me like I'm a long-lost cousin and the meal was on the house. It's been a while since I've been here, but I'm sure the food is still great."

About then, Frankie returned with our beverages, and we made our selections for dinner.

"What were you going to tell me that couldn't be said over the phone?" Caroline asked after our waiter left.

"I had a couple of strange things happen today. I was headed to the hospital this morning, but forgot my stethoscope, so I had to go back home to get it. As I turned into my complex, there was sedan with dark windows parked along the curb across the street. From the corner of my eye, the driver was typing into one of those new kind of laptop computers. When I entered my condo, my message machine was being played and the messages from you were being deleted."

"Kyle, are you sure?"

"Yeah, I am. And when I left, the sedan was gone."

"What do you think that means?"

"Well, I've got one more tidbit to add to that."

"What?"

"Before I headed to the office this morning, I wandered over to Medical Records at St. Jude to get all caught up so they wouldn't put me on the delinquent list. For reasons I won't go into, I reached into a trash can and found this."

I pulled the folded piece of crumpled paper up from my coat pocket and handed it to her.

As I watched her read it, I saw her face turn from calm to horror.

"Kyle, what does this mean?" Her voice rose to nearly a shout.

"Easy there, Cleopatra. It means that someone is very interested in my relationship with you. It also means that someone is very interested in my whereabouts and what I say to you. Otherwise, that slip of paper wouldn't be in the trash basket right where the stack of the medical records was put there for me to sign."

"Kyle, did you call the FBI like you promised me you would?"

"I sure did. Yesterday morning. They politely told me to contact the local police force instead. Seems like they weren't too interested in some crazy drug smuggling scheme."

Frankie reappeared with our salads, and we waited for him to vanish before continuing.

"Who do you think these people are?" she asked anxiously.

"Like I told you on the phone, I have a suspicion that somebody connected with the situation I was looking into is now turning up the heat. As I said, I was suspicious that someone was monitoring my phone calls. Now I saw in person that they are. If they can monitor my calls, they can monitor yours."

"What are we going to do, Kyle?"

"No more calls to our home phones. We got to check in

with each other every day and use only our mobile phones. I don't know; they may even have a way to listen in on us with them too, although I doubt it. And you are going to have to get a new phone message machine for your home."

We sat in silence for a while trying to understand the seriousness of our situation.

By then, our boy Frankie arrived with our entrees on large, steaming platters.

"Wow, smells great Frankie," I said.

He nodded and left without saying a word, completely different from the eager to please waiter when we first arrived.

That was strange.

A few minutes passed while we dug into our food. I was about to continue our discussion when the restaurant manager came to our table.

"Joey, great to see you. How's your sister?" I asked.

"You've got a lot of nerve showing up here Dr. Chandler," he said with a cold stare.

Whoa. Where did that come from?

"What do you mean, Joey? I know it's been a while since I've been here to eat, but it's not like I go out to eat that much anyway."

"I think you know what I mean."

"No Joey. I don't know what you mean. As a matter of fact, I really don't have any idea what you're talking about."

He paused with a silent look of danger in his eyes. I glanced at Caroline, and she was still as a statue.

"I got a call from my grandfather this morning. He says the word on the street is that there's been someone putting their nose into my grandfather's business where it shouldn't be. And they've traced that person back to Kansas City. Not so smart, Doctor."

"What are you saying, Joey?"

"I'm saying that my grandfather's not so happy that this someone knows a little too much for his own good. Grandfather Carmine told me that if I ran across the likes of you, that I should let you know to be sure and watch your back."

It was my turn for silence. I finally got up the nerve to respond to him.

"I think your family is getting me confused with somebody else. You tell your grandfather that I'd love to sit and talk with him. I know we can discuss whatever he thinks is reasonable. You'll do that for me, right Joey?"

"Whatever you say, Doctor. Enjoy the rest of your evening," he said as he turned and walked away from our table.

Caroline looked at me with an expression of alarm.

"What is he saying, Kyle?"

"He's saying that his grandfather not a happy camper with me right now. That's because he pretty much confirmed to me that Grandpa Carmine is right in the middle of what I told you about the smuggling of likely illegal substances in the flexible wine bladders. That pretty much confirms what I suspected."

"What are you going to do, Kyle?"

"Well, first off, I'm going to tell you how sorry I am that I got you involved in this."

"Me? How am I involved with this?"

"Caroline, I started sniffing around a scheme to most likely smuggle narcotics into the US. How did I know that it would ultimately involve the Mafia? Now I've got someone from their family business deleting your messages on my home phone message machine from a remote laptop computer. I told you, if they can get to me, they can get to you."

"There's a lot at stake here Kyle. I've got a business to run and my life to lead. What do you want me to do?"

I looked deeply into her eyes, hoping I could say the right thing.

"First off, if you have any feelings for me right now, or even in the future, you're going to have to trust me."

After a long pause, she slowly nodded that she

understood.

"Second, we got to make sure you are protected. These guys do not play by the rules. I think it's time we call in the cavalry. Remember Sergeant Wilkins from our case earlier this year? He's a specialist at surveillance and protection. I'm going to give him a call to see if he can give me a hand on how to protect you."

"That's all well and good for me, but what about you?"

"I been thinking that I might just have a way to neutralize this whole mess, but I got to run it past a certain someone first. Let's finish our meal and get out of here."

Somehow, both of us had lost our appetites since the jarring conversation with Carmine's grandson. We took one or two more bites and then signaled our boy Frankie for the check. After paying the bill, we headed out the front door. While walking to the car, it reminded me of an old saying one of my surgery professors used to recite.

If you kick the hornets' nest hard enough, there's a good chance that you're going to get stung.

23

CHINATOWN, NEW YORK CITY

Philip Hauser paid the cab driver and slowly walked towards the dingy Chinese restaurant entrance. Despite it being a weeknight, there were many Asian Americans scurrying along the storefronts in the always-busy section of Chinatown. Hauser normally wouldn't dare to be seen here in this tiny neighborhood of Manhattan, but he knew that making this business partner uncomfortable out of his element would give him an advantage.

He opened the restaurant door, entering a huge concoction of aromas and scents mixed with a beehive of activity. A quiet, white table clothed Italian restaurant in the Bronx this definitely was not. It was a dark, narrow room laced with tacky Chinese décor about fifteen degrees warmer than outside due to the open range flames bellowing in the kitchen. Hauser walked in where immediately the owner recognized him, coming over and bowing at the waist. The owner then led him to a reserved booth in the back for his meeting.

It wasn't the quietest or even the nicest place to meet, but he knew the owner with his gang connections made the location a safe place not to be overheard. Just the right kind of venue to make the guy he was meeting completely ill at ease.

Within two minutes, the owner was escorting the slender olive-skinned man in a dark gray overcoat holding his fedora hat in his hand. He took off his overcoat, threw it into the far end of the booth, and slid into his seat opposite of the CEO. The man put his elbows on the table and interlaced his fingers while staring silently at Hauser.

The waiter showed up promptly and asked if they would like to order drinks first before dinner.

"Johnnie Walker Black, neat," the olive-skinned man said without looking at the waiter.

"Dry martini, Bombay Gin, one olive," the CEO said calmly.

After the waiter left, the olive-skinned man exclaimed, "I don't eat Chink food."

Just by that opening comment, the corporate executive knew he had his opponent on the ropes, so he decided to push his adversary beyond the first stage of uncomfortable.

"You wanted to meet, so here we are," Hauser said. "You say your superiors are not happy. You say they are hearing about a possible breakdown in the transport system. Explain."

The man began looking around the narrow room cautiously while still silent.

"Are you sure this place is a safe place to talk? I've never trusted any gooks," the olive-skinned man finally said.

"I picked this place because I've known the owner for years. Let me tell you, he's more trustworthy at keeping things confidential than you'll ever be. This place is beyond safe for not being overheard. As I already said, explain," Hauser said.

"We have word from our sources that your transport

system for our product might be compromised. My superiors think the problem is with you and your system. One of your workers seems to have let the cat out of the bag. He very well could have already told the wrong kind of people about our little setup. That could be bad news for you and your take on things."

"Well, that's quite an interesting point of view," the CEO said. "It just so happens *my* sources told me they found out something completely different about the possible leak. And they have photographic and audio evidence to prove it."

The Italian American man's face didn't show a hint of emotion. But he also didn't try to immediately disagree. He stared straight ahead at the CEO, quietly waiting for Hauser to continue.

"My sources tell me that one of the heads of your five families declared there was a compromise in the transport system for a specific reason," Hauser said. "If the agreement for everyone on your end of it was to get an equal amount of product delivered, but the delivery system was suddenly shut down, then the agreement was no longer valid. And guess who planned on taking over the delivery system that would create a new and unequal distribution of product?"

The olive-skinned man waited in silence keeping his full attention on Hauser.

"That's right; it would vault that family out in front of the other four. There was a confidential meeting recently within one of the families. My sources say they couldn't get a video but have audio proof as well as photographs of the principal players leaving the meeting. You figure it out. Do you want us to continue to handle the transport of your product where things are running smoothly, or do you want to play instant second fiddle to one of your competitors?"

The business partner sat completely still for several moments.

"You can produce the audio tape and the photographs for me to show my superiors?" the olive-skinned man finally asked.

"By Saturday noon as long our transport agreement stays the same for all parties involved. Including one more condition."

"What is that?"

"That the source of the tape and photographs stays unknown. Now and forever in the future. Understand?" Hauser said, looking right into the man's eyes.

The olive-skinned man didn't move for a moment and then slowly nodded.

"Good," Hauser said. "I don't need one of your competing families interfering with my transport system. I'll expect my deposits for the transport of the product to continue on schedule. I'll call you and leave a message where to meet for the pickup of the photographic and audio evidence at Saturday noon. Got it?"

The Italian American man said nothing but got up with his overcoat and hat and left for the front door.

Hauser smiled. The contest was so easy to win if you made all the rules yourself.

24

KANSAS CITY

On Friday morning, I got to the hospital early just to make sure all was ready to go for my morning cases. Most of the hospital OR staff were pretty proficient in their work habits. There were an occasional few that seemed to get a serious case of "Friday-itis" on the last day of the work week. If their minds were wandering about what they had planned for the weekend instead of focusing on the surgery case at hand, it could make for a long morning.

Thank goodness the staff in my room that morning was dialed in and ready to get going. Taking really good care of patients in surgery took not only a lot of tactical skill, but a lot of empathy of the patient and the problem you were trying to fix for them. That is just as important from the surgeon in charge down to the orderly running for supplies when needed during the case.

While I was in charge of everything that went on in that room, I pretty much let the nurses choose the music we played during the case in the OR to keep them happy. Another old surgery professor used to remind me, "A happy crew means a happy you." Amen.

After finishing up my third outpatient case before noon, I talked to the patient's family in the surgery waiting room and headed for the physician's dressing room. I had about thirty minutes before the onslaught of Friday afternoon patients in my office who all wanted to be seen before the weekend. My Friday office scenario usually ended up somewhere between being in the middle of a rugby scrum and trying to herd a bunch of cats. I sat down on the bench in front of my surgical locker for a minute and went over the events of last night.

After dinner, I dropped Caroline off at her car at work, worried about her safety. I thought about any other way I could protect Caroline from whoever was so concerned about my interest in this puzzling smuggling scheme that I had blindly stuck my nose into.

Because of my worries about Caroline, I had called Sydney a little after 9:00 p.m. when I got home last night. He had always been like my long-lost uncle giving me advice on just about everything since I moved to Kansas City. I decided to get his take on my situation.

After three rings a voice came on the line, "Hello, this is Sydney Alfred."

Proper and precise as usual.

"Sydney, this is Kyle. I'm sorry to bother you this late."

"That's quite alright my boy. Is everything okay?"

"Just fine Sydney. I wanted to get your advice on something if you have a minute."

"I was just watching some old reruns of Ryder Cup matches that I have recorded on my VCR tapes. What can I help you with?"

I proceeded to explain my concern about the phone messages that were being deleted as well as the slip of paper I found in the Medical Records' trash can with all of Caroline's information listed.

After listening to my storytelling, he got right to the point and told me what I should do.

"Why young man, you need to find some help to protect that attractive woman you are so fond of," he said. "If you will jog your memory, you were in the same kind of situation just a few months ago."

It was interesting to me that although the subject of Caroline had come up several times before with him, Sydney could not bring himself to say Caroline's name out loud. I guessed that it was because he missed his niece Molly terribly, probably because she was so much like him.

Sydney knew about me going out with Caroline. Every time the subject came up, he seemed to be fine with me seeing someone other than Molly. Although in his mind, no one could ever replace his darling niece, he more than encouraged my pursuit of the striking antiques dealer. Probably a little too much so from my viewpoint, but he still wouldn't say her name out loud to me.

"Right now," he said, "just like back in April, you need to contact Sergeant Wilkins."

"I really don't want to bother him, Sydney. Particularly with all I drug him through on the last case."

"Nonsense. He protects important people for a living all the time. He'd be happy to talk to you again."

"You think so?" I asked with some hesitation.

"I know you have his number. Give him a call soon. You can rely on him. Say, when are we getting together for our regular golf outing again? You've been skipping out on me with all those work excuses."

"I'm so sorry, Sydney. You know I love playing golf with you, but work seems to be in control of my schedule since I got back from that conference in London. We'll get together soon, I promise."

"Well, it better be soon because with your lack of practice, I'll be outdriving you before you know it," he said.

"I'm sure you will Sydney. I'll be in touch and thanks for the advice."

"Sure thing, Kyle. Goodbye now," he said in his usual formal manner as he hung up.

After changing back to my street clothes, I decided to follow Sydney's advice and contact the one guy who really saved my hide from some bad guys on my first case. That was the one and only Sergeant Wilkins. Maybe Sydney was right. If anyone could, maybe Sergeant Wilkins could figure out a way for me to evade these people who were controlling my phone messages.

Ah yes, Sergeant Wilkins. He was an incredible six-foot four-inch specimen of muscle and know how. Over twenty years in the Marine Corps as a colonel, a super successful businessman, a scratch golfer, and now a part-time bodyguard for important visiting dignitaries. I called him a patriot who must have been part Pentecostal preacher and part John Wayne.

All together amazing.

Because of my suspicions of the phone lines being tapped throughout the whole CHS campus, I quickly made it to my clunky Volvo. I dialed his number on my mobile phone, only to get a generic voice on the line to leave a message. I knew that he never answered his phone right away as a standard precaution. I left a specific message for him to call me back.

About ten minutes later as I was pulling into my office parking garage, my mobile phone rang.

"Hello, this is Dr. Kyle Chandler."

"Dr. Chandler, John Wilkins here. Good to hear from you. What can I do for you, son?" he asked in an authoritative tone.

"Thank you for calling me back so promptly, sir," I said. "I have another situation that may need the use of your vast expertise, sir."

"After our last escapade, I thought you may have gotten a little gun shy of difficult situations. What can I do to help you, son?"

I proceeded to give him the short version of the laundry

list of my investigation over the past several weeks. I explained the predicament I was in along with my suspicion of the Kansas City Mafia's involvement. Most of all, I told him of my worries of Caroline's safety.

After I completed my roller coaster story, he was silent for a second and then calmly asked, "Is there anything else I need to know?" as his tone of voice had noticeably dropped an octave to mean that now he was all business.

"No sir, that's about it."

"Have you considered contacting the proper federal authorities, mainly the FBI?"

"I did sir, and they told me to contact the local police. A lot of good that'll do. Besides, I really don't want to spend the rest of my life constantly running away under their witness-hope-we-can-protect-you-program."

"This is quite an interesting position you've drifted yourself into since we last finished your previous case just a few months ago. And you say the Kansas City faction of La Cosa Nostra to boot?"

"Looks that way."

He paused for a second before continuing.

"Well then, I guess we'll have to figure out a way to keep that darling young woman you have seemed to have charmed out of harm's way. For the record, I still don't know how you managed to lasso that special of a lady. And I suppose that includes saving your backside also."

"That would be greatly appreciated, Sergeant."

"Let me discuss this situation with some associates of mine. I'll be back in touch with you very soon."

"Thank you, sir. Talk to you then."

Well, there were no rules in this game, so I had to do my best to be protected. Hopefully, it was the Black Knight to the rescue again just like last time.

So why not twice in one year?

I made it up to my office and managed to cram my brown paper sack lunch down as fast as I could before the torrential wave of patients was to begin at one o'clock. My administrative assistant Janice found me hiding at my cubicle. She assaulted me with a fist full of messages and tasks that needed to be taken care of that very minute. Another example of the not-so-thrilling things that they didn't quite explain of what private practice in medicine would be like after completing all those years of medical training.

I spent the rest of the afternoon bouncing like a ping-pong ball from one patient to the next during the quickly passing hours. Because of the hectic pace of the office schedule, my nurses helping me didn't have a fighting chance to even think about getting "Friday-itis" on the last day of the work week.

Just after seeing the last patient on the schedule, my cell phone buzzed. It was Sergeant Wilkins getting back to me. I made a beeline for the office emergency exit to answer the call outside while I put a small widget in the door so I could get back in. That area outside was where a few nurses would sneak outside at lunch to have a cigarette even through smoking was prohibited in or around the building.

"This is Kyle Chandler," I said.

"Dr. Chandler, John Wilkins here. I've spoken with my associates about your situation, and we think it is imperative right now to set up surveillance on Caroline for her protection and safety. These guys you are facing are not in the minor leagues. I will have one of my team members keeping her under strict, but unnoticeable surveillance for the next week. I will check in daily with you to report any situations that might seem unusual."

"That's a relief, Sergeant. Please keep me up to speed of what you find and send me your bill when you think surveillance is no longer needed," I said to the former military specialist.

"Don't worry about the bill. Now what are we going to

do about you?"

"I've been thinking about that myself. I spend most of my time at the hospital or my office, so I think it would be difficult for anyone to mess with me except to and from work."

"I totally disagree son, but we will respect anything you decide. Please do not hesitate to call me day or night if you think you might be getting yourself into a bind. Do you understand?"

"Yes sir, I will. And thank you for your help."

"No problem. I'll be in touch," he said and the line clicked off.

At least that was one domino finally falling my way.

I returned inside and told all the nurses to go home and not abuse their husbands after a long day at work. I don't know if they actually thought I meant it or not, but they gladly took off for home. After they left, I battled the stack of charts that needed dictations for all the patients I had seen that afternoon. Not the funnest thing to do, but oh well, that's part of what I had signed up for when I said I wanted to be a physician.

After gathering up all my stuff, I headed out to the parking garage just after 7:00 p.m. looking to get two things done: Immediately find something to eat and then getting some rest before my loads-of-fun shift on trauma call tomorrow. I knew that weekend trauma call was part of the job, but it really took a compartmentalized state of mind to accept what the reality of what I did for a living was really true. Like knowing I was going to be walking across a bed of hot coals tomorrow, but just how much of the heat can I stand all at once?

On my way home, I dialed Caroline's mobile phone to check in with her. I started to get a little nervous when she didn't answer until the fifth ring.

"Are you okay?" I asked when she finally picked up.

"I'm fine. What about you? No word from your restaurant manager's grandfather?"

"No news is good news in that department. What are you doing for dinner?"

"Well, Doctor Never-Plan, I had some yogurt and an apple at my desk after work. Now I am about to leave work for a twice a month hot yoga class at a health club not far from here."

"Hot yoga? What are you talking about?" I asked.

"It's this kind of yoga started by this guy from India named Bikram that got popular in the 1970s in LA. They put you in a room that's over one hundred degrees and super humid where you do twenty-six postures for an hour and a half. You come out exhausted and wringing wet, but I'll have to admit you do feel better after the heat torture is over."

"How did you get mixed up in this nonsense, especially on a Friday evening?"

"I promised a long-time customer that I would go to one of the sessions at her club with her after her husband passed away unexpectedly. She somehow talked me into going with her to this twice a month class. It's mostly divorced women who get together two times a month, sweat profusely, then go out for a drink or three to complain about their ex-husbands while feeling a lot skinnier from all the fluid loss. My friend and I pretty much skip that part of the ritual. You should come try it with me sometime."

"Oh, for sure," I said soaked in sarcasm.

"With your medical background, you'd especially like the part after sweating one-third of all of your bodily fluids away," she said. "At the end, the instructor proceeds to have you do these super deep breathing exercises that make you more than lightheaded."

"Well, I bet that's just unbelievably fun and sooo safe, too. Let's look at this a little closer for a second. What we have here is mostly middle aged, likely overweight humans, not you of course, with temporary hypovolemia, their heart rates of around one hundred and sixty, and then each person trying to top it off with hyperventilation to see if they can get as close as they can to an instant heart attack. What do you think about that?"

"You're just a spoil sport, you are Doctor."

"Maybe, but the fact is that I'm a *living* spoil sport is the difference."

"Whatever," she said in a huff.

"You haven't seen anything that might suggest that somebody has been watching you any more than usual?"

"How would I know?" she asked. "I've been at work all day. Unlike you and Elvis, I haven't left the building."

"Cute, real cute. Just keep an eye out when you go to your car and call me if you see anything strange. Got it?"

"Anything you say, my guardian angel. What about you? What's your deal tonight?"

"Well, I'm pretty beat from office hours this afternoon. I'm going to grab something to eat on the way home and get some rest before the slugfest of being on trauma call from tomorrow until Sunday morning."

"You describe it with such distain, yet you doggedly keep at it as your job. Why?"

I paused before answering her question that was so damn penetrating. I was still a little scared of divulging too much to this unique woman of insight.

"It's hard to explain really. I chose trauma surgery because of the here's-a-problem-and-let's-go-fix-it outlook. The whole grind of being on call isn't that bad at all once you define the problems before you and get caught up in achieving the solutions. It's very stimulating actually. What's hard is the anticipation of the uncertainty of what you're about to face next and the total lack of control of your schedule. Does that sound Freudian enough for you?"

"Believe it or not, that's more revealing of what's going on in that smart aleck brain of yours than I have heard in a while. I tell you what. Let's make a bet."

"What? Who are you, Jimmy the Greek's niece?"

"The next time you complain about being on trauma call..." she said.

"Wait a minute. I don't really complain. I just happen to casually comment on it now and then."

"Like I said before being interrupted, the next time you complain about being on trauma call and I call you on it, you owe me one session at hot yoga class with me on a Friday evening."

"Punishment by heat exhaustion? That's one I haven't heard before. Okay, if you get to challenge me, then I get to equally challenge you," I said.

"Now wait a second..."

I could tell she was starting to backpedal.

"Fair's fair. Let me think of something really devious that you really don't like to do."

"Who said that there's truly something that I don't like to do? I love trying new things. As a matter of fact, I plan on doing new things almost every single day of the week."

"That's it! You revealed it! A Freudian slip!"

"Oh no," she whimpered.

"It's you and your planning. Here's the bet. If I do not comment negatively, not complain note you, about being on trauma call for an entire week, then I get to declare a whole day, at my choosing not yours, where you have to absolutely not plan one single thing on your schedule in advance. And I mean not even one thing. If I find out that you secretly planned an activity on that day, then you must do whatever I tell you for that entire day. Within the limits of physical reason and sexual consent, of course."

"Real funny. But I guarantee that it'll be a piece of cake for me."

"Consider it official that the clock has now started until this time next Friday evening. Just remember, I will have my spies at your office watching out for me."

"Hope you have plenty of Gatorade at your place to replace all those electrolytes you're going to lose after going to hot yoga with me. I've got to go, but call me tomorrow Doctor Sore-Loser," she taunted.

"I will, with dreams about when I get to take away your

Day-Timer for a whole day," I said just before she hung up.

Despite the worsening unsafe situation I had put us both in, I was glad that she was the one that was ploughing through this with me.

Maybe Sebastian Clarke and Iris Kettleman both knew something that I didn't.

25

KANSAS CITY

By the time I stopped by a deli to get a sandwich to-go and swung by the grocery store for a few essential staples, I made it to my condo that evening about as tired as guy could be. I went to bed early with a giant question mark in my brain of how I was going to shake the KC Mob off my tail. And likely off Caroline's as well.

I awoke the next morning somewhat refreshed. I felt even better after a morning caffeine recharge. I turned my pager back on, grabbed a quick shower, and headed off to the hospital. On my way to the hospital, a fresh idea came to me that maybe could shed some light on how to find out more about if the KC Mob was really interested in me. My old friend Harold might know something. Maybe I could pay him a visit after lunch if I wasn't stuck at the hospital.

Oh well, first things first.

Parking at the hospital physician's lot, I made my way to the surgeon's lounge area that connected to the OR dressing rooms. We had a routine for the man on call to run down the list of inpatients to keep an eye on from the physician finishing up on call from the previous night.

"How'd it go last night John?" I asked Dr. Simpson as I sat on an overstuffed couch.

"Not too bad KC. I had two hot appendix cases early in the evening that I already checked on early this morning. They should both go home this morning."

John Simpson was a likable guy from New Orleans with an obvious Louisiana drawl. He and his wife always threw a big party every year around Mardi Gras with a crawfish boil and lots of beer. Where they got fresh crawfish in the middle of the prairie during February is still a mystery to me. He was a reliable physician who had been on the hospital trauma staff for the last four or five years. The thing I really admired about him was that he finished what he started and didn't dump unfinished work on the oncoming physician on call. We understood each other just fine.

"Other than that," he said, "the usual nursing calls about lab results and minor ER cases that required referrals, but overall, pretty good for a Friday. By the way, this weekend is the heart of the college football season and today's going to be sunny. And you know what that means for a Saturday in autumn, don't you?" he asked with a small smile.

"You bet I do. Overzealous football fans start drinking beer before noon cheering on their favorite teams in front of the TV. Everything stays calm until they realize that they are out of refreshments and have to make an emergency run at halftime to get more beer. That leads to an afternoon and evening of the continual bumper car jousting tournament."

"I see your wall of cynicism is ready to shield you from the on call demons," he said.

"I'll take an aggressive offense over a protective defense any day of the week. Have a good rest of the weekend," I said as he wearily got up to head home.

After running down a few lab values on two of my

patients, I made my way back to the physician's lot looking over my shoulder as a precaution. As I opened my car, I got in and thought for a second. My decent night's sleep last night didn't rid me of my apprehension about sticking my nose into a suspected smuggling scheme. Nor was I proud of the fact that it involved the far-reaching influence of the KC La Cosa Nostra. At least I was a bit calmer about Caroline since Sergeant Wilkins was keeping an eye on her.

Nevertheless, I left the hospital lot and proceeded to check off one by one from the list of weekly errands that I usually completed on Saturday mornings. Really exciting things like dropping my shirts off at the cleaners, going back to the grocery store to get the three needed items that I had forgotten to get last night. Probably because I was approaching total cerebral collapse from exhaustion at the time. Oh, and don't forget I had to fill up my Royal Swedish Chariot with gas for the weekend.

At every stop along my errands route, I looked 360 degrees for unexpected gorillas before I got out of my car. While the coast seemed to be clear at each place, I knew I was going to have to think of something soon to deal with my threatening situation. By the time I made it home around lunchtime, I was thankful to still be in one piece.

For now.

26

MANHATTAN – THE BRONX – MANHATTAN

Early Saturday morning, Philip Hauser awoke with a purpose to develop a plan to keep control of the transport of the product into the country at the current arrangement with his business partners. Moreover, he refused to be forced out by those greedy Italian morons. All he needed to do was execute his plan and that would keep the cash flow rolling in. The difficulty of trying to hide all of that tax-free cash in offshore accounts was a good problem to have. After all, he was nicknamed by all the business publications as the Blitzkrieg of Big Business.

That morning, Hauser needed to pick up the evidence so he could deliver it to the olive-skinned business contact without any hitches. Delivery of the convincing evidence would require a well thought out plan that was safe for him yet convincing to the distribution partners. Every aspect of the plan must be executed so that the evidence could not be traced back to him. And that would require thinking and doing things outside the box. Even if the execution of his plan was not a pleasant task for a distinguished CEO like himself.

Hauser absolutely detested taking the subway in New York. It was dirty, it smelled, and there were all kind of vagrant types everywhere you turned. How could anyone put up with such filth? He was sure he would catch some type of communicable disease if he rode it more than once a year.

Because of that conviction, he was not in his usual attire of a tailored suit and silk tie for today's journey. The CEO was wearing an oversized, ratty-looking jacket, old trousers, a ball cap, and wraparound sunglasses. Definitely not your standard power lunch threads. These vagabond clothes would immediately be double bagged and go into the basement dumpster the minute he arrived back at his apartment.

Hauser considered that taking a cab was an easy way for police to trace a passenger and where the fare was dropped off. Cabbies seemed to remember every fare and every passenger's face. That is why he decided to take public transportation on such a rare occasion as the one this morning. After all, he already had a busy early morning.

Hauser had left his spacious apartment to meet his contact at 10:00 a.m. on the nose at their backup meeting place at a Starbuck's off East Broadway on the Lower East Side. His Hispanic contact, Mango, brought Hauser two manila envelopes. The CEO carefully opened each one to check the contents to make sure all of the precious evidence was there.

The first envelope was filled with copies of eight by ten glossies of several men together exiting a social club onto the street. All the men were dressed in suits or sports coats while wearing sunglasses, and it was obvious several had their bodyguards with them.

These critical photos had been taken with a telephoto lens by a man hidden in the back of a van parked down the street. This talented photographer could alter photos like no expert Hauser had ever seen. The man had been referred to the CEO by a friend of a friend a few years ago. In addition, the photographer had a huge collection of photos to choose from, depending on the price willing to be paid. Yes, even photos of prominent Mafia family members together in groups. This was exactly what Hauser considered for his plan as a backup just in case.

A backup plan until now.

The other manila folder Mango picked up for him held two unlabeled cassette tapes. These had come from a recording studio technician Hauser used in the past with premier results. For a mere $3000 cash and a script that Hauser had written himself, the technician recorded a false meeting of one of the Mafia families explaining their desire to take over Hauser's transport system for product distribution. The accents and dialogue on the tapes the technician used in the past were pitch perfect. The CEO felt certain that there would be no duplicate recording or any other record of the tapes since he held a crucial amount of damning evidence concerning the technician's younger sister on some not-so-innocent activities. The extra tape became his insurance policy just in case.

After checking both envelopes, Hauser said, "I'll transfer payment as usual with a little extra for the double pickup. Don't call me unless I call you. I'll be in touch."

The young Latin American nodded in silence. Especially since he knew that he had a good thing going.

Hauser called his olive-skinned contact for the product distribution before he left his apartment that morning. The guy wanted Hauser to come all the way up to the middle of the Bronx to deliver the goods. The CEO told him absolutely no way. That was at least an hour and a half train ride each way, even if the trains were on time. They settled on a slightly closer spot further south outside the Bronx General

Post Office.

From Starbuck's on the Lower East Side, Hauser made his way for the nearest subway station on East Broadway. He got off at Lafayette, walking over to the Bleecker St. Station. Although he had to change stations, the train that went up the Upper East Side was way nicer than the one on the west side going through Harlem to Yankee Stadium. The CEO got lucky when he arrived at Bleecker St., catching the train just before it pulled out. He was headed to 149th Grand Concourse station on a forty-minute ride with multiple stops.

On the way, he put half of the photos with one cassette tape in each manila envelope. There was one for his olive-skinned contact with a blank label on the front and one for him. Always thinking about the next step in business, he never knew when he might need a backup get-out-of-jail-free card.

Upon exiting the subway and going up to street level, he stood at the top of the stairway looking around to get his bearings, his ball cap pulled down low and his sunglasses back on. Right in front of him across the street stood the huge Bronx Post Office building covering an entire square block. Just outside the building to his left was a drive through lane for mail. The olive-skinned man told him to drop the envelope in the third drive-through mailbox outside the front door of the post office exactly at noon. Hauser wondered how in the world the product distribution contact was going to find a single envelope dropped in a mailbox loaded with mail. Especially from what was considered US federal property.

He shook his head. Not his problem.

Hauser waited outside the subway stairs for a few minutes, checking his watch several times. When it was time, the CEO walked across the street and waited until there were no more cars dropping off letters. As instructed, he walked to the third mailbox and slid the manila envelope into the slot. Glancing around as he walked back to the subway stop, he didn't see anyone walking towards the drive through mailboxes.

When he started descending the steps to the subway, he stopped when only his head was above the surface of the street. Looking through the handrail vertical slats, he waited on the stairs, watching intently.

Sure enough, within fifteen seconds out came a postman in uniform who walked directly to the third mailbox of the drive through. Approaching the mailbox from behind, the mailman opened the back of the box with his key. With the first pull of the contents from the box, he snatched a manila envelope, quickly checked the front blank label, and then emptied the rest of the contents into a post office box with handles. He placed the manila envelope on top of the pile and walked towards a side entrance door. The mailman put the box of mail down and used another key to open the entrance.

Just as he did, low and behold the olive-skinned contact, who had been leaning against the building nearby, brushed by and made it look like he accidently bumped into the mailman. He patted the mailman on the back and smoothly whisked the manila envelope into his inside coat pocket. It just so happened that the partially opened entrance door conveniently blocked any security camera view. The mailman tipped his cap to the olive-skinned man and headed inside with the box of mail. A polished maneuver.

Hauser scurried down the steps to the subway, paid his fare, and walked, to the end of the subway platform away from the masses. He realized that he might have underestimated his business partners' sphere of influence. The CEO had just witnessed a federal government employee on federal property that allowed a third party to use a mailbox for a private transaction drop-off site. The mailman had obviously arranged the transfer to make himself look completely innocent. That way if he were ever questioned in the future, the mailman could claim innocence from tampering with any mail delivery, which everyone knows is a federal offense.

Hauser realized that the influence of the Mafia's control extended even as far as using federal employees to cover for their nefarious actions. That was more than he had initially expected.

On the subway back to the real world in Manhattan, Hauser began to wonder if he should devise some other backup plan in addition to the photos and fabricated audio tape. After all, one can't be too careful when dealing with shady characters who can control even postmen to do their dirty work.

But the more he thought about it, the more foolish it sounded. There's no way a bunch of uneducated hoodlums was going to outfox him. He was the one always two steps ahead of the competition. As all of Wall Street already knew, wasn't he the one the business publications labeled as the Blitzkrieg of Big Business?

27

KANSAS CITY

After finishing another male oriented Saturday lunch menu of a PB&J sandwich, raspberry jam, never strawberry, and a cup of soup, I went through the mail and paid some bills. Instead of waiting around for the weekend trauma games to commence, I decided to go pay my friend Harold a visit.

Harold was an energetic, sixty-something-year-old black man who owned Harold's Antiques and Valuables, a small antique store downtown. When I first moved to Kansas City, he was involved in a pretty bad auto accident. Harold was in a bad way when I first met him as his trauma surgeon. Despite the fact he ruptured his spleen and lost a lot of blood, he came through surgery like a champ. Ever since I took up the hobby of ferreting out French antiques, I gave him a ring from time to time to double-check the current going rate of certain items.

Harold not only knew a lot about antiques and their value, but he also had his finger on the pulse of what was going down in the metro Kansas City area. Not only in the field of antiques, but also in the underbelly of society. When I initially worked with Ian Griffin on the missing antiques case, it was Harold I tracked down first to see if he had any inside information that could help me. He was the one who told me to go look up Caroline, which led me to my acute interest in her.

I found a parking spot downtown on the street, parked my car, and ambled up to the storefront door. After pushing it open, I found seated behind a small desk a slender, middle-aged black woman with a large orange-red afro. I remembered the last time I came to see Harold the same woman was wearing a Nehru collared jacket with a miniskirt and had long, bleached blonde straight hair. This time she was wearing a midriff blouse covering up close to nothing of her prominent breasts and low-riding bell-bottom jeans. Quite a fashionista.

"How can I help you today?" she asked, snuffing her cigarette butt into a nearby ashtray.

"Is Harold around?"

"And who might be askin'?" she asked in a cautious tone.

"Just tell him 'Doc' is here to speak with him," I said.

She sat looking me over, like she might have seen me before, but she wasn't really sure. I figured the woman was trying to guess if I was some potential threat to her or her employer when Harold appeared through the beads hanging in the doorframe. One look at me, and he broke into his famous grin.

"I thought I heard trouble out front," he said laughing. "If it ain't the one and only Dr. Kyle Chandler, trauma surgeon and French antiques expert. I also heard that now you've added a third title of earth-shaking private investigator to your resume."

"You don't miss a trick, do you Harold? How's business these days?"

"Always a chance to make a profit, Doc. Roberta," he

said, directing his gaze to his receptionist, "this is the doctor that put me back together after my car wreck years ago. He came by here earlier this year in the springtime, wasn't it?

Roberta continued a look of total boredom at me as Harold spoke.

"Well, come on back to my office and grab a seat," he said, motioning me to follow him through the hanging beads.

We went into his office, and I took a seat in one of the two very comfortable leather Chippendale reproduction wingback chairs in front of his desk. I remembered them from before because they were completely out of place with the storefront appearance.

Strange what people remember and why.

As I sat, Harold walked around the desk to his large office chair.

"Well Doc, what brings you to this neck of the woods? I thought you only dealt with the fancy antiques stores down by the Plaza now that you and Caroline are a duo."

"A duo? Harold, you do remember that you're the one who told me to go see her earlier this year. I believe you said 'you tell her Harold sent you. She'll do you right.' I just didn't know you were sending me to meet someone that inviting."

"You don't trust my judgment? First, I tell you about my furniture refinisher Dan, and you've made him so popular I have to wait in line for months to get him to refinish something for me."

Dan was my special furniture refinisher. He was a mechanical engineer by day and a magician refinishing antique furniture by night. Harold had been using him exclusively several years. Now that word about Dan's talents had gotten out to the antique world in this part of the country, Harold had to wait in line like everyone else for Dan's services.

"Then," Harold continued, "I sent you to see Caroline, a really good businesswoman who's really smart as well as beautiful. And you still don't trust my judgment?"

I didn't know if he was really sore at me, or just pulling the wool over my eyes, so I waited a second to respond.

He pulled his pipe from the desk drawer and began to pack it with something. When he lit it, I don't know what it was, but I did know it wasn't tobacco.

"You still smoking that same crap as the last time I was here?"

"No, this is different from that special blend made up by my brother-in-law. I have this imported from the tropics."

"Right," I said as I started to cough.

"Now where were we?" he asked. He started to break into one of his famous grins and said, "Oh yeah. Word has it that you two are pretty tight these days."

"I got to admit, it's been interesting Harold. She's a one of a kind, so yes; I do trust your judgment. And that's what brings me here today to see you."

"Well, I'll give you a little credit since you did save my life way back when. So, what's on your mind this time?"

I paused before proceeding.

"Harold, you know that I know about your past. And I never have and never will hold that against you. But because of your experiences in the past, I know you know a lot more of what's going down in this city than meets the eye. Is that fair enough to say?"

Harold knew I knew about his past, spending some time in prison many years ago for writing bad checks. Because of his past, he always kept his antiques business with the appearance of nothing but squeaky-clean legitimacy. However, I knew about his connections with lots of shady characters, including the ones that sell antiques out the back door.

He looked me straight in the eye and said nothing as he stroked the short white hair on his bearded chin.

I took the lack of a response from him as a caution but decided to press onward.

"Harold, let me just throw out a hypothetical situation,

completely random, and you tell me what you think what should been done about the situation. Okay?"

Harold gave a little chuckle. "I thought you were the private investigator these days, not me."

"Let's suppose that someone mistakenly stumbled upon a scheme where an organization was smuggling illegal substances into the US. The substances were secretly brought in by freight containers, sent to New Jersey, and likely distributed from there nationwide."

"That kind of situation is quickly getting out of my field of expertise, Doc."

"I know Harold, but what I need to find out is whether there is any word on the street in Kansas City of some kind of organization who is looking for the guy who might have found out about the secret smuggling scheme."

"Doc, you know damn well I stay far away from any of those big organizations that deal in what you're talking about."

"I know you stay clear, Harold. I totally believe you, I do. But you do have information that comes your way from time to time you might have overheard while dealing in the antiques business. Am I right?"

Harold sat still. He looked as if he were deciding whether to answer the question or to play dumb about the whole thing.

"What if I sweetened the deal for the information with a few bills of legal tender?" I asked as I pulled out my wallet. I proceeded to put eight twenty-dollar bills on the front of his desk.

"That's only going to get you the bare minimum of rumors that might be going around. On a rare topic like that, it's going to take a few more bills to get some specifics," he said as he reached forward to scoop up the stack of money.

"As I told you before Harold, you evidently don't know too much about how managed care pays their physicians these days. That's all I got, so the bare minimum will have to do."

He nodded his head ever so slightly while putting the bills in his shirt pocket.

"It just so happens I had a noisy bird come by the store two days ago. Let me tell you, this guy was a talker. He showed me a bunch of photos of some stuff he stashed at his warehouse. The guy was trying to peddle some of it off as ancient European antiques. I could tell right off it was junk, and I turned him down on the spot."

"Anyway," he said, "somehow we were talking, and the guy starts bragging how he's good friends with Tito Fanucci. The Mafia don's kid. He said he just got a call from Tito and maybe he'll try to get him to take the stuff off his hands like he had in the past."

"This Tito character. Is he from here in Kansas City?"

"Yeah. He's a hot head. Stay away from him at all costs."

"Won't be a problem. I'm sure we run in different social circles," I said.

"The guy then starts to tell me some things that Tito had told him on the phone. He said Tito had just found out about someone who arrived back in town recently who could mess up their family business. The guy was going to say more, then all the sudden he clammed up about it. He didn't say anything more than that."

"So nothing else was said about who the someone might be?" I asked.

"No, but I got a feeling you might know who that someone is," Harold said while looking me straight in the eyes.

After a long pause I answered, "Maybe, Harold. Just maybe."

"Doc, you sure you know what you're getting into?"

"Maybe not, but it's looking pretty much like I don't have a choice."

I told Harold about my excursions around London and Rotterdam with the visiting gorillas followed by the wild goose chase to Long Island and New Jersey. I touched on the highlights of finding Caroline's phone messages being deleted, as well as the man in the sedan with the laptop outside my condo complex. By the time I told him about the slip of paper I found in medical records wastebasket that had Caroline's name and info on it, and the warning from Carmine Giacomo's grandson at the Italian restaurant Thursday night, Harold was starting to look worried. No more famous grin.

"Doc, I gotta tell you that you do *not* want to mess with these people. I'm no expert about these guys, but if they can follow you from New Jersey to Kansas City, they can follow you anywhere. And they don't fool around."

"I'm beginning to figure that out Harold. For the time being, I've got the retired Marine commander who saved my butt in the last case keeping an eye on Caroline. I've got to figure a way to take the pressure off me and put it back on them."

"Good luck with that because that's a tall order to fill," Harold said with the pipe still in his hand.

"We'll see, Harold. If you have any more noisy bird friends tell you something new, you give me a holler," I said, as I shook his hand and stood to leave.

"You'd better lay low for a little while until this blows over."

"Maybe I will. Always a pleasure seeing you, Harold, and stay out of car wrecks."

I always told Harold that every time I saw him. I headed for the beads hanging from the doorway.

"I'll try my best, but if f I don't, I'll know who to call," he shouted to me as I headed out to my car.

By the time I made it home from downtown, it was around 4:00 p.m. I decided to give Caroline a call to check in.

Well, not really check in like she was my chaperone or parole officer or something. More like to check in to assure me of her safety. And the realization in my hard head that I couldn't stop thinking about her despite all of our verbal skirmishes.

After the fifth ring on her mobile phone, she finally picked up.

"Hello, this is Caroline," she said cheerfully.

"Hey, it's me. I was just calling to see if you were needing me to take you in for any intravenous fluid replacement after last night's sweat-fest at hot yoga," I said.

"For your information, I feel just fine and dandy after my session last night. It's kind of like purging all of your body's toxins out through your pores, Doctor Doubtful."

"Oh, I'm sure that's the case. Especially if you can tolerate the smell afterwards of twenty to thirty humans maximizing the scent of their body odors in a small, contained room with zero ventilation."

"Trust me; it's not what you think. Have you been called into the trauma center so far today?"

"Not as of yet, but then I wouldn't even think of commenting on that particular subject since there is currently a minor wager in play. Nothing but joyful occupational cheer exuding from this humble servant."

"Oh my goodness," she groaned. "This is going to be an extremely testing week on my part with nothing but total BS coming from you."

"Why Caroline, whatever are you talking about?" I feigned.

"Drop the innocent act, Doctor."

"Your wish is my command. On to a more serious subject. Did you see any suspicious cars that might have followed you coming home from the yoga place last night?"

"Not that I could tell, but then again I wasn't looking for anyone," she said. "Have you heard anything from your buddy Carmine?"

"Like I told you last night, no news is good news in that department."

I hadn't told her yet about my conversation with Sergeant Wilkins and the guys he had keeping an eye on her. They must be pretty good if she didn't recognize anyone following her anywhere. And I didn't mention what Harold had said about staying away from the Mob. I wasn't going to tell her about either of them, at least until the time was right.

"If you ever see anything strange at all, you call me on my mobile phone right away. Got it?"

"And just what in the world are you going to do about it if you aren't with me? Especially if you are in surgery?" she asked.

"I have a backup plan, don't you worry Miss Hot Yoga Queen."

"You just keep thinking about that hot yoga because you'll be trying it with me sooner than you think."

"Well, you never know, but there is one other thing I hope to be trying with you sooner than yoga..." I said.

"You males have a one-track mind, you know that, right?"

"In my defense, it's not such a bad track to be stuck on. You should try to be stuck on it with me sometime."

"Keep dreaming, Romeo. Speaking of backup plans, Halloween is coming up. Do you ever go out on Halloween?"

"Not since I was in elementary school trick or treating back in the Dark Ages."

"That's one thing since I've known you that you never, ever talk about."

"About trick or treating as a kid?" I asked.

"No silly. You never, ever have said anything about your childhood or your family to me. We've been seeing each other since April, and I have absolutely no information whatsoever about where you grew up or about your family."

"Well, you're no different," I said. "We've talked some about how your folks practically disowned you since you called off your wedding once you found Mr. Right was cheating on you big time. You did tell me about your training in antiques in London and elsewhere, how you got your store going here, and about how you moved it to the high dollar district at the Plaza. But you hardly ever said anything about your family or your childhood either. I don't even know where your folks live."

Total silence from her.

"Do you ever speak with them?" I asked. "Do you ever see them? I assume they don't live that far away since your wedding was supposed to be the KC Social Event of the Year. I mean, do you even see them at Thanksgiving?"

After another pause, she said, "They live here in town. I see them occasionally, more than I used to. So yes, I see them at Thanksgiving and Christmas. You know, the required family holiday events."

"Don't sound so convincingly overjoyed," I said.

"We get along fine, but my parents, especially my mother, have never completely forgiven me for suddenly ending what would have been their reward from the upper echelon of Kansas City society."

"So what's your mother like? What does she do?"

"I can honestly say that she's not anything like me. I've always wanted to make it on my own in the world, regardless of my disadvantage as a woman. My mother is much more social, where everyone knows their place in life all the while jockeying for a higher rung on the status ladder. More of the Junior League, ladies' charity organizations, and country club luncheon set. There's nothing wrong with that, but it's just not me."

"What about your father? What does he do?" I asked while she was still willing to talk.

"He's basically a workaholic. My dad has always had his hands in everything. His commercial real estate company has skyrocketed. He's got eight or nine other businesses that he's bought and managed from the ground up straight into the clouds. I should know because he was never at home the whole time I was growing up."

"Siblings?"

"You are persistent, aren't you? Yes, one younger brother, Chance. Eight years younger than me. Kind of a surprise for my parents at the time. He was a sports star in high school. You name it; he played it. Scholarships and girls flooded his way. He went off to college on a full ride and found out the minor complication of having going to class wasn't for him. Since I was pushed to the rear of the bus with my calling off the wedding, he is the one in their eyes that can still do no wrong. Last I heard, he's a seasonal fly-fishing guide in Montana living the life. So that's enough from my side of the coin. Now, what about your family?"

"Not much to say. I grew up in a rural area outside Raleigh, North Carolina. My mom was a homemaker and my dad worked at a hardware store. He suddenly died when I was in med school. We got by. I did well enough in high school to get a partial academic scholarship to UNC at Chapel Hill. It was a preppy place to go to school, but I didn't have time for all that fraternity jazz since I had to work two part-time jobs during the week as well as on the weekends to make ends meet. I took out major league student loans to pay for medical school at UNC. Still paying them back."

"How'd you get to Boston for your surgery training?" she asked.

"I always wanted to go far away for school, but we didn't have the money. So I did some rotations in Boston during my senior year in med school. I guess they had their quota of Harvard eggheads and needed a southern farm boy to broaden their residency stats. And I already told you about Molly."

"Brothers and sisters?"

"One older sister. She's married in Raleigh and works as an elementary school nurse. Everyone loves the school nurse."

She paused for a second, so I decided to put the focus back on her.

"Are you going to see your parents next month at Thanksgiving?" I asked before she pummeled me with more questions. I quickly realized that I might have stepped out to the end of the diving board and there was no turning back.

"Probably. I have slowly learned to try to ignore my mother's verbal jabs every time I go over to her home. I also ignore her questions about why I am thirty-four years old without a husband and no multiple grandchildren by now for her to put their pictures on her Christmas cards. According to her, running a growing successful business is really no place for a woman."

"Easy there, Boss-Lady. I can see there might be a slight amount of tension in your relationship with your parental units."

"What about you? Do you head back to North Carolina to see your mom at Thanksgiving?"

"No, not anymore. She's had an early onset of Alzheimer's and I had to put her in an assisted living facility two years ago. She's only in her early sixties. My mother kind of shut down mentally after my dad died. Like the old saying goes, if you don't use it you lose it. It's a shame."

"I'm so sorry," Caroline said.

I could tell it was from her heart.

"It's okay. My sister is nearby if anything changes. And I usually have to work on either Thanksgiving or Christmas anyway."

"I don't suppose you would consider being a human sacrifice and come with me to my parents' house for Thanksgiving dinner?" she asked out of the blue.

Oh boy. Holiday dinner with her peeps. Scrutiny being belief. I guess I asked for it by bringing up the Thanksgiving subject with her.

"Where did that question come from? Have you been thinking about this for a while?" I asked.

"Honestly, no. I just thought of it now. Because you know I never plan ahead..."

"Give me a break. This will *not* give you any bonus points towards winning our bet."

After a pause, I said, "Let me check and make sure I'm not on the schedule for Thanksgiving. If that's correct, then

I'll go with you to be your sacrificial lamb for your familial pack of wolves."

"I hope you realize that you're going to find yourself getting bombarded by uncomfortable personal questions like you have never faced before."

"Well, the questions at my oral surgery boards were pretty uncomfortable, but as long as this doesn't involve any type of sigmoidoscope, then I think I can bear it."

"Sigmoido-what?"

"Don't worry about it. And the proper attire for this festive holiday occasion?" I asked with a sense of false anticipation.

"I'll coach you when it gets closer to the time. I wouldn't want you to constantly be worried about it the whole time before hand, especially after you get depressed by losing our bet," she said.

"I think that I'm the one who's going to have an extremely testing week from the BS that you're tossing my way. I'll let you go now. Be sure and think about that bad track we can get stuck on together."

"You never know what'll happen next. Bye," she said.

Thanksgiving with her family. What were you thinking Chandler?

28

ST. JUDE HOSPITAL, KANSAS CITY

After hanging up with Caroline, I decided to put my on call game face on and eat something early in case I got called in right away to work. Things had chugged along in a pretty benign manner for most of the day, but I didn't want to tempt fate. Finishing a typical single male's gourmet dinner of a tuna fish sandwich, some raw broccoli, and a can of fruit cocktail, I hunkered down with a cup of coffee waiting for my pager to go off and lead me back to work.

It was a weekend night in a major urban city, and I was on trauma call at the hospital, so just about anything could happen. Since it was a Saturday, I figured that eventually my luck of quiet solitude would probably play out by the early evening, which it did exactly around 8:00 p.m. I got a page from the ER triage nurse that a multiple trauma victim was on the way into the trauma center so I should head that way immediately. Without any angst, that's what I did.

After parking in the physician's lot, which seemed like

about ten miles from the hospital, I walked into Trauma Room One with my calmest demeanor in place. A quick assessment of the situation at hand made it clear to me that I had a multiple trauma victim where I was going to have to call all the king's horses and all the king's men to try to put Humpty Dumpty back together again. Such is life in the world of trauma care.

I quickly went to work.

The chart had listed the victim as a twenty-four-year-old white male whose driver's license listed his name as Steven Spiegel. He had been riding his motorcycle at a high rate of speed passing around an auto when a large delivery truck cut in front of him. In this case like most cases, whose fault was not important. It was a simple physics problem here. A large immovable truck versus a much smaller motorcycle at a high speed. Only one outcome would happen here.

The patient was currently unconscious and couldn't answer any questions at the moment. Thankfully, he been wearing some kind of helmet the transfer report had stated. No description of what the patient had hit or how far he had been thrown from the motorcycle, but a pretty good guess of what the results would be. His vital signs were a blood pressure of 178/98 with a pulse of 124 and shallow breathing at best.

Time to get going.

I got one nurse to start a large bore IV to run wide open to replace the kiddie IV that the EMS techs had started. I gave the order to another nurse to put in a Foley catheter to monitor the urine output. An oxygen facemask was put on his face and the O_2 saturation clip went on his finger to monitor the percentage of oxygen in his blood.

I asked the third nurse to get the usual tubes of blood for labs, including a type and cross for four units of packed cells. I began my evaluation of the patient like I always did, starting from the top of the head and working my way down to the bottom of his feet as the trauma nurses were cutting all of the patient's clothes off with big pair of scissors.

Standard procedure for all major trauma cases.

I started my usual physical exam, gently feeling and prodding every square inch of this poor guy's body from top to bottom. His pupils were a little sluggish to react to light, and that could indicate closed head trauma, but he was going to need a head CT scan anyway. I found multiple cuts of the face extending into his scalp on both sides, but luckily no obvious major bony trauma of the skull. Definite evidence that if he was wearing a helmet, it must have got thrown off in the process. His breathing was shallow, but it was difficult to tell with all the blood on his face and in his mouth due to soft tissue injuries. I quickly suctioned all the fluids from his mouth and noticed there were several teeth missing with lots of blood due to trauma, as well his left mandible loose most likely due to fracture.

Proceeding on with my exam, I kept his C-spine collar on until cross table cervical spine films could be shot to rule out cervical bony injuries. The exam of his neck inside the collar showed no crepitance or deviation of the trachea to either side.

Upon examination of his chest, a quick listen with my stethoscope showed decreased breath sounds on both sides probably due to his shallow breathing, with ecchymosis and a huge abrasion on the right lateral ribcage. I was unable to find any specific tightness or reactive pain when examining his abdomen, but since his was unconscious, he'd need that CT-scanned also.

I finished the rest of my physical exam while they were setting up for taking X-rays, finding his pelvis fairly stable and no blood by rectal exam. It was obvious that he had a right upper arm humerus that was probably fractured with lots of overlying skin abrasions. His other extremity trauma was going to be a bugger for the ortho doctors to fix with an obvious left open tib/fib fracture of his left lower extremity.

About this time, I looked up and in walked Bill, a big barrel-chested trauma nurse who was starting his evening shift.

"Well, well. I figured if a multiple trauma case came in this early on a weekend, it must involve the one and only Dr. Kyle Chandler," he said.

"I wouldn't want to spoil your evening by having you sitting around just reading some gossip magazine," I said. "Make yourself useful and put some gloves on."

"Aye, aye captain."

Everyone who worked in the trauma room had a specific job to do and went about it calmly, quickly, and in a business-like manner.

"I assume with closed head trauma he needs to go to CT," Bill said. "Want me to call to see when they can take him?"

"Please," I said while fixating on the EKG rhythm on the monitor.

After a few moments, Bill with his hand over the phone said to me, "CT says you'll have to wait for fifteen more minutes before they're ready for him. What do you want me to tell them?"

"If we gotta wait, then we gotta wait. Tell them we'll be there then."

After hanging up the phone, Bill ambled over and asked, "What are you going to do about his airway?"

"You're reading my mind. The patient is unconscious, his breathing is shallow, and his O_2 saturation is slowly dropping on 100% O_2 by face mask. We have to assume that he's got some kind of closed head trauma with all those lacerations extending up into his scalp. I sure as hell don't want to get over to CT department and the patient decides to take a nosedive on us. We'd best intubate him safely here before we head over to CT. He'll need a neurosurgery consult regardless of what they find on his head CT."

"I'll get what you need," Bill said, "and I'll find out who's on trauma call for Neurosurgery."

"Roger that," I said while keeping an eye on the monitor.

In about two minutes, Bill rolled in a small table with a fresh set of instruments I might need for intubation of the patient.

"Bill, open me a number eight endotracheal tube and have O_2 support ready. Give him one-milligram of Atropine IV and then call respiratory therapy to come set the ventilator parameters."

Using a curved Mac intubation blade, I smoothly intubated this nice patient whose O_2 saturation was previously slipping south and now was headed back up in the right direction.

Crisis averted for now.

"Has anybody tried to locate the family of this gentleman?" I asked out loud to whomever.

"I'll have the triage desk get on it," one of the techs said.

In about five minutes, a large entourage of people surrounded the stretcher and started down the hall toward the trauma radiology department. There was a respiratory therapist adjusting the controls to the respirator, a tech pushing the respirator, two more techs pushing the stretcher, two nurses minding the IV and recording vital signs, and me. It was crazy how much manpower it took to make the process chug along.

After what seemed like forever, the radiology technician completed the scans of the patient's head, chest, and abdomen. I had a quick look at the images of the abdomen and chest, and they appeared to be clear of any serious injuries. Next, the whole crew took the show on the road back to Trauma Room One. By then, the neurosurgeon on call finally called back into the room where I explained the patient's situation to him and to why he needed to not get into bed just yet on his Saturday evening. He was not overly thrilled, but too bad.

Pages had been made from the triage desk to the oral surgeon on call for the suspected mandible fracture, to the plastic surgeon for the facial trauma, and to the orthopedic surgeon for the humerus and open tibial fractures. As usual, the oral surgeon said he'd see him in the morning. The plastic surgeon said he'd take care of the facial injuries soon. The ortho guy was there in about fifteen minutes since those guys practically lived at the hospital anyway. Sure, they made a lot of money, but I really doubt that they ever got to spend much of it. And I know they didn't spend any quality time with their wife or kids if they were always at work. Maybe so or maybe not, but it was still my opinion.

I inquired again about contacting the patient's family without any success. There was no family contact information in the patient's clothes to be found. Oh well, maybe tomorrow I could speak with one of his family members to explain Steven's situation to them when they were tracked down.

By the time I reviewed the chart, dictated a trauma consult, and all the paperwork had been filled out, it was just after midnight before the patient was headed to the ICU. Just as I was about to leave, the triage desk paged me for two more patients to be seen in the ER before I could leave. Well, it was a typical Saturday night.

I went to the ER and consulted with both of the patients. After a thorough history and physical exam of each patient, as well as reviewing their charts and laboratory values, I assured them that neither of them required immediate surgery. Going through the whole process for each patient, I finished their dictations just before two in the morning.

Things were starting to slow down in the Trauma Center by this time of the morning. Trust me, they could heat up in a heartbeat, but it looked like John Simpson's prediction of college football fans going strong all night long weakened in the wee hours.

I headed for my surgery locker, put up my white coat, and started down the hallway for the door to the parking lot. That damn backache had come back again and getting more than a little aggravating. After stepping through the door onto a dimly lit area, I suddenly heard a crashing noise just in front of me. I immediately froze into a crouched defensive position.

I quickly looked to my right from where the crashing noise had come, with me frozen with fear. It was a janitor throwing used glassware and bottles into a dumpster causing an enormous crashing sound with each heave. I slowly caught my breath and straightened upright.

What in the world was I thinking? Just because I had been busy inside for most of the evening, that didn't mean that some Wise Guy had been waiting for my unprotected exit from the hospital right about now.

So much for the theory of an aggressive offense over a protective defense that I bragged about to Dr. Simpson.

I got to my car in one piece and drove home on autopilot wondering how to shed this growing sense of fear of getting assaulted.

Come on Chandler; you gotta figure out how to make all this right.

29

KANSAS CITY

After grabbing about four and a half hours sleep without any further calls, I awoke around seven Sunday morning. Knowing that my trauma call was over, it made my cup of coffee taste all the more flavorful. Even though I could have called the next surgeon on call to check on the trauma victim from last night, I didn't. I never dumped the responsibility of the care of my patients on anyone else unless I had to because I was out of town. Call me old fashioned, but that's the way I was taught and that was the right way to handle it.

I showered and had a bite to eat before heading back to the hospital. I met with the oncoming on call trauma surgeon in the surgeon's lounge and went over the patient list. Leaving there, it took a while for me to find what intensive care bed they finally found for the motorcycle daredevil.

When I finally tracked him down, I looked through the window of his room and saw he was still unconscious and intubated. I wondered how long that would be as I began to review his chart I grabbed from the nurses' station. The orthopedic surgeon had seen him in the trauma center for his open tibia fracture and closed humerus fracture, and temporarily splinted them both. It was hard to read the writing in his note, but it appeared that he was going to take the patient to the OR later today to further wash out the open tibia fracture.

Reading further, it looked like the oral-maxillofacial surgeon had yet to see him for his closed mandible fracture but would likely see him sometime this morning. All of the patient's lab values were as good as expected considering the multiple insults to his body.

I quietly entered his room. The patient looked much better since he had been cleaned up of all the blood and dirt from last night. Also, the plastic surgeon had done a nice job on all the facial lacerations that previously had made his face and scalp appear so bloody. I gently shook him explaining again who I was even though he was still unconscious and intubated. I reexamined his abdomen with a soft touch. No apparent tenderness. I listened to his heart and lungs with my stethoscope. All normal.

I told the patient that there would be a lot of physicians checking on him and that he was going to have to be patient with all the things that needed repairing. I said I would be speaking with his family if and when they arrived at the hospital. Maybe he could hear me, maybe not, because you never knew. I made my way to the nurses' station to write a note in the chart of my findings. I asked about the family and the clerical secretary said no family had been located as of yet. Well, I pretty much was going to be in the background on the rest of this case since it didn't any longer involve me directly. Now it was up to the other services to put the patient back together again.

I went by my surgery locker to drop off my white coat and headed for my car in the physician's lot. I could tell that the caffeine I previously had ingested was wearing off. The only things I was concerned about was to eat a bite of lunch then maybe get a few more hours sleep when I got home. It seemed like my shoes had lead weights in them as I walked up to open my car door. I guess I should have not been thinking about my shoes because it was right about then I felt the world come crashing down.

Literally, on my head.

The next thing I knew, I was barely conscious and being pushed into the back of some kind of vehicle with a huge throbbing headache. And I mean huge.

My head spun like I was stuck on the Tilt-A-Whirl at the county fair. When my vision slowly changed from outright blurry to partly clear, I realized a big guy was sitting on my back and my hands were tied together behind my back.

Perfect. You let your guard down KC when you were tired and look what happened. So much for that restful nap I had been thinking about.

In about what must have been ten to fifteen minutes, we reached wherever we were headed. I noticed a gradually increasing loud noise in the background, almost like a continual humming sound. The big guy on top of me finally got off and quickly dragged me out of the back of what seemed to be an old cargo van. A quick look around made me realize where I was—a sewage treatment plant. The noise of the surrounding loud machinery would make it impossible to hear anybody scream. And that included me.

The van driver got out and helped the big guy pull me into a small building that was some sort of ancient control room with all kinds of gauges and dials and a constant humming noise. The door was slammed shut and I was thrust upon a short wooden bench. The big guy stood by the door.

It was right about then when I thought to myself, "Okay genius, now why did I tell Sergeant Wilkins that I would be fine going to and from work and wouldn't really need his help?"

Finally, the van driver walked up and grabbed me by

my hair, yanking my head upward. He was shorter than the big guy, but still kinda stocky.

"We know all about you, Dr. Kyle Chandler," the driver said in an Italian American accent. "We know you have been snoopin' around London and Long Island and even New Jersey where you shouldn't have. We know what you have been trying to find out about our product delivery and distribution system. We also know where you live and all about that babe you've been sweet on. Do you know who you're messin' with here?"

I figured that I'd let him do most of the talking, so I kept my mouth shut for the time being.

"My name is Tito Fanucci, and in case you didn't know, I'm the heir to throne of the KC Mob, and don't you forget it."

Right about then this guy's chubby hand slaps me across my cheek so hard that it knocks me off the bench onto the floor. The big guy who tossed me out of the van was behind me and shoved me back up on the wooden bench. How convenient.

"You've got to understand that somebody like you does not get to challenge the rulers of Kansas City. We own this town. And some puke like you is not going to interrupt our business, understand?"

This was the guy that Harold had said to avoid at all costs. I nodded in agreement but continued to keep my mouth shut. Somehow, and pretty damn soon, I was going to have to find a way to buy some time to get out of this one.

"My father, Big Tony, runs our organization. He wanted to meet with you and ask you a few questions, maybe have some milk and cookies together. But as you probably can tell, I don't do things that way. If someone threatens to interfere with me, or my business, they are expendable. Nobody gets in the way of Tito's business. Understand?"

This guy was beyond histrionic, referring to himself in the third person. I slowly nodded, wondering how I could talk my way out of this more threatening by the minute situation. I had to think of something quick before they turned me into ground beef.

Then to my surprise, instead of further physical insults to harm me, Tito goes off on this long diatribe about all of the guys he's made disappear over the last five years. Whacked for this, whacked for that. Running his mouth off at me like I wasn't going to believe what kind of tough guy he really was. He must have babbled on for six to seven minutes before he came to a stop.

During his running commentary, I heard a faint sound over my left shoulder while Tito paced in front of me. At a time he turned his back to me, I quickly glanced over my shoulder for only a second to see a man dressed in black including a black cloth face covering. He was crouched low around the corner and had his index finger up to his closed lips indicating for me to keep quiet. I didn't know who he was, but I had an idea who sent him. Upon looking back to Tito, I wondered how to play this one.

"I tell you all of this to make sure you understand who you have been messin' with," Tito said. "Now before we say our final goodbyes to go dump your body tied to cinder blocks into the Missouri River, you're going to tell me who you've told about our product distribution scheme."

Time now for me to go on the verbal offensive to see if I could distract Tito from my new hidden friend.

"Let me ask you one thing, Tito," I said. "Why do you guys always call the stuff product? Why don't just you fess up and call it what it is—narcotics?"

Tito didn't respond, like that was not a question he was expecting from me. And he seemed to not have an answer for it.

"And another thing," I kept talking to see if I could get him confused without getting him too mad. "Why is it your father Big Tony, the head of your organization, wanted to give me milk and cookies but you want me six feet under? I think Big Tony has no idea what you are doing right now, that's what I think."

"Don't even try to bring my old man into the picture here," Tito said. "I'm handling this, not him, you stupid puke."

"From my viewpoint, you're going to get knocked down a few rungs if you don't let Big Tony have it his way," I said to make him think twice about who was really in charge. It was a longshot, but maybe this might make him change his mind from going against Big Tony's wishes.

When is my disguised friend going to get me out of this mess?

Tito's eyes started to bulge, and his jaw visibly tightened. I guess you could say I probably pushed the wrong button.

"Why you smart-mouthed..." Tito muttered in anger as started towards me.

Just about that time, the sound of a faint police car siren began and got louder and louder as it approached the building.

Tito turned to the big guy by the door and said, "Go look out front," as he looked away from me to the closed windowless door that we previously entered.

As the big guy opened the door a crack, the sunlight blinded our eyes for a mere second. It was then I heard a loud crash right in front of me, causing me to fall to my left off the bench, my hands still tied behind my back. I looked back over my shoulder while on the floor and saw Tito hit the bench with a crash. After that, I heard several more crashes just to my right. I tried to stay balled up in the fetal position with my eyes shut to protect myself, but that was easier said than done with my hands firmly cinched behind me.

Before I opened my eyes, I heard two muted sounds like air rushing out of some kind of tank or pipe for five to six seconds. Then everything went quiet.

About two seconds after that, the door shut, and I looked again over my shoulder. There were two men standing there dressed in black looking down at the zip ties around Tito's and the other big guy's wrists and ankles. Cotton rags were already stuffed into each of the two thugs' mouths. It was hard to see who the two rescuers were since I was somewhat prone on my stomach. I really didn't know if they were going to be friend or foe.

"Who the hell are you two?" I asked.

The shorter of the two muscular men slowly pulled off his face covering while looking straight at me.

"My name is Winston, and this is my associate, Jake. Sergeant Wilkins has had us and one other team keeping an eye on you since you called on Friday," the man said as he came closer to remove the ties around my wrists. His partner stood quietly nearby at a position of attention.

Winston helped me up as I sat on the wooden bench while rubbing both of my wrists.

"How long have you been inside this room waiting to pounce?" I asked.

"Well, we followed you from the hospital parking lot and were ready to intercede when they were getting you out of the van, but experience told us that the element of surprise would be greater inside than out," Winston said. "Reconnaissance revealed no back entrances, but I was lucky and found a loose window in the back I could climb through. We waited for the proper moment to take control of the situation and figured the bright sunlight shining right at the door would momentarily give us an advantage."

"Really. You make it sound so routine. And the bit about the siren?" I asked.

"A faint diversion to make your captors think a police squad car had arrived at the scene. You of all people should know that Sergeant Wilkins preaches to never leave home without proper alternatives," Winston said. "Now let's get out of here before these two come to," he said as he shuttled me out the front door.

As I got in the back seat of a plain sedan that had been parked just around the corner of the building, Jake got in to drive and Winston got in the back seat with me. Heading out of the sewage treatment plant, I had several more questions for my daring rescuer.

"Winston, did you know who was trying to nab me?"

"Our intel had a good idea of who was keeping tabs on you. To be honest though, we thought it would be Tito's dad and his guys who were interested in speaking with you, not Junior there."

"So what were the air rushing noises?" I asked.

"We use a small can of nitrous oxide with a face mask to make the targets stay down. Always after the zip ties, I might add," Winston said.

"Were you there when Tito went off on that long dissertation of all the guys he's had vanished? It was super strange, like he was trying his best to convince me that he was in charge."

"Not only was I there, but I got to try out my new play toy!" Winston said like an excited second grader. "It's a miniature camcorder that can record on a bare minimum of light with a high degree of resolution. It's awesome."

"So you got that whole speech down on tape?" I asked.

"You bet, but not on tape. That's so last generation."

"I don't suppose you recorded him knocking the crap out of me across my face?"

"No, sorry. That must have happened just before I made it through the rear window."

Great. No video evidence of who tried to dislodge my molars. Oh well.

I could have kept asking questions, but I decided to stop and be thankful for the "Good Sergeant" who didn't trust my judgment that I could make it on my own.

By the time Winston and his silent pal Jake dropped me off at my cherished old sedan in the hospital physician's lot, I started to realize just how lucky I was to escape the far-reaching tentacles of organized crime. I thanked them again and said I would call the "Good Sergeant" right away.

Thank God for guardian angels.

30

KANSAS CITY

As I got in my car, I concluded that staying at my condo after all I had been through today was out of the question. You might call it a little more than risky. I pulled out my cell phone and dialed Caroline's cell number.

"Hey there, sailor. What's up?" she asked in a cheerful voice.

"Remember the case we worked on earlier this year when people were breaking into my condo? And they were trying to track me down?"

"Kyle, what's happened to you now?" she immediately asked.

"Well, do you remember that I had to crash on your couch for a bit?"

"Kyle, quit fooling around and tell me the truth."

"Here's the deal. I think I might need to sleep on your

couch tonight. Well, not necessarily your couch, since I did sleep in your bed that one whole weekend. That was a really good weekend by the way. You know, we should do that again sometime..."

"Doctor Kyle Chandler, tell me the truth!"

"Caroline, relax. I had a slight encounter with a not-so-agreeable representative of the group that is doing the distribution of the products I have been investigating. I need to lie low for a day or two until I can figure out how to make this whole thing go away."

"Dr. Kyle Chandler, M.D., what happened to you?" she asked in a building rage.

"Easy there, Queen of Sheba. It's nothing major. Just promise me you'll call right now to get me past the protective gate guard at your palace."

"Okay, I will call him right now. Then I'm going to quit my errands this second just to make sure I get there before you. You have to promise to explain everything to me when you get to my condo. Do you understand, Doctor Hardhead?"

"Roger that, oh great female knowledgeable one. See you in a little bit," I said and hung up.

I made a quick call to Sergeant Wilkins' phone and left a message thanking him for his crew saving my hide at the right time. Again.

I waited around in my car for a few minutes, keeping my eyes open for any type of suspicious person. Like someone would have followed me just to irritate me after I barely escaped from being tortured by the Mob.

I cautiously drove to my condo and picked up all the necessary items needed for a few nights' stay away from home. No bogeymen as of yet. Two Tylenol and a quick ham sandwich also seemed to make things a little calmer.

I finally got the energy to head to Caroline's condo complex, which was guarded like Fort Knox. When I got there, one of the guards who had previously given me a hassle about coming in to visit Caroline earlier in the year recognized me right away.

"Good evening, Dr. Chandler. Ms. Martinelli called and said you would be arriving this evening. She's at her residence. She arrived about fifteen minutes ago," he said.

"Thank you, Officer Geffen," I said as I glanced at his name badge.

I drove through the gate and parked in the visitor's area, quite a distance away from her front door. Not so convenient. After ascending the front steps, I found the front door ajar.

Oh great. After all that had happened today, I was immediately on edge.

"Caroline?" I yelled. "Are you okay?"

Through the crack of the open door, I heard this relaxed response from her, "Come on in."

You pay all this money to live in a walled-off complex for privacy, and more importantly for security. Then you go and yell "Come on in" to the person at the front door who could be the next Jack the Ripper for all you know.

Go figure.

I proceeded into her condominium and closed the door behind me. Definitely locking it, as a precaution.

I walked into an empty living area and plopped down on the couch, presuming that she was back in her bedroom. At last, she appeared in the bedroom doorway, barefoot, decked out in tight black yoga pants with a tight sleeveless workout shirt to match. Oh, my goodness.

"Are you going somewhere?" I asked. "Cause if you are, every red-blooded male of age will be visually undressing you if you wear that outfit."

"No, I'm not going anywhere. I just changed into something comfortable so you can tell me the truth of what happened to you today," she said as she moved across the room closer to me.

She suddenly stopped and placed both her hands on her hips.

"Kyle Chandler, what happened to your cheek? There's

a big red mark that's starting to bruise."

I reached up to gently touch the stinging area just above my jawline.

"Oh, that. Just a little souvenir from one of my interested suitors today."

"What are you talking about? Does your cheek hurt? We need to put some ice on it right away," she said as she headed straight for the kitchen.

"Actually, Florence Nightingale, I'm going to need the ice for someplace else if you keep that spray-to-fit outfit on," I said.

"What did you say?" she asked as she returned to the room.

"It wasn't important," I muttered as I took the zippered plastic bag filled with ice cubes from her.

"Now tell me exactly what happened today, and I mean the truth," Caroline commanded as she sat at the opposite end of the couch, crossing both her legs underneath her.

"Well, as I told you on the phone yesterday that I was on trauma call at the hospital. And notice how I did *not* comment negatively about that just for the record. Things chugged along in a pretty benign manner until about eight when I had a multiple trauma victim. I had to call in multiple physicians to try to put Humpty Dumpty back together again."

"Kyle, you're so cynical sometimes," she said.

"Maybe. Well anyway, I got home sometime after two in the morning, again without any complaining note you. I grabbed a few hours of sleep then went back to check on the patient to make sure he was doing all right. Just when I make it back to my car, two tag team amateur wrestlers come out of nowhere and decide to enlist me as their next practice punching dummy."

"Kyle Chandler, this is not funny!"

"Yeah, I started to realize that the minute one of them smacked me on my head and stuffed me in the back of some beat up old van. Right there in the middle of the parking lot with security cameras. Can you believe it? So much for safety because of the hospital security cameras."

"Kyle Chandler, forget the hospital cameras. Tell me what happened!"

"Fine. By the time I came back around, I found myself being dragged out of the van by the two bozos inside some dark garage and onto a hard wooden bench. That bench was no La-Z-Boy recliner, that's for sure."

"Kyle, this is serious! We've got to call the police."

"No way, Wonder Woman. The police wouldn't help in this case. These guys were from the group in charge of the product distribution I was looking into. They were more than a little peeved about what I had found out about their scheme."

"Kyle, this is getting too dangerous. You've got to do something!"

"Well, I already had done something. I called Sergeant Wilkins Friday morning to make sure you would be safe. I explained the whole thing to him with this distribution scheme. He's had someone watching you since then ready to charge in if they saw anything suspicious."

"Watching me? What are you saying? I couldn't tell that anything was different. So what about your safety, Einstein?" she asked.

"Well, he told me that I could call him anytime, but the experienced surveillance expert didn't trust me, so he had someone keeping an eye on me, same as you. Kinda helped me out in the nick of time today."

"Imagine that, someone else wouldn't trust the word of a hardheaded surgeon," she said forcefully with a wry smile.

"Well, if you remember, the 'Good Sergeant' and I did work together on that last case."

"Yeah, the case where you refused to hand over the key to the psychopath who was just about to break both your hands."

"Minor details, dearie. Anyway, Sergeant Wilkins' helper Winston and his pal came to the rescue just as the two

Oxford graduates were about to show me their vast knowledge of S & M techniques they were about to try on me. The best part was that Winston supplied me with the evidence that I need to probably put an end to all this foolish business."

"What are you trying to say, Kyle?"

"Don't worry about it, Caroline. I'm a little more lucid this time as compared to when you and the 'Good Sergeant' pulled me out of the fire on that last case. Those two dunderheads who nabbed me are only the tip of the iceberg. The good thing is now I've got an idea how to play this situation to my advantage."

"And how are you going to do that?" she asked.

"Sorry, Caroline. I told you that I'm not dragging you into the mess like last time. Now that I have Sergeant Wilkins looking out for you, I'm going to try and fix this situation solo."

"Dr. Kyle Chandler, do you always have to think you're Superman and try to make things right without help?" she asked with her eyes piercing right through me.

"Well Lois, I guess if Clark Kent could dodge all those bullets, then so can I."

"One day, Doctor Lonely Heart, you're going to realize that you can't fix everything all by yourself."

Ouch. That one hit home.

"Well, changing the subject, I do know of one thing that only you can fix to help me to feel better…"

She cracked a small smile and said, "Sorry Romeo. Not going to happen while you are sleeping on the couch all alone tonight. Let me get you a pillow and a blanket."

Caroline got off the couch and went to her bedroom. She returned with the bedding and gave them to me.

"Are you going to wear that comfortable outfit to bed?" I asked.

She stopped and put her hands on her hips, revealing her magnificent curves. Then she looked right at me with a tiny grin.

"Well, there is one outfit which I like more that's a lot less confining, but too bad you won't get to see what it is. Sweet dreams, Doctor."

Sweet dreams, indeed.

31

COLUMBUS PARK, KANSAS CITY

“This is Carmine,” the older gentleman said when he picked up his mobile phone early Sunday evening.

He knew by the number on his cell phone screen that it was his boss Big Tony calling to check in. He knew because his boss called him every single day of the year to check in on the status of the operational aspects of the organization. Not that he needed to because Carmine always took care of everything. The underboss knew the real reason Big Tony called was to make himself feel better.

His boss would ask about the loan sharks, the take from the bookies at the racetracks, whether they would cover the spread on the sports games today, especially now that the college football season was in full swing. Big Tony would ask Carmine endless questions over and over until he was satisfied the things were running smoothly. Carmine found it easier to go ahead and answer the questions than to make a fuss about the daily inquiry.

There was a rock-solid reason why Carmine was where he was today. He had worked his way up through the organization over the years because he was a proven "fixer." Need a witness to disappear before an important trial? Carmine would fix it. Need a sports team to win but not by more than the betting spread? Carmine would take care of it. Need a police charge dropped on one of the foot soldiers of the organization? Carmine would resolve the matter.

Carmine was chosen to be the underboss when Big Tony made his move to be on the throne of the organization years ago. Not because he was special friend of Big Tony, not because he was Tony's older second cousin, but because he understood how Tony thought. He understood what Tony wanted and why. And more importantly, he was about the only one who would put an end to some impulsive response by the organization's boss before it got out of control. He could reel in his cousin back to reality, stressing that in all cases it wasn't personal. It was strictly business.

Because they had known each other for so long, they didn't need to verbally communicate when they were together in the same room conducting business. A simple look from Big Tony to Carmine would tell his underboss all he needed to know on how the boss felt about something.

Carmine was probably the only one in the whole world who would quietly downplay in public anything that had to do with his boss. He would then pull his boss aside in a private setting later and make sure Big Tony knew why the Mafia don could not take that approach ever again in the future. Like he always stressed; it wasn't personal; it was business.

"Have you talked to Tito today?" Big Tony asked.

"I don't ever talk to that son of yours Anthony. Every time I do, he flies off the handle and says I'm too old to understand how to run a business. So no, I haven't heard from him."

"The last time I saw him was at Rose's birthday dinner at our house Thursday night. I haven't heard from him since then."

"Well, I only get to hear about what he gets into. Then it's about what I need to do to get him out of a jam. And that hasn't been since last Monday," Carmine said.

"I told him to stay completely away from our suspect, that Dr. Chandler character, when I talked to him at my office mid-morning Thursday. I hope Tito's not doing something stupid with that guy right now that we might regret," the Mafia don said.

"Speaking of that," Carmine said. "My grandson Joey called me Friday afternoon. He told me that our Dr. Chandler came to his restaurant with his lady friend Thursday evening for dinner."

"Why didn't you tell me this earlier? What did he say to Joey? Because it's time to bring this guy in to stop the families in New York from breathing down my neck. You know what I mean?"

"Relax Anthony. Instead of us risking it by nabbing him, I just might have figured out a way for him come to us," Carmine said.

"How do you figure to pull that off?" Big Tony asked.

"Joey told me that our doctor friend wants to set up a meeting so he can talk to us about something he knows. Either this guy is really naïve or just plain stupid."

"Either way, we need to find out what he knows. How soon can you set up a meeting in a secure location?"

"Already taken care of Anthony. Tomorrow evening in our penthouse suite at the Crown Center. I left Dr. Chandler a message on his phone machine this evening. I'll have one of our guys follow him tomorrow to make sure his gets there. And I told your driver when to pick you up tomorrow evening."

"Good Carmine, good. Hey, if you hear from Tito, tell him to call me right away."

"Trust me, I won't hear from him. If you want, I'll have one of our guys track him down for you."

"Yeah, go ahead and do that," the Mafia boss said.

"See you tomorrow," Carmine said as he hung up.

The underboss shook his head slowly. That damn Tito. *That boy is, and always was, a fly in the ointment.* Even as a young child, the Mafia don's son never thought about what was going to come out of his mouth before he said it. When someone speaks before they think, that will lead to nothing but trouble. So, this was the next leader of the whole organization if something suddenly happened to Big Tony? Mother Mary help us.

Carmine had a funny feeling that the crazy son of Big Tony was likely going to be the downfall of the whole business one day. Just you watch.

32

MANHATTAN

"Excuse me Mr. Hauser, Mr. Sawyer for you on line one," the intercom voice said to her boss early Monday morning.

"Thank you, Mrs. Pennington," Hauser said.

What does that imbecile want now?

"Hauser here," the CEO said after punching line one.

"I just wanted to let you know that we finished installing all the new security cameras at the three companies where you requested updates. I've double checked with the head of security at each company and all units are already functional in sequence with our master control board."

"Fine," Hauser said curtly.

"Is there anything else you need from me right now?" the security chief asked.

"Not right now. As we previously discussed, I want you to make sure we are up to date on all software updates for our computer systems in the US. You let me deal with the ones in England and the rest of Europe since that involves different regulations and requirements in each individual country. You go over the list of each company we own in the US. Then, give me an estimate of software update costs and a timeline on how long it will take to make them all interactive as one system. Understand?"

"Yes, sir," Sawyer said.

"Meet me in my office tomorrow morning at 10:00 a.m. to discuss how we can speed up and streamline the process."

"Will do, sir. Can..."

The only thing Sawyer heard next was the sound of the dial tone after the line went dead.

The security chief knew there was no possible way in twenty-four hours to get an estimate on the costs and the amount of time it would take to unify the security systems of all those companies. His boss was far too impatient and expected the impossible not for tomorrow, but for yesterday. He was going to have to bust his backside to try to come close to finishing this one by tomorrow at 10:00 a.m.

Hauser smiled to himself after he cut the phone call short. He had no intention of spending all that money to make the security systems of every company Evolution Industries owned into one interactive system. He had sent his security chief on a diversionary snipe hunt to keep him busy for a while. The CEO made it even harder for Sawyer to be anywhere close to the security system of Hawthorne Containers since he told Sawyer to stick to the companies owned in the US.

Oh my, if the employees who worked for him only had the same intelligence as their boss. That certainly was not possible.

What made the business executive even more satisfied was the fact that his backup plan with his distribution partners had worked like a charm. He had not heard back from them since dropping off the fabricated evidence for his olive-skinned contact at the Bronx mail slot on Saturday. The CEO had learned in the past when dealing with them that no news was good news. Hauser's basic instinct was to switch tactics when there was any bump in the road. His distribution business associates had already tried that tactic on him. His foresight to be two steps ahead of the competition had saved his hide once again.

But the CEO wanted to ride this gravy train for just a little while longer. Then when the time was right, he would duck out of the whole thing smelling like a rose. Things this profitable never lasted forever he reasoned. Such is life, on to initiating the next business opportunity.

33

WESTIN CROWN CENTER, KANSAS CITY

When I awoke on the couch the next morning, I felt like a used punching bag. I looked down at my legs to see if I could find any tire tracks from the truck that must have run over me in my sleep.

No such luck.

I was stiff all over from sleeping on Caroline's slightly too short couch, which didn't make things any better. At least I had remembered to set the coffeemaker, a purposed gift I had recently given her. I poured a cup and sipped my coffee to hopefully regain my consciousness.

I figured if any bad guys had broken into my condo overnight, it would have been when I wasn't there to give the gorillas something to punch. It was unlikely by now they would be hanging around for me to show up.

Since it was still early and I had slept on the couch instead of being invited to share Caroline's sleeping abode, I finished my coffee in silence. I found a piece of paper and left her a note that I would call her on her cell phone later. She wouldn't be too happy about it, but life goes on.

On the way home, I reviewed my options to settle this foolishness with Tito Fanucci once and for all. None of which were foolproof in the least.

When I got to my condominium, the red light on my phone machine was blinking. I played it with a monotone voice on the message stating that I was scheduled for a meeting. It didn't say with whom. The message was from last evening and said for me to come to the #1A penthouse suite at the Westin Crown Center tomorrow evening today at six p.m. It said that I should come alone and be sure to bring nothing that could endanger me.

Endanger me. If I was right about who the message was from, just showing up could endanger me. I'll have to admit that I never got a phone message that said something like that before.

Still, it was obvious who the message was from. It was from Joey's grandfather, Carmine Giacomo. Therefore, my vague idea for a plan to sway this situation my way was really going to be put to the test. My fate was now held in the balance.

Yippee-ki-yay.

While I was getting ready for work, I spent most of the next thirty or forty minutes thinking about what my final plan would be to present to Joey's grandfather. Nothing was certain, but acting like I knew what I was doing would be three-fourths of the battle.

My day at the office was a typical Monday and flew by in a blur. Multiple phone calls, more patients to see than I ever remembered before. More paperwork than I could ever imagine, and I still didn't catch up all the way.

Ah, the joys of managed healthcare.

By the time I finished work, it was already 5:45 p.m. I

left my office and made my way across town to the always busy Westin Crown Center.

As scared as I was, I knew it was time to get to the bottom of this whole thing. It may not turn out like I wanted it to, but it was good that at least there would be no more constant dread. After parking my vintage Volvo in the parking garage, I walked into the lobby of the big hotel complex heading to the concierge's desk. I politely asked the nice lady at the desk which elevator I needed to take up to the penthouse suite I needed. She pointed me in the proper direction, and I rode the elevator to the top floor. Upon opening of the elevator door, I turned left like the lady said and proceeded down the corridor.

Time to play Truth or Consequences.

I knocked on one of the large suite doors that had #1A on the front. It was opened by a huge man, his muscles bulging in his tight-fitted suit. He didn't say a word. The gorilla pointed with his thumb for me to come in through one of the double doors. After closing the door, he then motioned me to raise both of my arms out to my sides. The huge man frisked me from my chest all the way down to my feet for any weapons or wires that might be on me. Again, without saying a word, he nodded his head for me to continue inside.

I walked through the foyer into a large sitting room with huge floor to ceiling windows looking out over the city. Sitting in one of the overstuffed chairs with a blank expression on his face was Joey's grandfather, Carmine Giacomo. What I didn't expect was the other participants present in the room.

On the adjacent couch with his hands tightly clinched together was the boss Big Tony Fanucci. And standing right behind him with his arms crossed was my previous attacker, his son Tito.

Just great. The gang's all here.

Carmine and Big Tony stayed seated while I walked up to the large coffee table in front of them and remained standing.

"Dr. Chandler," Carmine said. "My grandson Joey said you wanted to meet with us to explain something to us. Well, here we are. What do you want to tell us?"

"I thought we might have a reasonable conversation concerning possible conflicting viewpoints we might have of one another," I said.

"Conflicting viewpoints, you say?" Carmine said while Big Tony's glare felt like it was a laser piercing right through me.

"Yes, Mr. Giacomo, I think that's what you could call it. Your grandson Joey indicated to me that your family is presently not so happy about a certain someone. I believe he said, 'someone who knows a little too much for his own good.' And he indicated that someone was me."

There was a long pause before Carmine replied.

"We have a very thorough network of security in our business in order to keep all our enterprises running efficiently and legally. Our sources indicate to us that a gentleman similar to your physical description has been inquiring both in London and New York about the methods of legal transport of bulk wine into the United States. Which is interesting because our organization is not currently in the wine business. What do you have to say about that?"

It was my turn for a pause.

"I will not deny that I was looking into the transport of bulk wine from Europe to the US on a recent trip to London for a wine importer friend of mine. He was interested in finding out about the latest transport methods and had me look into it. However, it's the possible transport of something other than wine that has me concerned."

Carmine began tapping his fingers together before he gave his measured response.

"So, why do you think our business would be concerned with the possible transport of something other than wine?"

"I'm not saying that you are," I said slowly. "But if

there was any chance that your businesses were even remotely involved in the transport and eventual sale of something that was considered, uh…to be illegal, I would want to make sure that you would know there could be grave consequences."

"Tell me, Dr. Chandler, what kind of grave consequences would that be?" Carmine asked.

"Let me try to explain my viewpoint to you. As a physician, it is my moral obligation to try to teach and protect my patients, including your granddaughter, Mr. Giacomo, from harmful habits that could damage their health. If by an extremely unlikely chance I knew harmful products were being shipped to Kansas City for illegal sale and use, I would want to try to prevent patients from using such products. Because of my relationship with your family through your granddaughter, I would want you to know law enforcement authorities may possibly be involved in the investigation of the distribution of these products in the future."

Carmine leaned forward and looking straight at me, asked, "Is that some kinda threat?"

Big Tony sat perfectly still while he waited for his right-hand man to slowly carve me up.

"No sir, Mr. Giacomo. In fact, the authorities do not need to be involved in this matter at all. There could be a way to work this out between us to assure that the people of Kansas City may not be tempted to use such products. Especially if they were no longer available. And your businesses will go on successfully if they don't approve of the distribution of such products in the future."

There was a huge sense of unease that filled the room until it was suddenly shattered.

"This all a bunch of garbage! What if we just take care of you right here and now and go on with our business as usual?" Tito asked in anger.

Obviously, he was not thrilled by the fact I had escaped his grasp barely twenty-four hours ago. Moreover, I was now standing before his superiors answering to them and not to him.

A long, scary pause followed. Big Tony and Carmine didn't show one iota of expression while looking straight at me. You could cut the tension in the room with a knife.

Big Tony turned to give Tito a glare that could drop an elephant at a hundred yards. The Mafia chief slowly turned his gaze back in my direction.

"You'll have to excuse my son, Doctor. His mother and I have indulged him, and he has not learned to keep his emotions to himself. He has yet to learn that emotional discretion is vital in any business decision. Now what exactly did you have in mind?"

I was beyond puzzled at this point, but I wasn't going to rock the boat by straying from my plan.

"Your local business ventures will come out ahead if you tell your associates in New York they have a mole in their midst. You will tell them that you don't know who the mole is exactly, but that the mole has the potential to bring down their entire product distribution scheme. You can continue all your other ventures with business as usual."

"Carmine," Big Tony said, "I'm not having this punk or anybody else tell me how to run my businesses. If you think…"

"Anthony!" Carmine held his right hand up. "Let's give the man a chance to finish before we make any kind of decision here."

Carmine slowly turned back to me.

"Let's just say for the sake of argument," Carmine said, "that our businesses might know something about this product distribution that other businesses, not us, may be participating in. So, you think as an individual citizen here in Kansas City, you can stop the distribution of all such products? Surely you are not that naïve, Doc."

"Absolutely not. I know that product distribution of a result of supply and demand, and no one is going to stop either one completely. I just want you to consider to persuade whoever distributes this product to no longer use this one product source."

"And if we can't persuade this unknown distributor to stop, then what happens, Doc?"

"Well, federal authorities could be notified," I said. "That would bring a ton of pressure on the unknown distributor of this product. All of the other business ventures of the distributor would be investigated with a fine-toothed comb and that would not be overall good for business. Of course, that would lead to my ultimate disappearance and demise. But I have a better solution for the both of us."

"Really, and what would that be?" Big Tony asked.

"Because I saved Mr. Giacomo's granddaughter at surgery, he promised me a favor that could be cashed in anytime in the future. He told me it was a favor to be honored no matter what the circumstances. Honor is very important in your business. So, I'm cashing in that favor right now. You don't kill me and leave my body with cement shoes in the Missouri River, and I don't say a word. Not now, not ever."

Both Carmine and Big Tony grinned with a small chuckle. All Tito could do was look incredibly angry.

"I will be happy to honor that favor at this time," Carmine said. "But Doc, I can't guarantee if some kind of accident happened to you in the future, if you know what I mean. Surely you have more than that up your sleeve other than such a lame compromise."

"I see you've played this game before, Mr. Giacomo. You are correct. There are two pieces of insurance left in place to make sure nothing happens to me. Not now, not ever."

"And those would be...?" Carmine asked.

"If anything at all happens to me or Caroline Martinelli, now or in the future, multiple certified letters will be automatically mailed by five separate sources to the New York Times, the Washington Post, the Wall Street Journal, and the FBI, documenting in great detail the huge illegal narcotics distribution scheme directed by the La Cosa Nostra. Not just here in Kansas City, but nationwide. It's all ready to go. That will definitely not be appreciated by your associates with a certain five families in New York."

Both Carmine and Big Tony looked ready to jump across the table at me.

"He's bluffing. Let's just take care of this pinhead right now and move on," Tito said.

Big Tony shot his son a glance, which immediately made him cower and take a step back.

I decided to push the young bully back in his place once and for all.

"And the second piece of insurance is for the icing on the cake. Your son's attempt yesterday to keep me quiet in a permanent fashion, which I bet he hasn't told either of you, was filmed and recorded on miniature camcorder. It isn't that he threatened to kill me that makes the film so interesting. It's that he bragged about multiple other crimes, including several that gave specifics about murder, and the authorities would have a field day on that one. Tito will be eating prison food for the rest of his days if the authorities get ahold of one of the copies of that tape from one of the five separate sources."

"And I suppose each of your five separate sources would mail a copy to the FBI, or whoever, if anything would ever happen to you," Big Tony said.

"That pretty much explains the whole situation. As long as you make sure nothing happens to me, or Ms. Martinelli, now and in the future, I will be like a silent balloon floating up in the sky. As long as you convince the unknown distributor to cease distribution of the product from this one and only source, then I will not have any reason to tell any authority anything ever about this situation. I will float along silently forever. However, if the unknown distributor tries to shoot my balloon down, all the hidden damaging information will crash to Earth. It will be automatically unleashed, bringing your business more than a few headaches."

Big Tony shot a glance at his right-hand man and then turned to his son.

"I think you better head straight to my office and wait for me. Now," the Mafia don said, his words harsh.

Tito hesitated, started to plead with his father, and then apparently thought better of it. He took off down the corridor in a huff.

Big Tony glanced back at Carmine. Although no words were spoken, there was an understanding between the two.

"We need to make some inquiries, and we'll be back in touch with you tomorrow," Carmine said.

"I appreciate your honesty, Mr. Giacomo. I know I can't change the reality of illegal product distribution in this day and age. If I can at least make a dent in some of it, then I'll take it as a positive. Tell your granddaughter hello for me."

Carmine stroked his chin with two of his fingers before replying. "You would have made a good Wise Guy."

As I turned to leave, looking over my shoulder I said to him, "Thank you. I'll take that as a compliment."

After getting in my car at the hotel parking garage, I pulled out my cell phone and called Caroline.

"Hey there, where are you? You split awfully early from my place this morning," Caroline said.

"Kinda had a full schedule at work today, so I got going early. I just got through with a meeting that I need to tell you about in person. And I'm going to need to crash one more night on your couch. I think by tomorrow, it'll be safe again at my condo."

"How do you know?" she asked.

"I just have to get a phone call saying that it's all clear."

"What does that mean?"

"I'll explain it to you when I get to your place. Did you get my note?"

"You mean all six words of it? You're not big on poetic prose I take it."

"I like to skip the prose and go straight to the activities that really matter."

"And what activities are those that really matter?" she asked with a coy edge in her voice.

"Usually ones involving spontaneity, intrigue, and different positions," I said.

"And how difficult is it for one to learn those different positions?" she asked, playing along.

"Well, it takes an expert teacher, of course, and lots and lots of practice."

"I see. Would I assume that you are an expert teacher of these positions?"

"One of the best."

"And are these lessons better to try before or after dinner?"

"Almost anytime is fine."

"Have you eaten dinner yet?"

"Not yet."

"In that case, why don't you pick up some take-out from our favorite Szechuan place and bring it to my condo. After dinner, I think you may need to start giving me some advanced personal lessons on learning some of those new positions," she said, more than tempting me.

"That's sounds reasonable to me. Does this mean that tonight I will be subjected to the too short couch?"

"Why, surely these lessons involve positions in multiple places, not just on the couch?"

Her amorous response took me by surprise.

"I'm starting to like the way you think. You're going to make an excellent pupil."

I think this kind of teaching gig just might work for me.

34

KANSAS CITY

After fetching the take-out food, I had a long talk with Caroline that evening about the events of the day. All the way from the message on my phone machine to the resulting meeting with the three adversaries in their penthouse suite. She was none too happy that I hadn't told her what was going on at the time, but she was somewhat relieved that the whole episode was likely to be resolved.

At least for now.

We talked at length about our feelings and expectations of each other. That's not something I normally said out loud to anyone, including myself. Caroline explained her fears and uncertainties about our relationship while I mostly listened. Most guys want to put their opinions about anything out there to be heard. I figured in this case, it was better to let her do most of the talking if we were going to go forward. We addressed a lot of issues that were bothering her, especially about each of our conflicting schedules. Most important, we were up front and deadly honest with each other. It was the first time in a while that I felt that we had emotionally connected.

After finishing our take-out food, the verbal interaction between us somehow came to a stopping point. That's when the nonverbal communication took over. As for the lessons on different positions, boy, did we ever connect the rest of that evening, and in a bunch of places. I guess you could say things in our relationship were positioning back in the right direction.

Early the next morning, I snuck out of her bed and grabbed a cup of coffee before heading off to my condo to change for work. When I arrived home, I was hesitant to open my front door. With my past history of unexpected intruders who had gotten into my place despite the gated entrance and my condo alarm system, I had a good reason to be so timid.

You got to ride through the storm to get to the calm. I opened the door. I made it into the kitchen where everything thing looked normal. I turned to see that my phone message machine red light was not blinking, indicating there were no messages. Especially the one I was waiting on.

Not so good.

Out of the corner of my eye, I noticed on the kitchen table a small silver tray with a piece of paper folded in half lying on the center of it. I immediately recognized that silver tray. That tray was just about the only wedding gift momento I brought with me when I moved to Kansas City seven years ago. Without Molly.

A chill went down my spine. That tray had always been stored in a protective cloth in the back of one of the kitchen cabinets. Only I wasn't the one who had gotten it out.

After staring at it like it might jump out at me, I took a deep breath and walked over to the table. Anxiously lifting the note, I found it had four simple words and two initials:

Deal allowed
Debt even

CG

I stood there in silence. I was not thrilled knowing that they had access to everything in my life, including free access to my residence. On the other hand, a sense of relief came over me. Relief that for now the worst was over. And with that relief, I realized that it was definitely time to get back to reality. Time to get back to normal, whatever that was.

I tried to convince myself that this whole episode with Big Tony and Carmine was now over. Really over, finished, concluded. But down deep, I knew that it would never really be over. While Carmine and I were now even, there were no more cards up my sleeve to play in the future. And the big boys in New York wouldn't take it lightly that they were told that there was a mole in their midst. I had rolled the dice to get by on this one, for now at least. From now on, I had to keep my eyes open for anything that seemed even minimally unusual.

Yeah Chandler, on every single day of the rest of your life.

35

MANHATTAN

"Good morning, Mr. Hauser. How are you today?" the corporate security chief asked as soon as he entered the large executive office precisely on time for his scheduled appointment Tuesday morning.

"Not bad, not bad at all, Sawyer," the quirky CEO said.

"I tried to do my best to gather all the information you requested," the exhausted Sawyer said as he handed a thick folder to his boss.

"Well, now, let's have a look Sawyer," the busy CEO said as he took the massive folder filled with spreadsheets and descriptions of all the computer software systems that their many companies were using and opened it on his desk.

Sawyer had stayed up nearly all night compiling the information for his demanding boss. He could hardly see straight at this point despite nearly overdosing on coffee.

"It looks like you have accumulated a large amount of data. Is there a cumulative spreadsheet that explains what it would cost to consolidate the multiple systems into one centralized system?" Hauser asked

"If you'll turn to the back of the folder, Mr. Hauser," Sawyer said. "You'll find some rough estimates in broad terms of what the approximate costs would be. I can't project the true costs without further investigation of what the labor costs would actually be. I've used estimates from similar smaller jobs we had completed two years ago to fill in the labor costs on that spreadsheet for the time being."

After looking at the data his security chief put together, the relentless CEO tossed the folder on his desk with a sour look on his face.

"Sawyer, we cannot expect to remain a Fortune 500 company in this competitive environment if we base our decision making on *vague* estimates from two years ago. While this information is a start," he said pointing to the folder on the desk, "we *must* have precise, up to date data to make informative decisions that determine the positive forward growth of our company. Am I clear with that point?"

"Crystal clear, sir," the security chief said.

"We need to continue to stay ahead of our competitors in all aspects of our business. And that especially includes security. Technology is developing rapidly. We need to stay aware of the latest safeguards to prevent electronic swindling of our corporate secrets, which could have our competitors surpass us. Understood?"

Sawyer nodded.

"Let me expound on some ideas I've been thinking about. To start with..." the CEO began with an air of all-encompassing knowledge, as he began to explain his wisdom on the subject.

At that very moment, the phone intercom buzzed with Mrs. Pennington saying, "Sir, you have unscheduled visitors here."

"Excuse me, Mrs. Pennington. I'm in the middle of an important meeting. Please tell them that they will have to come back..." Hauser said.

"Are you Philip Hauser?" a man asked as he came through the office door unannounced with three others.

"Excuse me," the CEO said firmly. "We are having an important meeting right now, and you will need to come back some other time. My schedule is very booked, so if you will talk to my assistant out front, Mrs. Pennington, I'm sure she will be able to..."

"Mr. Hauser, I'm Special Agent Booker with the FBI. These are Special Agents Gutierrez, Wellington, and Stockbridge. We have the necessary warrants under federal law that allow us to search this premises and seize all necessary property, including electronically stored information that might be related to potential criminal activity," he said as he laid down multiple copies of the search warrants on Hauser's desk.

"What in the world are you are talking about?" Hauser shouted as he stood.

"Mr. Hauser," the FBI agent said, "the warrants also include the seizure of all telephone and computer records deemed necessary. Gutierrez, start making an inventory of all property seized, and be sure and document the removal of all the hard drives. Be sure and round up all cellphones and dictation equipment. Wellington, talk to this other gentleman and read him his rights," Booker said as he pointed to Sawyer.

"But..." Hauser sputtered.

"Mr. Hauser, I am placing you under arrest for the suspicion of illegal transportation with the intent of distribution and trafficking of narcotic substances under the jurisdiction of both federal and the state of New York laws."

At this point Special Agent Booker walked behind the stunned CEO and placed both of Hauser's hands behind his back, securing them with handcuffs. At the same time, Special Agent Wellington was doing the same to the sputtering corporate security chief Sawyer. Simultaneously, Special Agent Stockbridge was putting all forms of evidence into multiple boxes the federal agents had brought with them.

Hauser was speechless.

"You have the right to remain silent," Booker said. "Anything you say can and will be used against you in a court of law. You have the right to an attorney. If you cannot afford an attorney, one will be provided for you. Do you understand the rights I have just read to you?"

Hauser was shocked beyond belief and could not speak.

"With these rights duly read to you, do you have anything you wish to say to me at this time?" Booker asked.

It was then the fuming CEO realized what had just happened to him. Him, the Blitzkrieg of Big Business of all people. The chief executive always two steps ahead of the competition. He had been set up by the people he was transporting product for their distribution. They wanted total control of the operation and all the money. And they got it. They had made him the fall guy to take the blame.

Hauser remembered something the unknown olive-skinned contact had told him when the initial arrangements of their business deal were made, "You will never get your fair share when you deal with the Mafia."

"Mr. Hauser, with your lack of a response to my question, I'll take it that you do not want to answer any questions at this moment without your lawyer present. If you'll come with me please, we need to be going now," Special Agent Booker commanded, taking Hauser by the arm.

36

KANSAS CITY

Once the dust had cleared with the smuggling investigation, things for me had settled back into a routine again.

Thank goodness.

Work for me was up and down busy as always, but my relationship with Caroline was growing in a steady, positive direction day by day. Despite each of our hectic schedules, we were spending more time together and relying on each other more and more. We both began to know when each of us needed space and alone time.

And just to keep the peace, I had called the bet between Caroline and me a draw.

For now.

About two weeks after I had found the note on the silver tray on my kitchen table, I was going through my mail on a Saturday afternoon when I found a letter addressed to me from Sydney. That was strange. Usually, if he wanted to talk to me or tell me something, he would just call.

I opened the envelope. Inside was a copy of a negative article from one of the financial magazines with a small yellow Post-It Note with the written word "Tremont?" It made me smile that the septuagenarian had put two and two together about his half-brother.

That evening I went over to Caroline's condo to fix dinner together. We began doing that weekly when we first started seeing each other earlier in the year. That ritual abruptly ended when she got spooked after the long weekend we spent together at her place. On one hand, I was glad that the long talk that we had as well as the positions lesson had broken the ice between us. On the other hand, I was even more glad for the way we were back to being comfortable around each other no matter what the situation.

She had spent all Saturday afternoon at work doing some kind of financial stuff on her computer to make her accounting come out even for the end of the month. I'm sure it was important, but that's something that would have driven me absolutely crazy in no time. Despite the chaotic pace of my unpredictable work schedule, I got to actually do something to make people better. And that gave me something really good to hold on to. If you asked me, looking at columns of numbers all day was beyond boring.

After the guard at the front gate of her complex let me through, I parked and slowly walked up to her front door. Instead of going on in, I rang the bell and waited.

No answer.

The hair on the back of my neck started to tingle. My thumb pushed down the door handle mechanism. It was unlocked. I still could not believe that after all we had been through, even having Sergeant Wilkins' crew keeping a careful eye on her place that she still left the front door unlocked. Some things in life just cannot be explained.

I pushed open the door, locking it behind me. As I walked in the living room, Caroline appeared in the doorway to her bedroom dressed in her terry cloth bathrobe.

As she ambled over to me in her bare feet, she asked,

"Hey you, how was your afternoon?"

She gave me a quick kiss while keeping both hands grasping the front of her robe to keep it tightly shut.

Spoil sport, but I did not say it out loud.

"It was interesting. Did you just get home?"

"Yeah, after finishing up at the office, yoga class ran late this afternoon. If you can wait a minute, I need to jump in the shower to get cleaned up before we start dinner."

"It wasn't that crazy hot yoga today, was it?" I asked her as I sat down on her all-too-familiar couch.

"No, that's only every other Friday night with my widow friend. If it was today, I'd still be soaking wet with sweat right now. I'm still going to convince you to come with me to it since you lost the bet. One session, and you'll be hooked."

"Hold your horses there, Miss Delusional. I did not lose the bet," I said firmly. "If you can make that short term memory loss of yours go away for a second, you'll recall we agreed the bet was a draw. Fair and square."

"Okay, you may or may not be right about that, but I'm still going to get you to try hot yoga with me," she said as she turned to go back to her bathroom.

"Changing to a more immediate subject, I think you might need some professional help in there to make sure you get clean."

She turned back to me at the doorway with a sly grin and said, "Not this time, Romeo. Let me get cleaned up, and then I'll help you get things started in the kitchen."

"I was trying to get things started in the shower first," I muttered as she turned towards the bathroom.

"What did you say?" a shout echoed to me from the other room.

"Nothing," I shouted back at her.

When she reappeared from her bedroom, she had her wavy brunette hair pulled back in a ponytail and was wearing minimal makeup. Throw in the yoga pants and tight-fitting, long-sleeve T-shirt, her casual, yet stunning appearance made my heart skip a beat.

"You're going to have an insect fly into your mouth if you leave it open like that," she said as she strolled into the kitchen.

"Must you be in control of every situation that seems to involve me?"

"A sorceress's privilege," she said as she started getting all the ingredients for a salad out of the refrigerator.

"Would you like a glass of wine while we're cooking?" I asked.

"Only if you're having one. And make mine small. Still watching calories."

I opened a bottle of Merlot from the one of the kitchen cabinets and poured us each a small glass.

"I talked to my mother today," she said casually as she washed and dried all the salad ingredients.

"I thought you told me because of your cancelled wedding you two didn't communicate to each other that often."

"Here, start chopping up the mushrooms," she said as she put a large knife on the counter next to the plastic chopping board. "And you're right, we don't talk that often. But she called to ask if I would be coming to Thanksgiving dinner this year. So imagine her surprise when I said not only of course, but that I was coming with a special guest."

"Ah yes," I said as I took my first sip of wine. "The sacrificial lamb to the wolves event we spoke about."

"You can still bail out if you want."

"No, as I told you earlier, I requested to be off call on Thanksgiving and a deal's a deal."

"I've got to warn you she will ask you plenty of penetrating personal questions," she said as she turned on the gas range to brown the ground meat we were making for the spaghetti sauce. "Especially if it comes up that you have been previously married."

"I'm not too worried," I said boldly. "I had a professor during my surgical residency who could verbally skin a resident in nine point five seconds flat. If I survived that horror show, I can let your mother's tough questions bounce right off me like Teflon."

"Turn the oven on for me to 350 degrees. I hope you're not squeamish about conversation dominated by who all just got married or engaged," she said as put together the salad.

"Hey, are you going to let me make my special meatballs with Italian spices to go with the sauce?" I said.

"Sure but cook them in a side pan. We can add them into the sauce later."

"And I don't get squeamish. You haven't seen me in action yet where I have mastered the fake smile as true art form. So, what will be the expected attire for this monumental occasion?"

"Wear a collared shirt with a sport coat. No tie. And don't wear blue jeans. For some reason, my mother has this thing against blue jeans. Don't ask me why."

"I've got a sports coat that's slightly too big that I think I'll wear. That way my Kevlar vest will fit under it just perfect," I said while washing my hands in the sink.

I started to mix the spices with the meat, molding it with my hands into individual meatballs. I pressed extra garlic into the mixture for good measure.

"One more thing," she said as she stirred the meat browning in the pan. "Don't talk politics with my dad. He has tunnel vision for the Republican Party and won't listen to any other views."

"Aye, aye Captain," I said with a spatula salute. "This whole pep talk sounds like we're going into battle."

"More than you can imagine. You mentioned your afternoon was interesting?" she asked, changing the conversation with her question.

"Yeah, I did. In an odd sort of way."

"Didn't you say you were going to the driving range?"

"Yeah, that's where I ended up."

"How's that back thing you were concerned about?" she asked while drained some of the fat from the pan of browning beef.

"I got to tell you, it's really weird. The pain has completely gone away. Even while I was hitting golf balls today. But like I said, it was still kind of odd."

"What could be so odd about hitting golf balls?"

"It wasn't the hitting of the golf balls that turned out to be odd. After I left the driving range, I went home and picked up the mail from my mail slot. When I was going through the mail, there was a letter from Sydney."

"What did it say?" she asked as she put the loaf of Italian bread into the oven.

"Well, it wasn't a letter. It was a copy of an article from financial magazine that described what happened to that Hawthorne Containers Company. Here, see for yourself," I said as I placed the meatballs in a separate frying pan.

I washed my hands again, then pulled the folded-up piece of paper from my back pants pocket, giving it to her.

Caroline read the article to herself as I tended to the cooking meatballs.

"So the company that was making the transportation bladders got sold. That's not surprising," she said nonchalantly.

"If you read between the lines, it wasn't that Evolution Industries took a big hit after their CEO was hauled in by the FBI for arranging the transportation of narcotics in the smuggling scheme. It even wasn't that they had to sell off Hawthorne Containers, the company that was making the Flexitank bladders where they were hiding the drugs. What is interesting is that they barely got pennies on the dollar for that company according to the news source," I said.

"Okay. So what?" she asked, looking somewhat puzzled.

"Look at the attached yellow sticky note," I said as I started a pot of water to boil for the pasta.

"It says 'Tremont?' Who's that?" she asked as she stirred the ground beef.

"Where do you keep the olive oil?" I asked. "I need to

put some in the water for the pasta."

"Kyle Chandler, I'm trying to understand what you are getting at here, and all you can do is worry about the olive oil?"

"Well, Caroline, I'm not actually worried about the olive oil, but it will prevent the pasta from sticking together. If you really..."

"Kyle!"

"Well, in my research I found that my greedy ex-father-in-law had invested a chunk of money from Molly's trust into this company. He thought he would bingo his return on the investment. Needless to say, he must have lost his shirt on that bet."

"You've told me about him before. And that's his name, isn't it?"

"Tremont Williamson, business investor deluxe," I said as I turned over the meatballs.

"From what you told me about him, he's not a real nice man. I understand he has never been nice to you, but you really need to let go of your disrespect of him," she said as she took a sip of wine.

I kind of chuckled. How did this woman always know what I was thinking ahead of time? I remembered what Alfie had said to me while were together on the stakeout outside the port east of London. He had said, "The really good ones do that to you."

"Funny you should bring that up. I've been thinking about that," I said as I took out the meatballs out of the pan. "I wanted to tell you I think I'm going to head up to Boston at the end of next week to make things right with my ex-father-in-law. To touch all the bases and put this chapter of my life behind me."

It was then I realized that my back pain hadn't gone away because I went and hit golf balls. It went away when I decided to go to Boston to make things right.

"What are you going to do?" she asked as she poured the spaghetti sauce into her big pan of cooked ground beef.

"I'm still working on the final aspects of that. And be sure to put some extra garlic in the spaghetti sauce."

"Do you think that will help you to finally let Molly go?" she asked in a truly earnest voice.

That question hit home a little too close for me. I took a big breath.

"I'm standing here cooking spaghetti sauce and pasta with the only one I want to be with. Is that evidence enough that I've let her go?"

She didn't really respond to my flippant retort. Looking at it from her viewpoint, I knew this had been a weight on her heart for more than a while. I took another deep breath and contemplated how to word my response.

"Caroline, I'll admit, I don't express my feelings enough to you," I said. "You are an unbelievable woman, and I love you dearly. I have to be honest with you. I will never be able to forgive myself there was not a single way in the universe I could have prevented Molly's untimely death. That's my burden, I know."

She looked like she was on the verge of tears, so I took one more deep breath before continuing on.

"But after eight years, I have realized I have to finally let that burden go. I have found in you not only the person, but the soulmate I would not trade for anybody at any time. And that's about as open and honest I can be. Both now and in the future."

Caroline looked at me with an expression that turned from sadness to pure satisfaction.

"Well, Doctor Stonewall. I'm finally starting to believe there is a person with real feelings deep inside that smart aleck persona. I was beginning to wonder."

"Do not get overconfident with this," I said, pointing my spatula at her. "If you try to tell family or friends about this little truth episode, I'll deny every last bit of it. Especially your mother, even though I haven't met her yet. And by no means should you think this is going to get me to come to one of your Friday sweat fests at hot yoga."

She just smiled as she drained the pasta out of the boiling water and into a serving dish.

"We'll just see about that. We'll see..."

If you don't think women rule the world, then you're obviously deaf, mute, and blind.

37

BOSTON, MASSACHUSETTS

There was one more thing I needed to take care of to wrap up this whole chapter in my life. On the following Thursday after I had told Caroline that I had to go to make things right with my ex-father-in-law, I caught a flight from Kansas City to Boston. Autumn there had come and gone, and the trees were barren of their leaves. It was the first time I had ventured back to my old stomping ground since I had finished my surgical training over seven years ago. It was also the first time I came back to Beantown. Without Molly.

I caught a cab from the airport to a hotel at Copley Place. It was bigger and busier than I remembered, but I guess didn't get out much back then since I was always at the hospital. I checked into my hotel and decided to head out for dinner. I originally thought I might go to one of the out of the way places at the North End. Molly and I used to go to dinner there when we had a rare free night. Instead, I settled for a noisy sports bar with the Celtics game blaring on multiple TVs. As I had admitted to Caroline last weekend, I somehow knew that chapter was now behind me.

The next morning after breakfast, I caught the Green Line on the "T" to the Red Line, which dropped me off in Cambridge at Harvard Square. I had previously made an appointment with Tremont Williamson's secretary at the Harvard Business School saying I was a reporter for a big-league New York business magazine. I told her we were doing a feature on the current financial stars of Wall Street and academia. I said Tremont was at the top of the list. I knew damn well I would never get in his door if I had said I was his disgraced ex-son-in-law who had recently caused him to lose a bundle via Hawthorne Containers' demise.

Moreover, I had one more score to settle with him.

I found my way to the address I had of an office building on the Harvard Business School campus on the south side of the Charles River. I went up the stairs and found the office at the end of the hall. I arrived promptly at nine fifty-eight for my ten o'clock appointment. His secretary showed me into his office and offered me a seat. I had never met her before, so she didn't know who I really was. She told me he would be in shortly since he was coming from a class he taught on Friday mornings.

About five minutes later, in walked Tremont, expecting to put on a dynamic show for a New York reporter who was going to make his star shine even brighter. Needless to say, the smile on his face turned immediately to an angry scowl when he recognized that he had just been duped.

"What are you doing here?"

"Good to see you too, Tremont," I said with a blank expression on my face. "I just thought I'd drop in to see how my ex-father-in-law is doing."

"I don't believe you now, just like I didn't believe you when you married Molly," he said. "You know damn well that I will never forgive you for the loss of my beloved eldest daughter. If it wasn't for you, she could have gone on to a brilliant financial career instead of rotting away at some foolish nonprofit."

A solid but expected blow straight to my ego. I didn't answer him.

"Get out of my office before I have to call security."

"Tremont, you don't want to do that. Especially because if I leave, you won't get what I came all the way here to give you."

"I don't need any gifts from you of all people. Since Philip Hauser was arrested on charges of international drug smuggling, do you have any idea of what you have done to my reputation as well as the embarrassing financial loss you have cost me?"

"When I last called you, you told me that you knew Philip Hauser well and that he was a good guy. Sound familiar? You never did tell me if you knew they were hiding the drugs in the container bladders, Tremont."

"I didn't know a thing about the drug smuggling scheme," he said disgustedly. "All I know is that I invested early in a company that had a new ingenious idea of how to transport bulk liquids, particularly wine across the ocean. That company had a really good chance for a phenomenal return on my investment until you and your nosy inquiry turned it into a total disaster."

"They broke the law and the product they were transporting harms thousands of people throughout the world every day," I said. "But that's not why I came here today. I came to give you back what you think is yours."

He gave me a vicious stare as I continued to explain.

"It's about that large batch of securities that you gave to Molly, not to us, as a wedding present. To tell you the truth, I didn't even know about them until after she died. Now I get it that you've thought all along they should have reverted back to you upon her unexpected death. Although as you know, her will specifically left me everything, including those securities you desperately thought you deserved. And you already know that they are worth a bundle. Especially since none of it was invested in

Hawthorne Containers like you did with the money from Molly's trust."

He stood there with his arms crossed not moving a muscle. I could almost imagine seeing white smoke blowing out of both of his ears.

"I could keep those securities and ride off into the sunset right now, and there's not a thing you could legally do about it. Instead, I came here today to release the last tie between us," I said, as I paused to let that sink into his consciousness. "If you will give me the name and phone number of your investment manager, I will have my investment guy make all the necessary arrangements to have those securities moved by wire transfer or however they move them back into your account," I said.

"I take care of all my own investments," Tremont said smugly.

"Well, give me the number of who you want me to contact at Bain, and I'll make sure it gets done by the end of business today."

Tremont didn't move at all and didn't say a word as he contemplated how to handle my unexpected offer. For a split second I could tell it had taken him by surprise. After the pause, greed kicked in. He turned around to write a name and phone number on a yellow Post-It Note. He handed it to me as I stood to leave.

The irony of the moment finally hit me. I was giving away a pile of cash to gain my freedom from the perpetual resentment of Molly's family.

I extended my right hand to him, and he stood still without reciprocating the gesture. "Tremont tell your wife Margaret I said hello," I said as I slowly dropped my hand to my side and strode to the door.

Just before I reached the door, I stopped and turned around to look him straight in the eye. After a slight pause, I reminded him, "Like you always said, Tremont, we all have our own hidden agendas. Some more important than others."

CPSIA information can be obtained
at www.ICGtesting.com
Printed in the USA
LVHW040716230222
711784LV00004B/172